"Molly Harper writes cha___
you can't help but fall in lov___
—*RT Book Reviews*

Praise for the Southern Eclectic series

Sweet Tea and Sympathy

"This sweet tale of the city girl finding a home in the country launches Harper's (*Accidental Sire*) latest series and will go down as easy as honey on a deep-fried Twinkie."

—*Library Journal*

"Margot is a terrific lead for Harper's supporting cast of quirky characters. This is a promising start to Harper's Southern Eclectic series."

—*Publishers Weekly*

"This book is funny and the characters engaging. . . . Finished it in twenty-four hours and already looking forward to the next in the Southern Eclectic series."

—*Book Riot*

"A small-town romance with tons of heart, lots of laughs, and of course, kooky locals. . . . *Sweet Tea and Sympathy* kicked off Molly Harper's newest series in the best of ways."

—*Harlequin Junkie*

"Molly Harper is known for writing hilarious scenes, and her unique sense of humor is evident all throughout the story. . . . There are countless laughs in *Sweet Tea and Sympathy* along with an equal number of heartfelt moments."

—*AlwaysReviewing.com*

Nice Girls Don't Date Dead Men

"Fast-paced, mysterious, passionate, and hilarious."

—*RT Book Reviews* (4½ stars)

Nice Girls Don't Have Fangs

"A chuckle-inducing, southern-fried version of Stephanie Plum."

—*Booklist*

Praise for the *Naked Werewolf* novels

How to Run with a Naked Werewolf

"Harper is back with her trademark snark, capable heroines, and loping lupines."

—*Heroes and Heartbreakers*

The Art of Seducing a Naked Werewolf

"Harper's gift for character building and crafting a smart, exciting story is showcased well."

—*RT Book Reviews* (4 stars)

How to Flirt with a Naked Werewolf

"Mo's wisecracking, hilarious voice makes this novel such a pleasure to read."

—*New York Times* bestselling author Eloisa James

"A light, fun, easy read, perfect for lazy days."

—*New York Journal of Books*

BOOKS BY MOLLY HARPER

THE SOUTHERN ECLECTIC SERIES
Ain't She a Peach
Peachy Flippin' Keen
Save a Truck, Ride a Redneck
Sweet Tea and Sympathy

THE HALF-MOON HOLLOW SERIES
Accidental Sire
Where the Wild Things Bite
Big Vamp on Campus
Fangs for the Memories
The Single Undead Moms Club
The Dangers of Dating a Rebound Vampire
I'm Dreaming of an Undead Christmas
A Witch's Handbook of Kisses and Curses
"Undead Sublet" in *The Undead in My Bed*
The Care and Feeding of Stray Vampires
Driving Mr. Dead
Nice Girls Don't Bite Their Neighbors
Nice Girls Don't Live Forever
Nice Girls Don't Date Dead Men
Nice Girls Don't Have Fangs

THE NAKED WEREWOLF SERIES
How to Run with a Naked Werewolf
The Art of Seducing a Naked Werewolf
How to Flirt with a Naked Werewolf

THE BLUEGRASS SERIES
Snow Falling on Bluegrass
Rhythm and Bluegrass
My Bluegrass Baby

ALSO
Better Homes and Hauntings
And One Last Thing . . .

AIN'T SHE A
PEACH

MOLLY HARPER

G

GALLERY BOOKS

NEW YORK LONDON TORONTO SYDNEY NEW DELHI

Gallery Books
An Imprint of Simon & Schuster, Inc.
1230 Avenue of the Americas
New York, NY 10020

First Gallery Books trade paperback edition June 2018

GALLERY BOOKS and colophon are registered trademarks of Simon & Schuster, Inc.

For information about special discounts for bulk purchases, please contact Simon & Schuster Special Sales at 1-866-506-1949 or business@simonandschuster.com.

The Simon & Schuster Speakers Bureau can bring authors to your live event. For more information or to book an event, contact the Simon & Schuster Speakers Bureau at 1-866-248-3049 or visit our website at www.simonspeakers.com.

Interior design by Michelle Marchese

Manufactured in the United States of America

10 9 8 7 6 5 4 3 2 1

Library of Congress Cataloging-in-Publication Data

Names: Harper, Molly, author.
Title: Ain't she a peach / Molly Harper.
Description: First Gallery Books trade paperback edition. | New York : Gallery Books, 2018. | Series: Southern eclectic ; 4
Identifiers: LCCN 2017058066 | ISBN 9781501151330 (paperback) | ISBN 9781501151347 (ebook)
Subjects: LCSH: Man-woman relationships—Fiction. | BISAC: FICTION / Romance / Contemporary. | FICTION / Contemporary Women. | FICTION / Romance / General. | GSAFD: Love stories. | Humorous fiction.
Classification: LCC PS3608.A774 A74 2018 | DDC 813/.6—dc23
LC record available at https://lccn.loc.gov/2017058066

ISBN 978-1-5011-5133-0
ISBN 978-1-5011-5134-7 (ebook)

*For Darcy, who alarms
and amazes me every day*

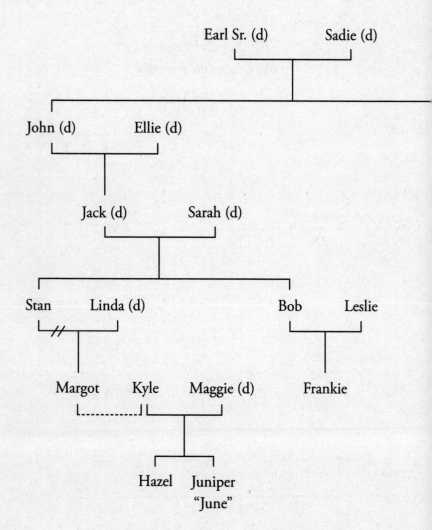

The McCready Family Tree

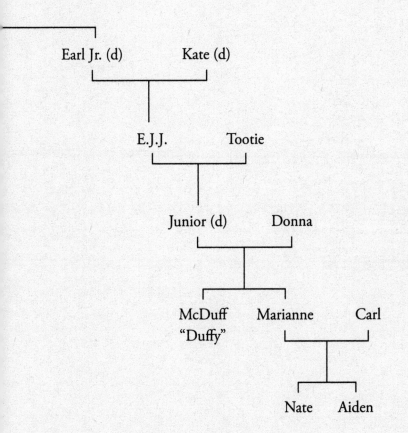

Earl Jr. (d)   Kate (d)

E.J.J.   Tootie

Junior (d)   Donna

McDuff "Duffy"   Marianne   Carl

Nate   Aiden

AIN'T SHE A
PEACH

FRANKIE McCREADY CAREFULLY dusted Maybelline blush in Light Rose on the curve of Eula Buckinerny's cheek.

"Now, Miss Eula, I know you've never been one for makeup. You've always been blessed with such a nice complexion, you've never needed it," Frankie murmured over the strains of the Mount Olive Gospel Singers' rendition of "How Great Thou Art." She liked to play her customers' favorite music in the background while she made them up, so they would feel at home. "But every now and again, a girl needs some help from a good foundation and blush.

"Do ya think I wake up every morning with this fabulous Elizabeth Taylor lash already in place?" Frankie gestured to her own carefully framed violet-blue eyes. "No, this is the result of a steady hand and some indecently expensive mascara that I splurge on every six months. But don't tell my mama. You know her. She gets downright indignant at the idea of spendin' more than ten dollars on anything you're just going to wash off your face every night."

Frankie studied her makeup kit and chose a lip color that, while just a bit pinker than beige, was still more risqué than anything Miss Eula had ever worn, even at the annual Sackett County Homemaker Society Awards Dinner. She painted a thin, careful coat across Eula's lips. "This will be our little secret."

Frankie dipped a smaller brush in a dark brown contouring powder called Hot Chocolate that would give Eula's features shadow and dimension. After a few strokes, Frankie leaned back and admired her handiwork.

"There. You look beautiful. And I really think that lipstick pops with your pretty pink suit. Trudy Darnell will spend the month trying to figure out how ya managed to go out looking better than her, even in your casket."

Smiling down at Eula one last time, Frankie bowed her head in a solemn gesture of farewell. She closed the frosted pink casket lid just as a loud knock sounded on the mortuary room door. "Frankie! Is it all clear?"

"Sure, Margot, I'm all finished up with Miss Eula."

Frankie's cousin stuck her blond head through the door. Margot Cary was just as sleek and polished as she'd been the day she stepped off the plane from Chicago a few months ago to take what was supposed to be a temporary job at the McCready Family Funeral Home and Bait Shop. And while her slick designer suits were still very much out of place in semirural Georgia, Frankie and the rest of the McCreadys were working like ants on a discarded Blow Pop to make her feel like part of the family.

"You comin' in?" Frankie asked.

"Nope."

Frankie snorted. Her cousin took no crap from the local PTA-based social terrorists, but she was still pretty creeped out by the concept of embalming. Frankie tried not to judge. After all, she was creeped out by the concept of gluten-free cupcakes and juice cleanses.

"Sheriff Linden is here for you, Frankie," Margot said, training her eyes on a spot over Frankie's shoulder, away from the form of Benjoe Watts, lying under a pristine white sheet on table two. "They're bringing in Bobby Wayne Patterson."

"Oh, that's a shame." Frankie sighed, frowning deeply.

"Yeah, my dad said that y'all—you all had been expecting this one for a while," Margot said, clearing her throat.

Frankie's momentary sadness over Bobby Wayne gave way to warm internal fuzziness over her cousin's casual use of *my dad*, something that wouldn't have happened just a few weeks before. After a lifetime of separation from the whole family, Margot wasn't quite ready to call Stan McCready "Daddy." But the two were able to stay in the same room and make pleasant conversation on a regular basis, which was a considerable improvement over when Margot had arrived.

Also, Margot had started to say "y'all," which made Frankie perversely proud.

"Could you tell *my* dad that Miss Eula's coming up on

the elevator?" Frankie asked. "All prettied up and ready for her party."

"Will do," Margot said, the corners of her slick coral lips lifting. "Your mom left your lunch in my office and said to remind you that you have to eat at some point. I believe the exact phrase she used was 'No excuses or I'll give her a whooping, just like when she was little.'"

"She's all talk. I never got whoopin's."

"I'd still eat the freaking sandwich, if I were you," Margot told her. "Your mother is a culinary genius, and bacon is her medium of artistic expression."

"Yeah, yeah," Frankie said, rolling the closed pink casket toward the elevator that led to the west chapel. She called after Margot, who was already halfway up the stairs to the funeral home proper. "Remind Daddy that Miss Eula ordered a full spray of white roses! She wanted them in place for her visitation. And she wanted to make sure Trudy Darnell saw them. She actually wrote it in her preplanned funeral paperwork: 'Make sure Trudy Darnell sees me covered in white roses.' They had a long-standin' feud over some pie-related incident at the 1964 county fair."

"The roses are already here. I'll place them myself," Margot promised from the stairwell. "Also, for the record, I did not expect the old church ladies to be *this* cutthroat. It's like *Game of Thrones* with less nudity and more denture cream."

"Just be grateful for the 'less nudity,'" Frankie yelled.

"Trust me when I say that I am."

Frankie snickered and then heard Margot say, "She's ready to see you, Sheriff," before click-clacking her way up the stairs on her scary ice-pick heels. Frankie had no idea how Margot walked in those things, much less did stairs.

Frankie turned to see a tall man in a dark green Sackett County Sheriff's Department uniform duck through the door. She kept her lip from curling in disdain, but it was a near thing. "Sheriff."

Blessed with a thick head of dark-blond hair and eyes the color of new moss, Eric Linden wasn't handsome in the classical sense. Frankie knew enough about bone structure to see that his sharp cheekbones and slightly crooked Roman nose didn't quite coordinate with his high forehead and square chin. His lips were oddly full and opened over white, but certainly not orthodontia-perfect, teeth. His top canines in particular were slightly off-kilter, which shouldn't have been charming but somehow was.

And damn, did that man know how to fill out a uniform. The fit of Eric's shirt alone was enough to make Frankie more than a little self-conscious. She liked to think that her sense of style made up for her own pale, under-toned physique. For instance, today's ensemble of a black tunic over tights printed with galaxies and comets lent her a certain air of quirky elegance. It would help her self-esteem considerably if she didn't turn to lady jelly in a lab coat every time she made eye contact with those big green eyes of his, while he seemed to remain unaffected. He was supposed to have been a fun highlight to an outstanding "self-care" weekend—a highlight she would never have to see again. But here she was, enduring regular awkward interactions with a guy who seemed to think she was some heartless sex marauder, all because she hadn't stuck around for postcoital pancakes a few weeks before.

"Ms. McCready," he drawled, his eyes catching on Mr. Watts. He seemed to blanch, and his speech faltered for a second. "I— Y—Your cousin was supposed to tell you Bobby Wayne Patterson is coming in. I think it's a possible homicide. Since you're the county coroner, I need you to give him the full workup before I can send him along to the state crime lab."

Jesus Herbert Christ. Not this again.

Eric Linden seemed to think that anybody who didn't die in intensive care surrounded by a circle of great-great-grandchildren was the victim of foul play. This was the second body he'd brought in as a "possible homicide" in the couple of weeks since he had taken over for the recently retired Sheriff Rainey. The first was Len Huffman, a poor tourist from Ohio who'd had no idea how to operate a fishing boat near a dam and ended up drowning. Sheriff Linden had insisted the boater's pretty and much younger wife had something to do with his untimely demise and refused to release the body to the family until he had evidence. While Frankie could see the motive in a woman forced to spend her precious vacation driving to Georgia for fishing, ultimately overconfidence and poor boatsmanship were the only killers in this case. It took Frankie's autopsy report, a statement from the bass boat's manufacturer, and affidavits from the man's sons regarding his poor swimming skills to convince Sheriff Linden.

Her relationship with Eric had suffered several episodes of tragic dickheadery in the short time she'd known him. What had been a very pleasant encounter that they'd both enjoyed—several times—on one of Frankie's lost weekends in Atlanta was ruined when Eric was introduced to her as Lake Sackett's new sheriff. Eric did not appreciate Frankie's no-nonsense approach to anonymous short-term relationships and was not pleased to find he'd moved to her hometown. He'd proceeded to act like an asshat every time their jobs brought them together. He'd managed to make her feel unattractive, unprofessional, and unwanted without really trying. And when she'd thought they'd finally reached some sort of understanding after resolving Len Huffman's case, he'd stomped all over it by accusing her of securing her evidence by inappropriately using her connections and natural charms.

Frankie considered herself a nice person, but she would dearly love to see Eric ugly-cry.

The buzzer by the back bay rang, letting Frankie know that a "delivery" was coming into her mortuary. She crossed the gray-tiled room and punched in the key code to electronically open the double doors. Naomi Daniels, the local day-shift paramedic, wheeled a gurney through the sunlit doorway. Poor Bobby Wayne was safely tucked inside a standard-issue black body bag. Frankie's heart ached for his long-suffering mamá.

"Hey, Naomi," Frankie said, a note of finality in her voice, as if she'd been expecting this delivery.

"Hi, Frankie." Naomi's voice was resigned as she handed over the clipboard. Her messy brown hair hung limp around her cherubic face as she bent over the body. "Unresponsive at the scene. No breath, no pulse, cold to the touch. Pretty sure the cause of death is that big ol' missing spot in the back of his head, but you'd know better than me."

"Who found him?" Frankie asked, taking the state paperwork that assigned her official stewardship of the body.

"The Clay boys. Poor things skipped school to squirrel hunt and found a dead body for their trouble."

"Well, they'll never play hooky again," Frankie muttered. She checked over the paperwork one last time before signing and handing it back to Naomi. The paramedic used her considerable upper-body strength to transfer the body bag onto Frankie's central treatment table. Frankie noted that the sheriff hadn't even offered to help her.

"No, they will not," Naomi said, shaking her head. "Little Brody Clay threw up so much I thought I was going to have to drop him off at the ER before I brought Bobby Wayne in."

Frankie grimaced. "Sheriff, this sort of thing can be pretty traumatic. You might make sure the boys get referred to the county's mental health services for follow-up counseling. You'll have to talk their daddy into it, because Allan Clay doesn't buy into that sort of thing."

"Already done," the sheriff said, his square jaw stiff. "I know my job."

Frankie pressed her poppy-bright mouth into a thin line, exhaled through her nose, and counted to eight. He didn't deserve ten.

Naomi saw the grim set of Frankie's normally cheerful mouth and took a step back. "Okay, then. I'm going to head out. Sheriff, you have my statement. If you need anything else, let me know."

Sheriff Linden offered her a curt nod and Naomi carefully wheeled her gurney out into the sunlight. As she closed the double doors behind her, she mouthed the words *Good luck* at Frankie.

Frankie took the necessary report forms out of the filing cabinet by her desk. The little Funko Pop! versions of the Avengers, plus half the Lannister family, standing sentinel over her desktop monitor didn't cheer her up like they normally did. She wanted Eric Linden and his big-city cop attitude out of her work space, yesterday. He was a condescending ass in a town that had already met its condescending-ass quota. They didn't need to go importing them from Atlanta.

Frankie cleared her throat and turned carefully on thick-soled sneakers printed in cosmic blues, pinks, and purples. She thought they were a nice complement to the purple and blue streaks in her hair. "Can you explain to me why you think that Mr. Patterson's death is a homicide?"

The sheriff cleared his throat and several beads of sweat appeared on his brow. "If you would open the body bag, I'll show you."

Frankie shook her head. "After the deceased come through my doors, I don't like to let other people see them until I've prettied them up for their services. It's a little more dignified."

Eric frowned at her. "Do you understand how police investigations work? This isn't optional. I'm the sheriff. You're the coroner. I don't want to use the phrase 'chain of command,' because it's too damn early and I've spent my morning up to my ass cheeks in chiggers. So please, just open the damn bag."

"I might, if you would explain to me how you could possibly think this is a homicide investigation."

"The gunshot wound to the head doesn't seem suspicious to you?" he drawled.

"Not when you consider that Bobby Wayne Patterson drank *at least* a twelve-pack of Bud Light every day and he was an avid hunter who built his own deer stand about twenty years ago. Also while drunk. And he called the safety on firearms 'the sissy button.' So no, when I add all of those factors up . . . I'm not seein' homicide."

"Just because the man had a reputation as a drunk doesn't mean he couldn't have met with foul play!" the sheriff exclaimed. Frankie noticed that he'd gone oddly pale. "Every case deserves our full attention."

"I absolutely agree. But how many times have you pulled Bobby Wayne over for DUI in the weeks you've worked here?"

Sheriff Linden grimaced, which was answer enough for Frankie. He fumed, "So you're just going to sign off on it as an accident without even looking into it? Is that how you normally handle things around here, Ms. McCready?"

"No, I'm going to do my due diligence, just like I do with each and every body that comes through my doors. But I'm not going to waste the county's limited budget on expensive, unnecessary tests when we need to save it just in case there's an actual murder in our town . . . for the first time in more than twenty years."

Sheriff Linden glowered at her with those icy green eyes of his and she rolled her own in response. "Okay, do you have pictures of the scene?"

The sheriff took a mini tablet out of an oversize pocket in his cargo pants, tapped in an access code, and handed it to her without looking at the screen. She scrolled through the photos of the body, the deer stand, and the ground surrounding the scene, until she found one that featured the dry-rotted wooden steps Bobby Wayne had nailed into the broad oak tree when he was in high school. Frankie noted that the fifth step up was broken and dangling from the trunk by a loosened nail.

"That broken step's, what, eight feet off of the ground?" she said, manipulating the screen to zoom in on the step. Sheriff Linden frowned at the screen and nodded. Frankie snapped on a pair of sterile exam gloves.

"Excuse me, Bobby Wayne," she said in a polite but brisk tone. "I just need to take a quick look."

"You talk to the dead bodies?" Eric asked.

"I was raised well. Just because they're not breathin'

doesn't mean I shouldn't be polite," she shot back as she opened the body bag and gently extended Bobby Wayne's hand. The sheriff took a rather large step back and she showed him the dark brown material packed under Bobby Wayne's ragged fingernails. "And this looks like tree bark, doesn't it? And those stains on his sleeves?" Frankie sniffed delicately at the green camo jacket. "Smell a lot like beer."

The sheriff nodded, his lips going the color of day-old oatmeal. "McCready, don't *sniff* the body. I gotta draw a line somewhere."

"From that height, given the scratches on the tree trunk and the bark under his nails, and what looks like a Bud Light can at the base of the tree, I think it's pretty safe to say that Bobby Wayne was trying to climb into his rickety old deer stand while holdin' a beer, because I'm pretty sure Bobby Wayne was born holdin' a beer. The step gave way under his foot, he dropped the beer, tried to keep hold of the trunk, but fell onto his back, with his rifle barrel right under the base of his skull, and the rifle went off. It's a terrible tragedy, but these things happen. Haven't you ever heard of the Darwin Awards?"

Sheriff Linden shook his head. "How would that even happen?"

Frankie took the sheriff's tablet and opened the photos from the crime scene. She noted the way he instinctually turned his eyes away from the images. She tapped the screen. "Bobby Wayne always used his granddaddy's rifle. He thought it was good luck."

"Okay."

"Well, modern firearms have that firing pin block thing that prevents a gun from firing accidentally if it's dropped."

"I'm familiar with the concept."

"Bobby Wayne's granddaddy's rifle didn't have that. So . . . not good luck after all." When he shot her a disappointed look, she added, "But just to make you feel better, I'll run tests on the back of Bobby Wayne's jacket to show the patterns of gunshot residue and determine how the rifle was situated against his back when it was fired. And I'll send the bullet to the state lab for comparison to his rifle."

"You can run GSR tests here?" Sheriff Linden asked, eyeing her work space.

"As I've told you before, Sheriff, this is technically the county morgue. There's no major hospital for fifty miles. I've been the county coroner since my uncle, the last coroner, died. I know what I'm doin'."

"You ran unopposed," Sheriff Linden shot back, a tiny bit of color returning to his cheeks.

"No one else wanted the job," she told him. "Because people around here enjoyed dealin' with Sheriff Rainey about as much as I like dealing with you."

"Well, that's hurtful." He placed his hand over his heart. For the first time since he'd entered the basement, Sheriff Linden offered a hint of a smile and she saw a glimpse of that charming, adventurous soul she'd spent quality naked time with all those nights ago.

"I'm not tryin' to be hurtful. Just honest." Frankie carefully tucked Bobby Wayne's arm back in the bag and zipped it. The sheriff took a deep breath and his shoulders relaxed. Frankie rounded the table and he took several steps back toward Mr. Watts's table.

"I get that you're used to murders by the hour, but you're going to have to pump your brakes just a little bit. This is Lake Sackett. Not every non-natural death is going to be suspicious. Sometimes alcohol and outdoor sports are going to combine in awful, permanent ways."

"Look, I'm an interim sheriff. I took the job knowing I would only have it until the special election in November. That doesn't make it any less demoralizing to campaign for the job I have. And difficult, since, as you like to point out at every possible opportunity, I'm an outsider. I have to make a good impression with voters or there's no hope of me getting elected." He pinned her with those frank, incredibly dilated green eyes. "Besides, I saw what happened to the last sheriff. I would like to retire without the words 'gross incompetence' written on my cake."

"Well, don't let your evidence room become a hoarder nightmare and you'll already be way ahead of Sheriff Rainey."

Eric wiped at his sweaty brow. "So, what, you're saying I should relax? Take up a hobby?"

Frankie opened a mini-fridge she kept near her desk and handed him a bottle of water. "No, I'm sayin' you're going to burn yourself out if you're not careful. And you're going to become the 'boy who cries murder,' which will make people laugh at you when you walk into the Rise and Shine. They'll pretend it's something else, but it will be you. Not to mention, it doesn't look great to the tourist trade if every hunting accident and drowning is investigated as the possible work of a serial killer."

The sheriff sagged against the autopsy table behind him. "You're right. But for the record, I want to do a good job, not just 'cause I want to be elected, but for my own reasons. I *have* to do well here."

"Um, I really appreciate this new level of emotional openness between us, but maybe you shouldn't touch Mr. Watts like that," Frankie said, timidly gesturing to the table he was leaning on.

The sheriff turned, saw the covered body on the table, and stumbled away, dragging the sheet with him in his haste. The barest hint of Benjoe Watts's gray hair became visible. And then Eric Linden did the last thing Frankie would have expected.

His eyes rolled up like window shades and he fainted dead away on the tile floor.

ERIC WOKE UP with a cold cloth on his forehead and Frankie's hand waving a broken smelling salts capsule under his nose.

Inhaling sharply at the harsh ammonia scent, he blinked at her a few times and a dreamy smile parted his lips. And then his brows drew down hard over his eyes.

"I'm on an embalming table, aren't I?"

Frankie nodded, her purple- and blue-streaked ponytail bobbing over her ear in a jaunty fashion that seemed obscenely out of place. Eric yelped and launched himself off the slab. His boots skidded on the tile and he landed in a heap on the floor.

Despite her general lack of damns about Eric, she understood a good panic faint. She'd had them off and on for years—usually while she was waiting on test results from her physicals or felt some pain that didn't feel normal for a woman in her midtwenties. On the rare occasion when she'd done it in front of her parents, she'd played it off as low blood sugar and long hours. Still, waking up on the floor, not knowing how you'd gotten there and how long you'd been there, was scary and humiliating. She was willing to cease hostilities until Eric was on his feet. A battle of wits was no fun with the unarmed.

"I wanted you to be more comfortable while I worked. Besides, I could hardly lift your heavy butt all the way over to the elevator," she huffed. "I only got you this far because the table lowers all the way to the floor."

"The table . . . where you embalm people."

"Oh, calm down, it's disinfected at least three times a day," she said, slapping his bottle of water into his hand. "So, you've got an aversion to dead bodies. A way-more-serious-than-the-average-person's aversion. I should have noticed before, at the Huffman drowning site, when you refused to make eye contact with, well, anybody. But I thought you were just being a jerk."

"It's a long story. I don't want to talk about it," he snapped.

Frankie raised her hands in a defensive pose. "Fine. I did GSR tests on the back of Bobby Wayne's jacket while you were 'nappin'.'" She made sarcastic air-quote fingers. "In my professional opinion, the pattern looks pretty consistent with someone who was lying on top of a rifle when it fired, but I'm sure you'll want to send it along to the state lab to confirm."

He cocked his head to the side and his eyes narrowed. "You let me stay unconscious on an embalming table while you ran forensic tests?"

"It was only a few minutes. And I wanted to wake you up with good news," she said with a cheeky grin. "Well, that's not true, I wanted to wake you up with the news that I was right and you were wrong. But it's basically the same thing."

"What the—what?" he spluttered.

She placed a large evidence envelope in his hands. "Bobby Wayne's jacket. Scrapings from under his fingernails. I'll send you the blood alcohol content results, plus photos of the wound and the bullet as soon as I remove it."

"There is something very wrong with you."

"You're not the first one to say so," she said cheerfully, though his words stung a bit, even in his low honeyed-whiskey tones. "But gettin' back to the subject we were discussin' before you took your little floor nap, yes, I do think you need to relax a little bit and take up a hobby. Preferably one that gets you out of the house and into the community, so people see you as an actual person with feelings, instead of a cyborg sent from the future to accuse innocent people of murder."

"Let me guess, you're going to recommend I take up fishin'?"

"What's wrong with fishin'?"

"It's just a little self-interested to recommend I take up fishin' when your family runs the local bait shop."

"You aren't one of those outdoor superstore guys, are you?"

"No, I'm just not that into fishing," he said, shrugging.

Frankie scoffed. "I wouldn't tell anyone here that."

"I told you I'll get a handle on it. A little trust wouldn't hurt this uncomfortable workin' dynamic we have going."

"Okay, fine," she said. "I'll stop expressing concern for your well-being."

"Can you tell me where Margot's office is?" he asked. "I'm supposed to give her some reports about emergencies and incidents at the Founders' Festival. I tried telling her there were none, but she said she wants me to fill out a form and give some sort of sworn blood oath for a report to the county commissioners."

Frankie frowned at the tone of . . . intrigue in Eric's voice. She swallowed thickly. She'd given this guy some of the best . . . hours . . . of her life, and he wanted her to draw him a map to Margot's office? She'd never envied Margot her polished good looks, the always-smooth blond hair and the kind of skin that came only from good genes and fancy spas. But now, seeing her former hookup showing interest in her cousin, Frankie kind of wanted to shave Margot's head. She would feel bad afterward and apologize, but still, she wanted to do it.

This was a bad sign, in terms of her character. Nice Southern women didn't turn on family members when a handsome-but-judgmental law enforcement officer showed interest in them.

And what was Eric thinking, showing that much interest in her cousin? Surely he had to know that Margot and the local elementary school principal, Kyle Archer, were Facebook-official. Then again, being an outsider with no family in the area, he was cut off from most of the traditional channels for "local news"—the kitchen table, the beauty parlor, the church parking lot.

Oh, what did she even care? She didn't have any claim on Eric Linden. She didn't think she even *wanted* a claim. She just didn't want him looking like Christmas had come early when he thought about spending time in Margot's office. Because of reasons. That had nothing to do with Eric's face. His stupid, beautiful face.

"Just up the stairs. And she was only kidding about the blood oath," Frankie said, rolling her eyes. As soon as Eric relaxed just the tiniest bit, she added, "She'll accept tears."

Eric's mouth dropped open, making Frankie laugh as she turned to Mr. Watts. When she heard Eric move toward the stairs, she called over her shoulder, "Sheriff?"

His boots scraped against the floor as he stopped.

"The dead, they aren't scary. Even if they were scary in life, they're not any particular way in death. Not angry, not sad, not happy. They're nothin' at all. They're not there," she said.

"And yet you talk to them."

She turned and smiled at him. "Just because they're dead is no reason to be rude."

She told herself the little shudder in Eric's shoulders was due to the air-conditioning.

A FEW HOURS later, Frankie walked down the rear hallway, past the gallery of paint-by-number Jesuses, to the office Margot shared with Frankie's daddy. The rigidly structured religious art had given Frankie and her cousins nightmares when they were kids. But as the paintings had been done by their lovely but untalented ancestor Sarah McCready, no one had the heart to throw them out. So the family hid them here in the back hallway, where customers never ventured.

Frankie knew that most people didn't grow up running around a mortuary like it was a playground. The McCreadys had lived in Sackett County since the 1840s, long before the Army Corps of Engineers created the lake by damming the Chattahoochee River at Sackett Point. Her whole extended family lived on what could only be called a compound of cabins on the original family homestead, which happened to be lakefront property now.

The funeral home and bait shop was founded by a pair of McCready brothers, John and Earl Jr., nearly a century before. Earl came home from World War I injured but determined to work to support his bride, Kate. He built a little bait shop on a scenic boat-friendly spot on the river, selling night crawlers, cork bobbers, and Kate's famous sandwiches to fishermen on their drive to the river. John made up for his lack of interest in fishing with carpentry skills, a talent he hoped to turn into a cabinet shop. Then Spanish flu hit and the county's dwindling population needed coffins a lot more than they needed fine sturdy cabinetry.

With all the coffins the town needed, John had to have more space, and Earl let him use the back of his store as a workshop. The bait shop flourished, and the coffin business boomed, because no one had managed to find a cure for death. And when the river was dammed, the lake's edge ended just at the shop's back door, as if the business was always meant to be right on the shore.

The McCreadys added on to the business as they had more children, and soon it didn't seem at all strange for the tourists to launch their fishing boats from the same spot where the locals mourned. Frankie's cousin Duffy and her aunt Donna ran fishing tours out of the dockside bait shop. Her mother's snack stand was the centerpiece of the back docks, feeding eager fishermen her deep-fried masterpieces before sending them out on the water.

While the cozy collection of cabins far down the shore was where the McCreadys lived, the McCready Family Funeral Home and Bait Shop was *home* to Frankie. This was where she contributed to her community. This was where she had a purpose, like a cog in a great big machine, working with her family to do what no one else in town could do.

And if there happened to be readily available deep-fried Oreos at Sarah's Snack Shack, well, every job has its perks.

Margot had taken over a corner of Bob McCready's office, but Frankie's cousin was spending more time on the sales floor lately. As a former big-city event planner, she was much better at dealing with people who were breathing than . . . other McCreadys were. While Bob had a talent for the logistics and paperwork of funeral planning, he somehow managed to blurt out the most unintentionally offensive thing possible when faced with non–family members. So far, the arrangement was working out just fine, though Margot seemed to be filling Bob's swear jars much faster than Bob these days.

And it seemed that her fair cousin was in the office, by the sound of the shrieking. "Tootie, we have talked about this!" was followed by a deep, rumbling bark.

Double dammit.

Frankie jogged down the hallway in time to hear Margot continue. "Tootie, you know I support the work you're doing at the shelter. I helped you *set up* the shelter. But you cannot keep bringing your strays into the funeral home. It's not sanitary! Not to mention, it doesn't exactly present a professional image to have packs of wild dogs roaming the hallways while people are trying to mourn their dead."

"I've read up on this," Tootie said as Frankie poked her head through the door. Small in stature but large in mouth, Tootie McCready stood in the middle of Margot's office with her hands on her hips. Her purple sweat suit set off the snow white of her hair and the gleam of her still-sharp blue eyes. A large German shepherd lay at Tootie's feet, his gaze switching between Tootie and Margot as they spoke.

"If I tell you that this is an emotional support animal, you can't ask me to prove it or you're in violation of federal law. You just have to take my word on it. Or I'll sue you."

"You'll sue *your* family business?"

"This is my emotional support animal." Tootie's eyes narrowed. "Don't mess with me on this, junior."

It had been Tootie who brought Margot back into the McCready fold a few months before, tracking their long-lost cousin down after a very public firing involving flamingos and society matrons. She'd offered Margot a job, a place to live, and a connection to the family Margot had never known. In return, Margot had turned Tootie's penchant for animal hoarding into the county's only no-kill animal shelter. That appeared to be where the bond of familial gratitude ended.

Frankie gently nudged Tootie aside, stepping into the line of fire. "Tootie, stop believing things you read on the Internet. And stop bringin' your animals into the office. She's right. It makes us look like a bunch of yahoos. Margot, dial it back a notch. The vent is open."

Margot grimaced up at the air-conditioning vent in her office ceiling. While the central air provided much-appreciated defense against the Georgia heat, it also served as a funnel for noise from Margot's office to the chapel upstairs.

"The last dog she brought by my office chewed my Jimmy Choos!" Margot protested, eyeing the German shepherd warily.

"Shoes shouldn't have names anyway," Tootie scoffed. "Besides, Hercules here is so well trained, you don't have to worry about your shoes. He used to work at the Atlanta airport as a bomb-sniffing dog."

"Well, good for you, Hercules," Margot deadpanned. Hercules harrumphed lightly.

"Well, he's a cute little guy," Frankie cooed, slowly reaching her hand out for Hercules to sniff. In response, he folded in on himself, flopping his head down on his paws and letting out a sad little *whuff*. "And by that, I mean an extremely manly dog who knows no equal."

"Don't mind him. He's been a little depressed since his handler died," Tootie said, stooping down and scratching behind his ears.

"Poor buddy." Frankie bent to give his head a pat.

Even Margot softened a little bit, but she did not coo.

"Did you just come by to threaten me with frivolous lawsuits or is there a point to this visit, Tootie?" Margot asked.

"Marianne told me I should drop these with you," Tootie told her. "Something about puttin' up the animal shelter as the designated charity for the community Trunk-R-Treat. The county commission has to approve. And since you're now the designated muckety-muck around here, I'm handin' them over to you."

Frankie burst out laughing, bending at the waist and propping her hands on her knees to keep from falling over.

Margot frowned at her. "What?"

Frankie straightened and cleared her throat so she could answer, only to collapse on herself laughing again.

Margot groaned. "Did I step in Lake Sackett politics again?"

The Trunk-R-Treat was a Sackett County tradition. Because the residents' houses were spread so far across the county, the local Baptist church offered use of its parking lot on Halloween night. Volunteers parked their cars in a huge semicircle and filled their trunks with candy, so instead of going from door to door over dangerous, curvy country roads, the kids went from trunk to trunk. It was safer, the kids walked away with buckets of candy, and some of the pushier church ladies wrapped the treats in little strips of paper printed with Bible verses so they didn't feel like they were supporting a pagan festival.

It felt like a win-win, except Sackett Countians being who they were, it was a total pain in the ass to organize. People argued over whether the kids should have to earn their treats by playing carnival games. They argued over what sorts of games the kids should play. They argued over how much of Leslie's chili to prepare for the chili dogs. They argued over which brand of hot dog buns to buy. And then they argued over whether chili dogs were really necessary when all the kids wanted was candy.

The Lake Sackett Elementary PTA was usually designated as the recipient of Trunk-R-Treat's dollar-per-kid cover charge. Sara Lee Bolton had organized the Trunk-R-Treat as part of her duties as the PTA president . . . but after a spot of embezzlement during the Founders' Festival a couple of weeks ago, Sara Lee had other problems to contend with at the moment. So apparently the Trunk-R-Treat had fallen to Margot.

"Just when you thought you were out of the fryin' pan, you get tossed right back in the grease fire." Frankie laughed so hard, she bent over at the waist and had to prop herself up against her knees. Margot made a very rude gesture with her carefully manicured middle finger. Tootie clutched imaginary pearls at her throat and gasped, "In the presence of the paint-by-number Jesuses!"

Frankie jerked her head toward the door. "I don't think it counts. They're out in the hall."

"This is what I get for being a competent event planner," Margot muttered.

"People are still talkin' about how much they enjoyed the Founders' Festival," Tootie told her, patting her shoulder. "Everywhere Stan goes, folks tell him what a good job his girl did puttin' it together. Biggest festival in forty years."

"They mean they enjoyed the money they made," Margot said archly, though her lips quirked into a soft smile.

"Well, that's just the same as enjoying it," Tootie insisted. "The Marcums and the Courseys, they made enough in a week that they were able to catch up with their mortgages. They tossed out their plans to move. People are going to remember that."

"Good. I'll need it when I'm looking for volunteers for the Trunk-R-Treat," Margot muttered, making Tootie grin.

Frankie cleared her throat. "So, um, did Sheriff Linden come by and give you those nonexistent incident reports?"

Now it was Margot's turn to smirk. "Why do you ask?"

Frankie shrugged and tried to look as nonchalant as possible. "Oh, I just wanted to give him some test results for Bobby Wayne's case."

"Test results. On top of the test results you already gave

him a few hours ago," Margot said, doubt *and* smugness coloring her tone. "You're a miracle worker."

Down the hall, Frankie could hear the harsh whisper of an adult over the giggles and thumping footsteps of children. She heard a man say, "Girls, please, there's a funeral going on right now. Be respectful or other people will know I'm raising a pair of adorable hooligans."

Frankie blew out a breath. Saved by the hooligans.

A blur of green tulle and yellow sequins rushed through the door. Hercules chuffed and sat up on his haunches, but made no move toward Kyle Archer's younger daughter, June, as she threw herself around Margot's leg. Kyle and his older daughter, Hazel, appeared in the doorway. Hazel, whose fairer complexion and darker hair favored her late mother, wore a bemused expression that was far too mature for an eight-year-old.

"Margot!" June shrieked, hugging Margot tightly. "I took a spelling test today! And I fed Marco Polo, the class fish. And I drew a picture!"

The little girl flung open a folded poster-size piece of construction paper, on which she'd drawn herself and Charlie, the family's newly adopted dachshund, and an orange pony with a purple tail.

"Well, that sounds like a very full day," Margot said, hesitantly brushing June's thick hair back from her little elfin face. Frankie knew it took considerable internal struggle for Margot not to peel June's grubby hands off her designer suit. Single up until her thirties and the only daughter of a mother who wasn't exactly child-friendly, Margot didn't fall naturally into the role of nurturing the Archer girls. In fact, her near-clinical fear of not being able to nurture them had nearly kept her from a relationship with Kyle in the first place. But she was trying, and for the Archers that mattered a lot.

Frankie was pleased for Margot. She knew how hard it had been for her cousin to go from living in one of the biggest cities in the world with practically no family to living in tiny Lake Sackett surrounded by a biblical legion of relatives. But Frankie suffered a second jealous twinge toward her cousin for the day and felt even worse for it. Margot's "career first, children no-thank-you" stance was something they had in common. Frankie had never thought she'd live long enough to have kids, so marriage and babies and a white picket fence had never fit into her childhood dreams. At first, Frankie'd thought she and Margot could be the last two old maid aunties at the holidays, handing out rock-hard homemade fudge and scaring the kids with their dentures. But now Margot had a ready-made family and Frankie was going to be alone in the rocking chair, flipping her dentures upside down in her mouth as a solo act. She'd been left behind again, and the burn was just a little more bitter than it had been when Marianne married and started her family with Carl the magical redneck unicorn.

Once again, Frankie was the sole McCready chick in the nest, which bothered her a lot less than the "pathetic" factor. The guys she dated weren't very choosy, but they did make slightly judgy faces when she mentioned they couldn't go back to her place because her parents lived there. Not that she brought many of her partners anywhere near her home, because her parents didn't need to know that much about her sex life—or anything about her sex life, at all. Ever.

Even Duffy had managed to get married and move out on his own. He'd moved out to what turned out to be a toxic, awful mess of a marriage to a sociopath, but at least he wasn't sharing a roof with his mom. He'd divorced the sociopath, built his own cabin on the McCready property, and gotten on with his life.

Frankie was twenty-eight years old. She was employed and had a healthy savings account. There was no reason for her to still be sleeping in her childhood bedroom. Honestly, she'd wanted to move into Marianne's old cabin years before, but her parents always got so agitated when she talked about moving—even though she would be only a few doors down. If she wasn't under their roof, they would worry about how she was eating, whether she was sleeping enough, whether she was working too hard. It was like they thought she couldn't get cancer again if they worried enough. So instead of moving out and forcing them to work through their anxieties, she stayed. It was an unhealthy cycle fueled by love and worry, and Frankie didn't really know how to pull out of it.

And none of this internal turmoil mattered to June, who was trying to find a space on Margot's wall for her classroom masterpiece.

"You're going to put it where everybody can see it, right?" June demanded, hopping up and down and making her green tulle square-dancing-style skirt flounce.

"Sure. You and Hazel pick the best place." Margot handed June her tape dispenser. While June threw herself across the room to find a blank wall space among Bob's civil service awards, Hazel slowly sidled up to Margot. Margot offered her fist and the pair of them did some sort of secret handshake that Frankie could barely follow. Margot nodded toward the wall and Hazel joined her sister.

While Hazel was more conservatively dressed in jeans and a T-shirt that read MERMAID HAIR, DON'T CARE, June had paired her John Deere–themed puffy princess skirt with neon purple Keds and a yellow cardigan covered in iridescent sequins.

"That's a very pretty outfit you have there, June. I see you're wearing the shoes we picked out," Frankie said. Kyle narrowed his dark eyes at her. Kyle had almost gotten June through her "eclectic sense of fashion" phase before he and the girls started spending time with the McCreadys. But when June saw Frankie's outfits, she not only continued her mix-and-match approach to dressing, she began demanding "rainbow streaks" in her hair, just like Frankie.

"I will find a way to get you," Kyle murmured, in that New York Yankee accent of his that instantly marked him as different from any other man in Lake Sackett. Frankie suspected the accent was half the draw for Margot. The soulful brown eyes and Ryan Gosling ass probably didn't hurt, though.

Kyle added, "I realize working with small children all day doesn't make me that intimidating, but Margot is way meaner than I could ever dream of being. She'll help me."

"Hey, I think that hurts me. I'm delightful," Margot grumped as Kyle gave her a quick kiss. Frankie noticed that neither of the girls snickered or yelled "Ewwwww" like they might have a few weeks ago.

"It shouldn't. Your terrifying nature is what drew me to you in the first place. I like to live on the edge," Kyle said, slipping an arm around Margot's waist as she rolled her eyes. Kyle nodded toward the German shepherd, who was perfectly still at Tootie's side. "Miss Tootie. New pack member?"

June slapped enough tape on the drawing to secure it to the wall through a direct nuclear blast and turned, noticing the dog for the first time.

"PUPPY!" she cried. In all caps.

Hercules took a step back behind Tootie, clearly conveying the canine version of *NOPE NOPE NOPE*. Kyle caught June around the waist before she could launch herself at the poor dog.

"Honey, we talked about this, remember?" he said, effortlessly shifting her onto his hip for a face-to-face talk. "We don't touch dogs we don't know. Not all dogs are nice like Arlo and Charlie. And they don't know that we're not going to hurt them or scare them, and that makes them nervous and they can bite. So we wait until we're invited, right?"

June nodded, mumbling, "Sorry, Daddy. Sorry, Miss Tootie."

"It's all right. But Hercules is a bit shy yet, honeybun. He's got good trainin', but we need to give him more time to get used to little people," Tootie told her. "But tell me all about Charlie. How's my favorite wiener dog doin'?"

June and Hazel both launched into tales of their latest canine adventures, assuring Tootie that Charlie was the most amazing, intelligent, and brave dog to ever live.

Frankie stepped out of the room, watching from the doorway as her cousin was surrounded and absorbed by Kyle's little family. An odd, fluttering pain squeezed at her chest. Was it loneliness? The desire for a relationship that lasted more than a date or two? Or could it be something else?

The alien sensation sent a ripple of panic through Frankie. Could her heart be out of rhythm? Was it her blood pressure? A tumor pressing into her chest cavity? Frankie swallowed thickly, wondering at the sudden catch in her throat. Her last checkup was three months ago and her doctor had assured her that she was perfectly healthy. For someone who'd spent a good bit of her childhood in a cancer ward, she was in remarkable shape.

Dr. Langdon had suggested that she might want to consider medications to help her cope with these little spikes of anxiety over her health. And the much larger waves of angst that kept her up at night, unable to fall asleep for fear that she might not wake up. She refused the meds in favor of repeatedly reminding herself to stop being such a self-involved worrywart.

Frankie was fine. She'd already lost the health probability lottery once. There was no reason to believe her body would turn on her again. She was an adult, surrounded by people who loved her. She needed to breathe and get over herself.

Frankie felt a strong, warm hand close over her shoulder, and instantly her disquiet eased. Her uncle Stan, whose big brown eyes were a little less hangdog these days, smiled down at her and pressed her into his side. She leaned into the hug and took deep breaths as her heart rate settled.

"Doin' okay, kiddo?" he asked, a wry smile deepening the furrows around his eyes.

Frankie nodded.

The corner of Stan's mouth lifted as he watched his daughter through the office door. Toddler Margot had been the apple of his eye, at least when that eye hadn't been focused on a bottle. And then his ex-wife had decided to move Margot away from Stan's drinking, to no one's surprise. What *had* shocked the McCready clan was Linda's total break from Lake Sackett and anyone who lived there. Even after Stan sobered up, there was no communication between him and his daughter. None of the McCreadys knew what had become of Linda or Margot until a few months ago, when a hilariously bad video from an event Margot had organized went viral and Tootie tracked her down. Stan still looked at her like he was afraid she would evaporate if his eyes strayed away for too long.

"So, what did I do to deserve this spontaneous side hug from my favorite uncle?" Frankie bumped him with her hip, and to her surprise, he responded with a frown. Stan never frowned at her—90 percent of the general population, yes, but not her.

"We need to talk," he said quietly, jerking his head toward the back exit.

Frankie chuckled. "Well, that wasn't at all cryptic."

Stan led her through the parking lot, still muggy despite the autumn cool, to the back bay of the funeral home. The door under the awning, where caskets were loaded into the hearse to be transported to the grave, showed scratches, as if someone had tried to use a screwdriver to force the lock open.

Frankie hissed out an annoyed breath. Previous attempts to break into the funeral home had usually concentrated on the front door and the side entrance. Oddly enough, most people ignored the direct basement entrance to the morgue, assuming it was connected to the marina. But not her nemesis. He knew the layout to the funeral home all too well from years of trying to breach the walls.

Stan grumbled, "They tried the chapel window, too, I guess, before the numb-nuts figured out that stained-glass windows don't open."

Frankie glanced up at the camera mounted on the eave, pointed at the door. The lens was covered with a heavy coating of what looked like black spray paint.

"Sonofabitch!" Frankie drew a long breath through her nose. She was going to have to buy and install another set of security cameras, and most likely route the feed through her computer in the morgue. "I wish I'd seen this before the sheriff left. I could have talked to him about it."

"Sorry, I just noticed it a little bit ago, and then I got wrapped up in transporting Heck Porter," he said. "I checked the security feeds in E.J.J.'s office and all you see is a hand comin' up in the camera view and painting over the lens, then nothing."

Frankie frowned. Despite his advancing age, her uncle E.J.J. was sharp as a tack. "E.J.J. didn't notice that one of the security feeds was completely blacked out?"

"Well, Gray Tolar passed yesterday, and his kids are raisin' seven kinds of hell over whether he would want a full military funeral or a full Masonic funeral. All four of them think they were the favorite and they know 'exactly what Daddy wanted,' so E.J.J.'s distracted by grown-ass adults having tantrums in his office. Plus, when he saw the blacked-out feed, he thought that the camera had broken or something. He's not exactly a techno wizard."

"Aw, I liked Mr. Gray," Frankie murmured. "He had standards. Always kept molasses candy in his pocket, but only gave it to polite kids."

"Well, his standards should have included detailed funeral plans, instead of telling his kids, 'Y'all just do what ya think is best.'"

"E.J.J. will figure it out," Frankie said. "He always does. He is the master at making chicken salad out of chicken shit."

"Language. Your mama hears you talkin' like that, she

blames it on me," he said, looking around furtively, as if Leslie were looming nearby with a parabolic mic.

"Because you're the one who taught me the curse words in the first place."

"That's what your mama says. Also, you owe the swear jar a quarter." He nudged her with his elbow.

"I don't know what you're talkin' about. I'm the picture of ladylike restraint," Frankie said, gently shrugging off his arm and dropping to her knees to pick up a shiny object fluttering in the grass. It was a candy wrapper, ripped right through the fiery red logo for Atomic Mouth-Burners, one of those super-sour candies that combined the caustic quality of high-concentration cinnamon extract with citric acid that could actually dissolve dental enamel. It was thoroughly disgusting and Frankie knew only one kid in town who ate them.

"Lewis," she hissed, crumpling the candy wrapper in her fist.

"Frankie," Stan said, holding his hands up in the same sort of gesture a lion tamer would use to avoid becoming a feline chew toy, "just calm down, now. You're already on edge. You don't have any solid proof that it was the Lewis boy, and you don't want to do anything rash."

"I'm not going to do anything rash," Frankie said, shrugging. "I'm going to go have a very *calm* discussion with the sheriff, just like you suggested."

Stan gestured to the left side of his face. "I'm havin' a real hard time buyin' that, considerin' the way you're clenchin' your jaw. Look, hon, don't get all wound up about this. We've tried handling it on our own for the last few weeks, and now we need to call in the sheriff and tell him what's happening. It's his job to deal with junior jackasses-in-training, not yours."

"I'm taking my lunch break!" Frankie hollered, holding the candy wrapper over her head as she stomped over to the funeral home van.

"Could you at least pretend to listen to what I say before running off half-cocked? Besides, you don't have your purse—" Stan yelled as she raised her other hand to show she'd fished his keychain from his pocket. "When did you take my keys?"

THE SCENIC DRIVE through the hills that surrounded Lake Sackett did little to calm Frankie. Now that autumn had set in and the leaves were starting to fall away, one could see much more of the strangely fern-shaped lake. Damming the Chattahoochee had created a series of irregular inlets with the occasional tiny island of trees breaking up the steely expanse of water. That water was still heavily occupied by sailboats and fishing boats of all sizes, even with the tourist season hurtling toward its end.

Seeing the busy boaters did a *tiny* bit to ease Frankie's grip on the wheel. Busy tourists meant more money in town, being spent at the local shops and restaurants. It meant businesses staying open and families staying in Lake Sackett, something that had been more of a challenge ever since some newb at the Sackett Dam had released enough water to significantly reduce the amount of lake they had to offer. The "water dump," as it was called by locals, had coincided with an unprecedented years-long drought. The lake and the town had started getting pretty shabby, and people didn't want to spend their vacation looking at shabby. Tourists booked their rentals in towns where the water was abundant and the locals seemed less desperate.

Margot had helped turn this nosedive around by planning the best Founders' Festival ever just a few weeks before. The town was already seeing the benefits. They just had to keep pushing through the slower fall season. Distractions like Jared Lewis, and the havoc he tried to wreak at the largest marina in town, could only hurt their efforts.

Frankie couldn't pinpoint the exact moment her war with Jared Lewis started, probably because there was a cascade of moments over the years that had cemented their enmity. Her mama blamed a Halloween costume contest when Jared was eight. Frankie was an honorary judge and gave first prize to another kid, who'd made his own Iron Man costume out of cardboard and duct tape instead of having his mama buy one online. There was another incident when Jared was ten involving her taking his Jet Ski keys from him when he kept trying to tip over a younger boy in a canoe.

But honestly, their mutual dislike probably started when Jared, unlikable even as a small child, demanded that Frankie's late uncle and mortuary mentor, Junior, take him to the morgue during his great-uncle's funeral so Jared could "see a dead body." A then-teenage Frankie caught Jared trying to sneak downstairs to the morgue level. She blocked the door and told him to get his bony butt back to his mama. He tried to shove past her, and she used a pinching technique she'd learned from Marianne to grab him by the scruff of his neck and drag him back to the chapel.

The little shit had tried to kick her in the shins all the way down the hall, which prompted her own parents to make a rare public fuss. Frankie had always bruised easily. Bob McCready had not been pleased to see Jared kicking his girl with his full soccer halfback strength. Then again, Marnette Lewis didn't appreciate Frankie depositing her son in her lap and announcing his bad behavior in front of all of her kin.

The very public interparent skirmish in the chapel had made relations between the McCreadys and the Lewises tense ever since. The fact that Jared's father, Vern Lewis, was the head of the county commission, and technically Frankie's supervisor, didn't exactly ease that tension.

Jared was an annual pain in Frankie's ass. Every October for four years, he'd tried to break into the mortuary using increasingly annoying means, like throwing a brick through the front window of the chapel or distracting Stan with a flamin' bag of dog poo while trying to sneak through the back. But this year, Jared had started his charming shenanigans early. And he'd changed tactics, going after the businesses attached to the marina. He unleashed a plague of bait crickets in the bait shop, emotionally traumatizing one of Duffy's charter clients. He'd replaced the ketchup in the Snack Shack with hot sauce and inflicted gastric chaos on some poor tourist. He'd screwed around with Aunt Donna's fishing equipment, which made Aunt Donna react like, well, Aunt Donna.

The only things that had stopped the series of pranks were installing the security cameras near the back door and Stan sitting vigil on the dock at night. Because nothing is as terrifying as the sound of a McCready shucking a shotgun full of rock salt while shouting threats against your ass cheeks.

Once the cameras went up and the pranks stopped, Stan hadn't felt the need to stand guard every night. But it seemed that Jared had found a way around the cameras and was back to his usual tricks-and-treats. Of course, Frankie didn't have any actual proof that Jared was the one who had done these things. But it had to be him. In all the years the family had been running McCready's, no one else had ever tried to break in. The creep factor of a mortuary had served as its own security system for generations.

It seemed unlikely Jared had a plan for what he would do when he finally got into the funeral home. Frankie had told him that he wasn't welcome there—*gasp*, she'd told him "no"—and that had given the funeral home the appeal of forbidden fruit.

Breathing through her rage enough to safely use the voice commands on her phone, Frankie called the sheriff's department and was informed by Eric's dispatcher/secretary that he'd gone to the Rise and Shine for lunch. Nestled in the "business district" on Main Street, the Rise and Shine was a traditional circa-1963 diner with worn red vinyl booths and a shiny black-and-white tile floor. The mustachioed owner, Ike Grandy, kept Hank Williams Sr. on a continuous loop on the jukebox while he slung hamburgers and waffles at the same families who'd eaten there for decades. No one left Ike's place hungry, even if they couldn't pay for months at a time—a situation that had come up frequently during the tourist-season doldrums.

Frankie parked the van in her regular spot, passing a rather bland red-white-and-blue election sign announcing LINDEN FOR SHERIFF in the Rise and Shine window. Frankie supposed that you didn't spend a lot of money on election advertising when you were the only candidate running.

The diner was packed as usual with the lunch crowd. Ike waved at her with his spatula from the grill as she spotted Eric sitting in a booth in the back, picking at a bowl of chicken and rice soup.

Frankie greeted several people as she wound her way between the tables, most of them lifelong family friends— George Pritchett, Sweet Johnnie Reed, Dobb Cunningham. They smiled, squeezed her hand as she walked by, asked after her parents and E.J.J., passed along messages and little tidbits of news.

Others, though, avoided eye contact, and some even scooted away from her as she passed. She blew a breath through her nose, keeping a slightly less genuine smile plastered on her face. This was the problem with small towns. Everybody had an opinion about how you lived your life and thought they had a God-given right to express that opinion. Frankie had been informed from a very young age that her interest in the more practical aspects of the family business was unseemly and unladylike—by everybody except the people who Frankie actually cared about. Little old church ladies, elementary school teachers, clerks at the gas station—they all felt the need to tell her that nice Southern girls did not spend their time with dead bodies. That was "men's work"—the art of mortuary science lumped together with traditional male activities like changing flat tires, lifting heavy objects, and killing spiders. The fact that Frankie had devoted years of college and additional specialized training to become skilled at this manly task did nothing to convince her fellow Lake Sackett residents that this was not just a creepy teenage phase.

And so some of her neighbors chose to avoid Frankie as if she carried a communicable social disease. Some of the local kids even called her "Dr. Frankenstein," which, Frankie admitted, was an unfortunate but not unexpected result of her parents' choice of name. She tried not to let it bother her. She armored herself in her bright colors and odd pop culture interests, because if she was going to be considered "other" by the people she'd grown up with, she was going to go for broke. She had a family who adored her, a select few neighbors who understood her. She figured that put her ahead of a good number of people in the world.

Borrowing a smile from someone who gave a damn what her neighbors thought, Frankie slid into the booth seat across from Eric and waggled her eyebrows at him.

"No, please, join me," he said, frowning at her. "I insist."

As if by magic, Ike Grandy appeared at her side with a double bacon cheeseburger platter, complete with onion rings and a strawberry shake. "Your usual, Frankie."

"Thanks, Ike," Frankie said, grinning at him as she popped an onion ring in her mouth.

"Finish it all," Ike told her, wagging a stern finger at her. "There's a lot of essential nutrients in that bacon."

"I promise." Frankie winked at him. Ike's mustache swept up at the corners and he ruffled her bright hair.

"Do you call ahead?" Eric asked, watching her repair the damage to her do. "Or does he just keep bacon cheeseburgers waiting for you in reserve, just in case?"

Frankie shrugged. "No, he probably bumped a few orders when he saw me walkin' through the door, because he knows I rarely take a lunch break outside McCready's and he's been tryin' to fatten me up like a Christmas hog since I was a toddler. It's called being part of a community."

"Are you aware that there's an epidemic of diabetes and heart disease affecting our country?" he asked as she swirled a healthy dollop of mayonnaise on the top of her burger.

"Everybody dies," she told him. "I could eat kale and run ten miles every day and still walk out that door and get hit by a semi. I'd much rather go with a belly full of onion rings and my veal-like calf muscles."

Eric shuddered as she tore into the thick burger. "But how can you eat that after dealin' with all that blood and gore?"

"After a while, you don't even think about it," she said,

wiping ketchup from the corner of her mouth. "Look, I give people dignity. I give their families comfort. That's my purpose in life. But not the purpose for me comin' here."

"That was a strange conversational lane switch," he told her, pushing his soup bowl away.

Frankie slapped the foil candy wrapper on the table between them, then took a respectable-for-a-caveman bite out of her burger.

Eric lifted a sandy brow. "Thank you for the garbage on my lunch table?"

"This is evidence. I found this wrapper outside the back entrance of the funeral home. Right under some brand-new gouge marks on the lock. And someone took the time to spray-paint over the lens of our security camera, so all we have is footage of a hand aiming a can at it. And this candy wrapper proves exactly who it was."

"Okay, let's pretend for a second that I believe this random litter you found in your parkin' lot is a smoking gun. In the interest of our workin' relationship, I'll humor you. Who do you think tried to break into the funeral home?"

"Jared Lewis," Frankie spat. "He's been trying to get into the funeral home after hours for years. At this point, I think it's about beatin' me and Stan more than the cool factor of breakin' in. He's in high school, and I have two more years of this crap to look forward to until he goes off to college, flunks out in a tragic 'bought a paper off the Internet' incident, and comes right back to mess with me some more."

"So, your archenemy is a teenager?"

Frankie nodded. "Ours is an epic battle of wills."

"Do you have any proof, beyond the litter, that it's this particular teenager?"

"No, because he's a small-town criminal genius, like a penny-ante Lex Luthor. He's been getting away with this bullshit for years."

"What did Sheriff Rainey do about it?"

"Chalked it up to anonymous but mischievous 'kids.' Never approached Jared or his parents. Never spent any time watching McCready's to catch Jared in the act. Never opened a case file. Hinted that maybe if I were married with children, I would have less time to worry about people breaking into my workplace."

Eric was halfway through a shrug, as if he was considering his predecessor's point. Frankie pointed her finger at him. "I know how to end you and get away with it."

"You don't think it's possible you're blowing this out of proportion?"

"No," she said, dipping an onion ring in ketchup. "And I'll tell you why. One, because if you don't stand up to people like Jared Lewis, no matter how old they are, they learn that they can walk all over you and you won't do anything about it. So they escalate."

"It sounds like it's escalating anyway."

"Oh, hush," she told him. "And two, if you don't stand up to people like Jared Lewis, no matter how old they are, other people *like* Jared Lewis will see that and know that *they* can walk all over you and you won't do anything about it."

"Wait." Eric grimaced. "Jared Lewis . . . why does that name sound familiar?"

Frankie turned as the bells over the diner's front door jangled. She jerked her head toward the woman walking through the entrance. "That's why."

"Are you ever going to say something straightforward?" he asked her.

Frankie took a long draw from her strawberry milkshake, hoping its nostalgically sweet flavor would improve her mood as Marnette Lewis clipped her way across the diner. Marnette was tall and greyhound-thin, with a razor-sharp streaked blond bob and a permanently pinched expression on her face. She approached their table and folded her arms in such a way that her knockoff Coach bag nearly smacked Frankie in the face.

"Sheriff. Frankie, fancy seeing you here." Her voice was honey over ice, cold and sickly, and she was ignoring Eric altogether. Her dark blue eyes stayed entirely focused on Frankie.

Eric nodded and fidgeted with his soup spoon. "Mrs. Lewis."

"Marnette, how are you?" Frankie asked, her expression neutral.

"I'm just fine," she said, smiling without showing any teeth through her thin lips. "I hear your cousin is going to be settin' up the Trunk-R-Treat this year."

"Oh, she's *real* excited about it," Frankie said, smirking around her straw. Eric's eyes seemed to follow an invisible tennis ball between the two women, an expression of uncomfortable dread spreading over his features. "You know, she was just cuttin' her teeth on the Founders' Festival, but now that she's comfortable, I think she's really going to pull out all the stops."

Marnette's face soured, like she'd just swallowed a wasp.

"Yes, little Margot has made quite the impression around here. It must be so nice for her to come home and spend time with her daddy after all those years they missed," Marnette simpered. "It just seems so odd to me that her mama up and moved and never told Stan where they went so he could see his own daughter. Why was that again?"

Frankie's eyes narrowed. It was no secret in Lake Sackett that her uncle Stan once had a drinking problem. But given how long he'd been a sober, productive member of the community, most people were polite enough not to bring it up.

"Oh, it was such a long time ago, no one with any sense cares," Frankie said.

Marnette made a shallow attempt at a smile while she internally regrouped for her next attack. "Well, I hope we're not going to have any *confusion* this Halloween. You will try to keep control of yourself, right? You won't go telling wild stories about burglars and bumps in the night?"

"Oh, bless your heart, Marnette, I'm sure we won't have any *confusion* as long as you supervise your son," Frankie said, smiling sweetly. She nodded toward the candy wrapper on the table. Marnette's eyes landed on it and her face went two shades paler under her makeup. Frankie smirked.

Clearly, Marnette was aware of her son's penchant for tongue-dissolving confectionery.

Marnette spat, "My Jared has never gone near your silly funeral home! Not for years! Ever since the *unpleasantness* at Uncle Murney's service, we bury all of our people with Oakerson's."

Frankie rolled her eyes. Several people were turning in their seats, staring. This had escalated quickly.

"I'm aware that you don't bury your people with us. Thank you for saving us the trouble."

"Just be sure you remember who signs your checks, Frankie. My husband, that's who."

Eric's eyebrows lifted, even as Frankie snorted and sipped her milkshake. "Yes, I will keep that in mind, Marnette. Always a pleasure."

Marnette turned to Eric, all sweetness and light. "Sheriff, are you all settled in?"

Eric cleared his throat. "Um, yes, ma'am."

"Well, we hope you make yourself right at home for as long as you're in office. And that you make friends with the right sort of people," she said, glancing at Frankie. "Might help you hold on to that office a little longer."

Eric's brow furrowed. "Thank you. I'll think on that."

"Say hello to your mama for me." Marnette sneered at Frankie and then flounced away.

"She does not find you to be quirky or delightful," Eric noted.

"Picked up on that, did you? Good for you." Frankie

shoved her burger into her mouth and took a bite that was larger than was advisable.

"Is it because you think her son is a criminal mastermind?" he said, nodding toward the candy wrapper.

Frankie chewed, and around a mouthful of burger she said, "No, it's not that. Well, it's not *just* that."

"It's one of those complicated small-town web things I'm going to need a flowchart to understand, isn't it? Should I get out my notebook?"

Frankie laughed. "Remember Sara Lee Bolton? The lady who was charged with embezzling funds from the PTA?"

"Yeah, um, happened right before I was brought in. She's awaiting trial?"

"Well, Marnette is Sara Lee's cousin, and she's married to the head of the county commission. And he is pissed because Margot, and by extension the McCready family, is getting credit for the Founders' Festival going so well and he is not. Everybody knows it was Margot's planning-ninja skills and magical contact list that made the festival a success after years of it just sucking. Also, Margot is the one who brought Sara Lee's creative bookkeeping out into the open, which sort of compounds the whole 'McCreadys casting the Lewis extended family in a bad light' theme. Add to that, Marnette knows I'm watching her little delinquent son like a hawk, because she has not managed to convince me that he's as innocent as a unicorn's sneeze. So basically, that's three marks against my family in Marnette's eyes.

"Add to that, the Martins—that's Marnette's maiden

name—held the homestead right next door to ours goin' back generations, but they built at a slightly lower elevation, closer to the river. That little difference meant that when the Corps of Engineers dammed the river to make the lake, Martin land was flooded while ours stayed dry. They've been kind of bitter over it ever since. Between keepin' our house and the lake buttin' right up to the bait shop, Marnette's great-grandmother claimed we had the devil's luck or some such nonsense. And after an . . . incident . . . at a service a few years ago, they refuse to have their people buried at McCready's. They go two counties over to Oakerson's for funeral services. Because that'll show us."

"So, what, it's a blood feud?"

"No, no one's died. They're just very frosty to us in public and make it very obvious that they want nothing to do with our business. And insult us at church-related activities."

"All this over their land flooding sixty years ago?"

"They watched their home get washed away while their neighbors just continued living in theirs like nothing ever happened. That's the kind of resentment that builds up. Life in a small town, Sheriff."

"What was that bit about 'who signs your checks'?"

"Oh, as the county manager, Marnette's husband signs my coroner paychecks, just like he signs yours. But it's not much of a paycheck, to be honest with you. It's basically gas-and-pizza money. I don't depend on it like I do my salary from McCready's. Still, Marnette likes to hold it over my head, like she can have me thrown into the streets if she whispers in her husband's ear."

"Well, he can fire you if he wants."

"Yeah, he can try to impeach me if he can prove gross incompetence on my part, which he can't. Also, my daddy sits on the county commission, so Vern would have a hard time gettin' me voted out. Plus there's the small problem of no one else in the county wanting my job or being qualified for it."

"As opposed to my job, which apparently everybody thinks they can do better than I can," Eric grumbled.

"Yeah, but no one here is qualified for your job, either," she said. "Your only competition is Landry Mitchell, and no one is fool enough to put him in charge."

Eric shuddered, clearly horrified by the idea of his only deputy taking over the sheriff's position. Landry was best known for the mishaps he caused for both himself and others, like the time his shoddy porch swing repairs sent his mother to the hospital. Landry was a perfectly nice guy, just not very bright and completely unaware of how underqualified he was for his job.

"So, Jared Lewis. What should I do? Because most of my plans involve elaborate booby traps and YouTube, which I think would be illegal."

Eric reached across the table and wrapped his fingers around her wrist, which was awkward, because she was in the process of dipping another onion ring in ketchup. "You will do nothing. I'll take care of it. You just stay out of trouble, for the sake of both of our jobs."

Frankie leaned back slightly. She realized this was the first time since moving to Lake Sackett that Eric had voluntarily touched her. It was rare that anyone local, much less a man, touched her or told her that they were taking charge. Most people assumed that because of her job, she was suited to unpleasant tasks. Her family had a tendency to take those tasks out of her hands because she was so "fragile." Seeing someone strike a pleasant balance between the two moved her more than she expected. And because she was not ready to feel anything but wary disdain for the good sheriff, she stared pointedly at their joined hands.

Eric glanced down and realized he was millimeters away from a ketchup manicure. He cleared his throat and released her hand, resuming fiddling with his spoon.

"So you believe me? Inadmissable candy evidence aside?"

"Well, I've found that parents generally don't get that aggressive over *false* allegations about their children," he said. "So I'm giving you the benefit of the doubt. I'll come out and take a look around. If I see anything unusual, I'll open an official case file. And if I feel like the situation warrants it, I'll talk to Jared and his parents."

"If, if, if—if a bullfrog had wings, it wouldn't bruise its ass," Frankie told him.

"I think you mean, 'thank you'?"

"Thank you," she repeated, then smiled sweetly as she

picked up her burger. She nodded toward his bowl. "Aren't you going to finish your lunch?"

"I'm not very hungry. I think I'll get back to the office."

Frankie glanced around the crowded diner. "You ashamed to be seen with me?"

Eric followed her eye line. She noticed that several people were watching the pair, some less obvious than others. Frankie rolled her eyes. Before dinnertime, her mama would have people calling her, asking whether the sheriff was courting Leslie's only child. Oh well, she hadn't given her neighbors something to talk about in a while.

Eric cleared his throat. "No, it's just we're not really at a lunch-sharing stage in our relationship."

"We don't have a relationship," she reminded him. "We barely have an acquaintance, despite previous events, which seemed to affect you a lot more than they affected me."

"Hey," he shot back, glaring at her.

"You have to agree it's made our workin' relationship more than a little awkward," she said, shrugging.

"Right."

"So, you ever going to tell me why you moved out here?" she asked. "We get visitors from Atlanta, not full-time transplants."

Eric shook his head. "No."

"Why not?"

"Because it's none of your business."

"If you're wondering, this is why you don't have any friends," she told him.

"A woman took time outta her day to stop into this diner and cuss you out and you think I'm the one who has problems makin' friends?"

"Fair point," she admitted, nodding at his bowl. "Finish your soup."

Eric grumbled, poking at his half-eaten lunch.

"I'll call Ike."

Eric cut his eyes toward the kitchen. Ike pointed two fingers at his eyes and then at their table.

"The friends you do have are scary," he told her.

"Yep."

4

FRANKIE STEERED THE van through the inky blackness
of a moonless Georgia night. She'd meant to drive straight
home after lunch, but she'd been called out on the case of a
fifty-eight-year-old who'd had a heart attack in the middle of
a family reunion. Paul Harner's family had rented a remote
cabin off Copperback Bay for the occasion. Unfortunately, it
was so remote that he passed away before Naomi could arrive
with the ambulance to help.

And unfortunately for Frankie's afternoon, the Harner
family didn't get *less* argumentative after the death of their
beloved patriarch. She'd spent the rest of her day fending off
one brother declaring total control of the situation and an
aunt from insisting she receive the only copies of the official
coroner's paperwork. It seemed that Mr. Harner had quite a
bit to leave to his family, and they wanted their hands on it
as soon as possible. It was behavior Frankie had dealt with
before, but that didn't make it any less exhausting.

Getting Paul out of the rental cabin had taken hours, and then the family tried to follow her into the mortuary, making it take even longer to process him. It was good that she knew the curves of these hills like the back of her hand, because she was this close to nodding off behind the wheel. All she wanted was a shower and a bowl of the Brunswick stew her mama would have waiting for her. And then maybe two or three episodes of *Jessica Jones*. It would take that long for her brain to wind down enough to sleep.

What she did *not* want was to pull the van onto the McCready compound only to find Lana "Divorced out of the Family but Won't Take Her Own Damn Maiden Name Back" McCready's dented purple El Camino parked in front of Duffy's cabin. And as the topper to an already exhausting evening, the she-beast herself was sauntering out to that tacky-ass car, waggling her fingers at Frankie's headlights.

Throwing the van into park, Frankie rolled her eyes and dropped her head onto the steering wheel. She was not prepared to deal with this bullshit. Lana had married Duffy right out of high school, a hasty decision based on a false "pregnancy scare," the timing of which Frankie always considered suspicious. Lana was the only person who had ever made Frankie's mama utter the word *bitch*. Leslie had prayed over it later, but still, she'd meant it.

Leslie's breaking her curse policy had a lot to do with Lana's throwing Duffy aside for his best friends—yes, *friends*, plural—filing divorce papers, then trying to sex-bait him back into a relationship when she realized that neither one of her affair partners planned to marry her.

So far he'd resisted the marriage but not the sex.

Lana climbed behind the wheel of her car and sped off, making sure to gun her engine so the other McCreadys knew she was leaving at one in the morning. Classy.

Frankie slid out of the mortuary van. Duffy ambled toward his front door in bare feet, jeans, and an old Bulldogs T-shirt, drinking from a long-neck beer. Seeing Frankie, he disappeared back into his cabin and emerged with another bottle.

"For heaven's sake, McDuff," she said as he handed her the beer. "Why do you keep doing this to yourself? I will not handle your funeral when whatever alien parasite Lana's harboring bursts out of her chest and eats you."

Duffy lounged back on his porch swing, wearing a strange expression somewhere between sheepish and smug. "Lana was feelin' down because she got passed over for a promotion at the Jet Ski dealership. She just needed someone to talk to."

"Talk." Frankie snorted. "Right. She's a real conversationalist. Talk of the town."

"Who pissed in your Wheaties?"

She took a swig from her beer. "Sorry, it's just been a long day."

Duffy patted the swing seat next to him. "Yeah, Mom told me about the video cameras. Do you really think the Lewis kid's back to his old tricks?"

"Duff, if I knew how to teach him that lesson . . . I would probably be in jail."

"You're going to end up in jail anyway if you keep pokin' at the sheriff the way you do," Duffy told her.

"I'm not pokin' at him. I actually managed to have two conversations with him today without one of us yellin'. I mean, he did lose consciousness, but that wasn't my fault. I'm just tryin' to understand what's goin' on in that man's head. How in the hell did an outsider with his attitude get appointed to a job in Lake Sackett?" she asked, flopping down on the porch swing. "I can't find anything on him on the Internet, other than at one point he worked for the Atlanta PD. He's not on Facebook or Tumblr or Twitter or even Myspace. What kind of person has no digital footprint at all? It's like he's in the witness protection program for cranky law enforcement officials."

Duffy propped his feet up on the porch railing. "Have you asked your dad?"

"He says he can't discuss official county commission business with me and I should stop asking him. He also started locking his commission meetin' materials in his safe at the office, which I find insultin'."

"Maybe the sheriff doesn't have a story. Maybe he just wanted a quieter life at a slower pace with fewer crazy people."

Frankie thought about it for a second. "Nah, that can't be it. Can we stop talking about my professional difficulties and go back to your romantic jackassery?" she asked. "When are you gonna leave Lana in the dust and start datin' someone you might be able to bring home to your mama?"

Duffy snorted. "I can't bring anyone home to my mama. For their own protection."

"I just mean someone you can have a future with that doesn't involve high-test antibiotics."

"You want to have some difficult conversations? Because we can talk about the fact that for the third month running, you have failed to tell your parents that you want to move out of their house."

"Well, it's not my fault that Margot moved into Marianne's cabin before I could tell anybody I wanted to move in!"

"The apprentice apartment at the funeral home is open, now that Stan's moved back to his cabin. Why don't you move in there? It's a bit tight, but you'd have your own space for the first time in your life. Or, hell, move into one of those apartments on Langham Drive. They're always turning over. There's no rule that you have to stay here on the compound. It just makes things easier for everybody."

"I was worried about my parents freaking out over me moving into the cabin *next door.* Do you really think they'd accept me moving all the way into town? Or worse, living at the funeral home, without another soul for miles? What if I pass out? What if I get sick? What if I don't have someone there to remind me to eat a deep-fried grilled cheese every four hours?"

"I accept your point, but not your bitter tone," Duffy said, grimacing.

"I'm sorry, Duff. I know I sound like a spoiled brat, complaining that my parents love me too much and want to spend too much time taking care of me. I love them. I'm proud of them. I like spending time with them. But I think I would like that time even more if there was less of it. I'm just frustrated with the situation and feeling it today in particular. Most damn-near-thirty-year-olds don't have to plot this much just to move out on their own. I hate that I have to approach this like it's some military maneuver. Adults shouldn't feel like they have to ask permission to be adults. Then again, a real adult probably wouldn't ask permission. A real adult would just do it."

"Try not to take it personal, Frankie. You know your parents just worry about you."

"That doesn't make it okay. Their worrying isn't going to keep me healthy. It's not going to keep me safe. What's the plan here? Am I going to be a forty-five-year-old woman whose retired mother still leaves labeled Tupperware meals in the fridge? What's it going to take for them to finally feel like they don't have to watch over me twenty-four/seven?"

"Well, my parents seemed to see me as an adult after I got married."

"Yeah, because only an adult capable of making his own dumb-assed decisions could fuck up his life that bad."

"Easy."

"We both know I'm about as far from getting married as your mama is from winning a Pillsbury Bake-Off. I don't think I'm the marrying type. And I'm not going to drag some innocent bystander into this just because I'm not strong enough to tell my parents I don't want to live with them."

"At this rate, they might try to get you to stay in their house even after you get married," Duffy said. "Make one of those multigenerational-home deals."

Frankie's expression was so horrified, a little bit of beer trickled out the side of her mouth.

"Not helpful." Duffy nodded. "You are in a pickle, Frank."

"Thanks. That's why I came here, for your folksy wisdom."

"Look, your parents will eventually accept that it's time for you to move out. You just have to find the right time to approach them and have a place to move in completely ready. You might even wait until after you've already moved to tell them. They'll be upset, but eventually they'll see that it's for the best."

"Or *you* could tell them for me. They've always liked you."

"Oh, hell no." Duffy drained his bottle, stood up, and opened his screen door. "There isn't enough beer in the world."

"Good night," she called after him.

"Good night!"

Frankie heaved herself off the porch and walked to her family's cabin. She went into the kitchen to ferret out something for a late dinner. As predicted, Mama had left her helping of stew in the microwave, ready to heat, with a little Post-it note that read *Don't forget to eat.*

Frankie rested her forehead against the cool metal of the fridge. "Maybe the apprentice apartment wouldn't be so bad."

WHILE THERE WERE some perks to living with her parents, there were other things Frankie refused to put on the family shopping list. She usually shopped for those items late in the evening, when most people were zoned out in front of the TV or recovering from big family meals.

She pushed her cart full of sugary snacks and "personal items" through the Food Carnival, enjoying the relative quiet of the store. Her mama had these crazy ideas about serving Frankie oatmeal for breakfast in the morning, which was the one thing she made that Frankie hated, so she'd taken to keeping little boxes of cereal in her desk at work.

Standing in front of the display of Cocoa Puffs, Frankie pondered how grown-up she could really be if she was sneaking forbidden cereal into her parents' house to avoid her mother's lovingly prepared meals.

Probably not very.

Frankie knew she would eventually have to move out of her parents' place. She was twenty-eight years old. It was time for her to leave the nest.

Maybe now that Margot seemed likely to move out of Marianne's cabin and in with Kyle's family at some point, Frankie could slip into the vacant spot without making a big deal out of it. Her parents would just wake up and see her van parked in front of Marianne's old place.

That probably wasn't very grown-up, either.

"Is it really takin' you that long to read a cereal box?" a smug voice cracked from behind her. "I thought you went to college."

Frankie whipped her head around to see Jared Lewis standing behind her, his arms crossed over his orange polo shirt. Jared had his mom's weak chin and small dark eyes, which gave him a weaselly appearance. He was short for his age, and thin, eye level with Frankie, though she was wearing flats. He had the collar of his shirt popped so hard he looked like a villain in a ski comedy from the 1980s.

She rarely saw Jared in person if she could help it, and sometimes she wondered if she allowed her mental image of his adolescent awfulness to become exaggerated in his absence. It was nice to be reminded that she wasn't wrong.

Frankie glanced around for Marnette Lewis, but it seemed that Jared had made a solo trip to the grocery store now that he had a driver's license and a shiny new SUV from his parents. Jared was shopping for a giant bag of Atomic Mouth-Burners and two cans of black Krylon paint. She frowned at the contents of his cart, which only made him smirk harder.

He was taunting her with hateful cinnamon candy and spray paint.

"Oh, wait, you didn't go to college, did you, McCready? You went to one of them creepy 'learnin' to cut people up' schools."

Frankie's bright blue eyes narrowed. She had gone to college, but she wasn't about to argue fine points with a jackass-in-training. "Well, I did learn enough grammar to know to avoid phrases like 'one of them schools.' Which is good for me, really. Not all of us can go on lame little crime sprees and have their daddies clean it up."

Jared flushed beneath his acne scars. "You can't talk to me like that. My mama says that you're not allowed to accuse me of things I haven't done."

"Which is convenient, because I haven't accused you of doing anything. I'm just observin' that some people in this life are held accountable for their actions, while others are allowed to destroy property and cause problems for hard-workin' families for no other reason than being entitled little creeps."

"I told you before. I didn't have anything to do with the problems you've been having at your crappy little funeral home. My mama said you're kissing up to the sheriff, trying to get him on your side. But maybe you'd like to do a little more than kissing up, huh?"

Frankie made a noise somewhere between a groan and a growl. "Do you realize how many sentences you start with the words 'my mama'? It's a little unnatural at your age."

Jared continued as if she hadn't spoken, but based on the clench of his jaw, she knew the insinuation had landed. "She saw you trying to flirt with the sheriff, said it was the saddest thing she'd ever seen."

Frankie rolled her eyes. Marnette hadn't seen Frankie

doin' anything close to flirting. Frankie wasn't sure she knew how to overtly flirt. The guys she normally hooked up with were susceptible to overtures as simple as "How 'bout it?"

"You wanna know the saddest thing about you?" he asked, crowding her against the shelf, as much as a boy shaped like a banty rooster could crowd anybody. "You're too much of a freak for anybody in this suck-town to like you, but you're not even smart enough to get out of here. Nobody here wants you around, but you don't get the hint. You're just gonna die alone in that basement of yours with nothing but a bunch of cats and body parts in jars."

Frankie didn't want to admit that the words of a sixteen-year-old imbecile could cut deep, but they did. She was alone; among all of her family, she was the only one who was single except for Uncle Stan, who had been married once upon a time . . . and Duffy and whatever the hell Duffy had going on with Lana. She wasn't like Marianne, who had been brave enough to flee to a faraway college at the first opportunity. Frankie could have moved away years before, but she was scared. She loved Lake Sackett and its people, even if they didn't always love her back. But she also knew that a big part of her sticking close to home was being unsure if she could make it out there in the world on her own. But she wasn't about to admit that in front of Jared Lewis.

Instead, she stared at a spot in the middle of Jared's forehead, as if she could burn it like a laser using only the power of her mind. She did this long enough that he started to squirm under her gaze. And when she smiled, he flinched. She stepped forward and he backed away, suddenly not so interested in crowding her.

"Jared," she said, smiling like butter wouldn't melt in her mouth, "tell your mama I said hi."

ERIC HAD PROMISED back at the diner to stop by the next day to look at the blacked-out security video and camera equipment, but from what Frankie heard, he got delayed by the discovery of an actual moonshine still about a mile from the dam. Finding a still wasn't that big of a deal—the more rural residents of Lake Sackett had made shine for generations. Local law enforcement tended to overlook it as long as they were discreet about it and didn't blow anything up. The problem with this particular still was that, being so close to the dam, it was technically on federal land. Feds didn't find that sort of thing very amusing.

When he finally arrived at McCready's a few days later, he found Frankie sitting on the dock, enjoying the cool autumn afternoon and one of her mother's Turkey Day Rolls—a full Thanksgiving meal in a crispy fried shell.

"I don't want to know, do I?" he said, pointing at the enormous fried ball of holiday goodness.

"Mama's tweaking her breading recipe again. You hungry?"

"No," he said, helping her to her feet. "Don't tell your mama. She'll see it as a challenge."

"So you've had an interesting week, huh?"

"Moonshine stills," he said. "We did not get those in the city."

"Is that why you left the city? Not enough moonshine action?"

Eric didn't answer, so Frankie added, "Well, I don't want to be a narc, but you're gonna want to talk to the Dawsons. Carl's cousins are the only locals dumb enough to build a still on federal land. My cousin-in-law is a magical unicorn exception to his extremely shallow gene pool."

"Thanks, that is . . . very helpful," he said, casting his eyes sideways at her as she led him across the parking lot. "What's your angle?"

"I'm tryin' this new thing where I don't needle you without reason."

"I don't think I like it," he said. "I got used to being the target of your snark. It was like my mornin' coffee, but for the parts of my brain that make sarcasm and spite."

"I'll throw in a snarky insult every once in a while," she promised. She pointed toward the camera mounted over the bay door.

Eric took off his sunglasses and inspected the Krylon-covered lens. "Yep, that's spray-painted, all right."

"How many weeks did you have to spend trainin' for that expert opinion?" she asked. He frowned at her. "See? Your recommended daily allowance of snarky insult."

"Thank you. I can get through my day now." He turned and scanned the parking area. "You know, you're pretty lucky you haven't had more security problems. Remote location like this, open access to the water, multiple entrances . . ."

"Yeah, we kind of inherited it like that. Not much we can do about the setup."

"And people don't find it weird, showing up to fish where other people are goin' to a funeral? Or havin' a funeral when there's boat engines gunnin' outside?" he asked.

"No, my great-grandfather set up the parking lot so the two groups wouldn't cross paths. And it's not so weird, once people get used to it. Everybody tries to stay respectful of each other."

"Must be nice, havin' your whole family around," he said, nodding to the Snack Shack. "Y'all seem to get along pretty well."

"Sometimes it's the greatest thing in the world. Other times I wanna take a run right off that dock."

"I can see that, too. I never had much family to speak of, but I guess it can be a 'careful what you wish for' sort of thing."

"Right. Off. The. Dock," she said again.

He laughed, flashing her a million-watt smile she'd never seen before. She swore her knees turned to pudding. Just *whoosh*, right out from under her. If not for the thunderous rumble of a pack of dogs scrambling across the gravel, she might have death-dropped *RuPaul's Drag Race* style.

"What the hell?" Eric said, stepping between Frankie

and the pack. As usual, Tootie's entrance was heralded by her ever-changing rotation of stray dogs. Lulu, a sable pit bull wearing a pink tutu, led the pack, barking sharply at a tubby bulldog who attempted to usurp her front position. An older Dalmatian with a spade-shaped ear scrambled to keep up with two fluffy mutts of indeterminate breeding. Frankie couldn't make out the others because they were moving too damn fast. Since Tootie had opened her dog shelter, the pack had shrunk to the county-enforced eleven dogs. They sniffed and herded and chewed the shoes of anyone else who crossed their paths, but Tootie was the unquestioned alpha.

"That's just Tootie's entourage," Frankie told him as the lady herself walked around the corner of the office building.

"What are you two up to out here?" Tootie called.

"Hey, Miss Tootie," Eric yelled back. "I'm just checkin' out your camera situation."

The largest dog in the pack, the handsome but depressive German shepherd, Hercules, had perked up the moment he saw Eric. He trotted right up to Eric and barked sharply, then sat on his haunches. And if dogs could have expectant expressions, he would have had it in spades.

Eric took a step back. The dog took a step forward and sat on his haunches, then barked again. Tootie watched, her head tilted at an intrigued angle.

"Um." Eric looked to Tootie. "What is happening here?"

Tootie cocked her head and considered for a long moment. "Hercules is a retired airport security dog. His handler died and a friend of mine at one of the bigger city shelters sent him out here because he wasn't coping well in crowded quarters. To be honest, he's not coping too well in my quarters, either. He does not like sharing me with this many dogs, real anxious and fretful. This is the calmest he's been since he got here."

Eric took another step back and the dog stood and followed, stopping again and sitting as if awaiting orders. "This is gettin' sort of upsetting."

Tootie chewed her lip, considering. "He's probably reactin' to your uniform. His handler must have worn something similar."

"Aw, poor thing." Frankie clucked her tongue sympathetically, but she knew better than to pet one of Tootie's dogs when he was having a "moment."

"Have you ever had a dog, young fella?" Tootie asked.

"When I was a kid," Eric said. "But I've never had the time as an adult. I've always worked a lot."

Tootie pulled a tennis ball out of her enormous shoulder bag. Because of course she had both an enormous old-lady shoulder bag and an "in case of emergency" tennis ball.

"Throw this for him," Tootie commanded.

When Eric hesitated, Frankie told him, "You should just go ahead before she gets forceful."

Frowning, Eric tossed the ball across the parking lot. Herc took off after it like a lightning bolt, catching it midbounce and bounding back to Eric to drop it at his feet. When Eric didn't pick it up for another throw, Hercules whined and pushed the ball with his paws.

"Herc was only allowed to fetch for his handler. That's how they train the dogs, so they're completely dependent on the handlers for food, approval, play. And once they're trained, they only get to play when they find drugs or explosives or whatever they're being trained to find. It seems that Herc here has picked you as his handler. Nate and Aiden tried throwin' the ball for him for hours and he wouldn't budge."

"What does that mean?" he asked. "I don't know how to be a handler. The K-9 unit at the department *hated* me. Growled at me every time he saw me. Hell, he peed on my leg while I was standing at attention at a memorial service."

"But that was one dog, not all dogs. *This* dog clearly likes you. How would you feel about taking Herc home with you?" Tootie asked.

Eric shook his head, taking another step back. Herc followed again. "Not great. I still work a lot. I wouldn't be able to walk him or play with him the way he needs. I couldn't take him to work with me or anything."

"Well, Herc is pretty self-sufficient. Do you have a fenced-in yard?"

"Yes."

"Are you allergic to dogs?"

"No," he said, sounding resigned.

"Are you emotionally attached to your couch?"

"What?"

Tootie tried to pull her best "innocent old lady" face. "Nothing."

"Look, I really don't think this is a good idea."

"What if you just take him home on a temporary basis?" Tootie suggested. "Until I can find a forever home for Herc. Think of it as a foster situation."

"I . . ." Eric was still shaking his head when Herc put his wet nose in his hand. The dog looked up at the sheriff with his shiny wet brown eyes. Eric's rigid face softened ever so slightly.

"But Frankie says that you're really particular about the families who take your dogs home," he protested weakly.

"Well, if Frankie is fond of you, that's enough for me."

"I'm not all that fond of him," Frankie said. "I just learned to sort of tolerate him a little bit ago."

"I'll bring the paperwork by the sheriff's department for you to sign. Marianne says we have to keep things official for the county. Come on, dogs!" Tootie whistled as she walked away, and the pack followed in a gamboling swarm of fur and slobber.

Eric looked at Herc and then at Frankie. "What just happened?"

"I can't believe Aunt Tootie gave you one of her pack!"

"Yeah, it was a shock to both of us, I think."

"Doesn't he seem kind of young to be a 'retired' working dog?" she asked.

"Not really. Some K-9 units have a pretty limited window to work because they burn out fast. Also, Herc's handler died, and it can be difficult for a dog to switch handlers. Given the amount of money they spend training dogs, I imagine the airport's police department tried every solution to help him work before putting him out to pasture."

"That's sad."

"It is," he said. "I kind of understand how he feels, going from the prime of your work life to being sent to a strange place full of weird people."

Frankie snickered. Eric bent to scratch behind Herc's ears. The dog leaned into the scratch and rubbed his face against Eric's leg. Frankie smirked. Herc would have his own embroidered dog bed in Eric's bedroom by the end of the month, or she would dye her hair back to its natural brown.

E.J.J. REFUSED TO have birthday candles on his cake after an "incident" in which the sheer number of tiny flames turned one of Tootie's favorite tablecloths into a sputtering inferno. So, for the past ten years, his birthday had been cake-free, but consistently involved chicken and dumplings, simmered all day in an ancient boulder-size iron pot in a stone pit near the shore. Because one source of meat for any meal was never enough, Bob and Stan spent most of the day using a cabinet smoker to roast a pork shoulder. E.J.J.'s birthday dinner was one of Frankie's favorite days of the year, the perfect time for all-day outdoor cooking. Cool, mostly bug-free, with enough breeze to carry the smoke across the water. While she was Southern to the bone, Frankie would take the charms of autumn over bone-softening heat and humidity any day.

The only drawback was that Tootie and Leslie insisted that the family *had* to have cornbread with their chicken and dumplin's, which only continued the never-ending debate between her mother and her great-aunt about whether it was permissible to put sugar in cornbread. Honestly, as much as Frankie loved Tootie and her mama, she was considering stealing the cornbread skillets in both their kitchens and blaming it on a Sasquatch.

Standing at the kitchen counter, Frankie arranged the pulled pork artfully on a platter with potatoes that had been wrapped in foil and roasted in the stone pit. It was going to be difficult to find room for her platter on the family's enormous picnic table between all the dishes and the little decorative pumpkins Margot had arranged. McCreadys tended to go a little overboard on . . . well, food, really.

Her only regret was the lack of peach pie. (Because Mc-Creadys never had just one form of dessert.) It was way past peach season, and Leslie refused to bake with anything less than fresh, peak-season peaches. Leslie McCready had standards, so Frankie had to make do with pecan pie. It was still phenomenal, of course, but not as good as peach.

"Hey there, doodle bug." Bob gave her a kiss on the temple and managed to snatch a bite of pork without losing a finger.

She gave her dad a mock glare. She knew it was a little weird to think of one's father as handsome, but Bob Mc-Cready had a matinee idol's jawline and the forget-me-not eyes Frankie had inherited. He and her petite strawberry-blond mother made a downright adorable couple.

"So you and the sheriff seem to be spendin' a lot of time talkin'," he said, attempting—and failing—to sound casual.

"Yes, because our jobs tend to smack us together like two marbles in a Tilt-a-Whirl, despite my trying to keep him at arm's length," she said. "I also spent a lot of time with the guy who installed new security cameras around the McCready's property this week. You think I should date him, too?"

"I don't think you should date anyone," he said with a shrug. "I mean that literally. You should only date people who deserve you, and no one deserves you. I don't know how Junior managed giving his baby up to some boy. I like Carl and all, but if I saw somebody pawing at you the way Carl puts his hands on Marianne, I'd have to shoot him."

"You mean the appropriate way that Carl expresses physical affection for his wife, letting her know that he still loves her after all these years and serving as a good role model for their sons?"

"Yeah," Bob said, shuddering. "It's awful."

Frankie pursed her lips. This was why she needed her getaway weekends in Atlanta, and why her parents could never ever find out about them. Or the travel brochures for Peru and Iceland and Australia she'd been hoarding since she was a teenager. Or the tattoo of a phoenix on her hip. Or the other tattoos of flaming feathers over her ribs—one for every chemo treatment she'd received as a child.

Hiding the tattoos was particularly important.

"Anyway, back to the sheriff. I'm just sayin', he seems like a nice boy."

Frankie made a disinterested noise. "Not even sure the sheriff likes me that much."

"Oh, honey, everybody likes you. What's not to like?" Bob asked with a grin.

"Do you ever think that sometimes you two overestimate my charms?"

"Not possible. Who would put such an idea in your head?" he exclaimed. "Duffy?"

"No, Daddy, it wasn't Duffy. Trust me, my self-esteem is perfectly intact."

"Well, you haven't really dated anyone from around here for a while."

"Because *men* my age in Lake Sackett think that I'm creepy and off-puttin', Daddy."

Bob chuckled, but his eyes were a bit sad as he ruffled her hair. "Whatever you say, honey."

Frankie found space by edging aside the glitter-covered swear jar Tootie had placed in the middle of the table as a precaution. Family dinners were rife with opportunities to add to the quarter stash, and Tootie had been looking for alternative means of extra income to fund her planned cruise to Aruba with E.J.J. Her weekly poker games had slowed down considerably since Lucille Bodine broke her hip.

Frankie stretched her arms, enjoying the sensation of her soft Xavier's School for Gifted Youngsters sweater against her skin. She needed a bit of comfort. She hadn't slept well the night before, tossing and turning with worry over a mild twinge in her side she'd felt most of the day. Even though she knew in her head that it was likely just a muscle she'd pulled when helping Stan unload Paul Harner from the hearse, the throb of it was more worrisome than painful. She glanced over at her parents, straightening her shoulders. She couldn't let on how tired she was or why she hadn't slept. Her mom and dad would worry themselves sick over it, and that wouldn't do anyone any good.

It was pretty easy to fake well-rested cheer when her family was making a Hallmark movie come to life before her very eyes. With the table set and the sun setting, her relatives began filtering out of their cabins to take their seats, the very picture of familial harmony. Marianne's boys, Nate and Aiden, were occupied with chasing Kyle's daughters around the yard. As the fun uncle with the most energy, Duffy was trying to herd the lot of them toward the table with the promise of pie. Tootie's pack lounged on her porch, eyeing the food with hopeful gleams in their little doggy eyes. McCreadys were bullheaded and unruly, and Lord knew they were odd, but at times like this, Frankie was grateful as hell to be one.

Kyle wrangled June and Hazel into their seats while Margot fixed the girls' plates. Frankie noted that Margot not only put an appropriate balance of proteins and vegetables on the plates, but remembered that June preferred broken crackers on her chicken and dumplings (and everything else) while Hazel considered foods touching to be a threat to democracy and kittens and all things decent. Both girls thanked Margot sweetly when she put the plates in front of them at the "kids' end" of the table, but only June offered her a kiss on the cheek for her efforts. Hazel, as the older child and the only one who remembered their late mother, was a little slower to accept Margot's place in their lives. Still, it was progress from Margot's child-related reticence that'd had her questioning whether she could even have a relationship with Kyle.

Frankie was envious of Margot's bravery, in making her life in a place so different from everything she knew and risking rejection from the family, who were basically strangers. Frankie admired her willingness to open her heart to children, even though Margot had barely considered herself qualified to take care of her adopted dog, Arlo. But she did not admire Margot's look on this particular evening, because . . . yikes. Margot did not look as put-together as she normally did, and not just because she was dressed in a comfy sweater instead of her usual business suits. Dark circles bracketed her wide hazel eyes. Her golden hair was slicked back in a ponytail and there wasn't a lick of makeup on her face. Not even tinted ChapStick.

"You look exhausted," Marianne told her, sliding the German chocolate cake out of Nate's reach without even looking. Carl distracted their rambunctious youngest child by making a smiley face on his chili in shredded cheese. "You feelin' okay?"

Margot slumped slightly against the table and pointed a fork full of chicken at her cousin. "I blame you."

"Me?" Marianne scowled. "What did I do?"

"You were the one who duped me into the Founders' Festival with your adorable children and their big eyes and precocious sense of civic duty. And of course, I did an amazing job because I'm incredibly good at what I do. And now I'm in charge of the Trunk-R-Treat, and planning the Trunk-R-Treat is like some sort of psychological torture designed for one of those really awful prisons for political dissidents."

"It can't be that much harder to plan than a big festival," Duffy protested.

"Yeah, it can, and you know why? Because there are Lake Sackett moms involved," Kyle said, scrubbing a hand over his sandy beard. When Marianne squawked in protest, Kyle added, "You know I respect and admire you, Marianne, but you're all crazy."

Marianne pursed her lips together for a moment while she considered. "Fine. So what are the moms giving you trouble over?"

"They want to have a series of meetings about which costumes should and shouldn't be allowed."

"Which costumes do they not want allowed?"

Margot ticked off her list with her fingers. "Anything involving witches, demons, or the devil. No 'deliberately scary' costumes. Nothing violent or bloody, so no ghosts or vampires or zombies. You can be a princess, but your belly button must be covered. You can be a pirate or a ninja, but you can't carry a sword or weapons of any kind. Then again, if Karen Coleson gets her way, ninjas will be out, too, because *she* doesn't want any costumes involving ethnicity or homelessness."

"Homelessness?"

"She finds the whole hobo thing to be offensive."

Frankie jerked her shoulders. "Well, it is, a little."

Marianne asked, "So basically, the kids will be able to be dinosaurs and butterflies and that's it?"

"Not meat-eating dinosaurs," Margot muttered. "But of course, there's another group of moms who think this whole thing is silly and the kids should be allowed to wear whatever violent and culturally offensive getup they want. And after we settle the issue of costumes, we have the debate over appropriate treats and whether peanut allergies actually exist. If I get through this damn festival without getting arrested, I'm buying myself a bottle of Cristal and hiding in my cabin for a week."

"Jar!" Tootie crowed, rattling the glittery container at Margot.

"I barely cursed!" Margot exclaimed.

"But it was in front of the babies. So it counts," Tootie insisted as Margot dug a quarter out of her pocket.

"You're reaching," Margot told her.

"That couples' massage in Aruba won't pay for itself," Duffy told her. Margot shuddered.

"I'm sorry the Trunk-R-Treat is spiraling into, well, what community events always spiral into in Lake Sackett, but in the long run, it will be worth it, because it will make the kids happy. And those kids are awesome." Marianne nodded toward the end of the table.

"They are. I never thought I would be the sort of person

who looked at a child and thought, 'I want to kiss her face off,' but I totally do," Margot said as June shoved overbuttered cornbread into her mouth. "But don't tell them that, because then they'll know they have all the power and I'm toast."

"One of us . . ." Marianne intoned.

"Don't go crazy. I said I liked Kyle's children. Not all children."

"Still progress," Frankie insisted.

"I'm sorry that I sucked you into our community by forcing you to organize public celebrations. Even though you're really, really good at it," Marianne said.

"Don't guilt me and try to prop up my self-esteem at the same time," Margot said, though there was a hint of a smile quirking her lips. "But, according to my informal poll, the town already has a steady stream of hotel and rental bookings since the festival. And now that there's a concerted effort to advertise fall activities and events around here, it's going pretty well.

"So, enough about me. Frankie, how are things going with the highly attractive and yet astonishingly single sheriff?"

Frankie shrugged. "Fine."

Marianne smirked. "Just fine? That's all you're going to say?"

"There's nothing going on with me and the sheriff," Frankie said. "We're on friendly terms, which is nice. But that's it."

"Friendly terms? Is that what they're calling it now?" Marianne asked her.

"Look, Eric is a tolerable enough guy, and there's no denyin' he's good-looking, but I know almost nothing about him. And not because I haven't asked, but because he won't tell me."

Marianne made a noise suspiciously close to "Hmph."

"What do you mean, 'hmph'?" Frankie asked.

"It's just that 'knowin' almost nothing about' someone has never stopped you from seein' the guys you've—"

"Let's call it 'casually dated,'" Frankie told her, glancing at her parents. She was grateful that they were distracted by the kids' Viking-style table manners. While it was refreshing to talk to people who knew about her . . . extracurricular activities, Bob and Leslie didn't need to overhear details.

"Okay. You've never really cared about knowin' any of the men you've 'casually dated.'"

"Exactly. And I'm not dating or anything resemblin' dating Eric Linden."

"Right, because there's clearly no attraction there at all," Marianne said, her tone arch.

Frankie picked at her chili and made a raspberry noise.

"There is a distinct eye-sex vibe," Margot agreed.

"There is no eye sex!" Frankie insisted.

"Who's havin' sex with people's eyes?" Bob asked from the opposite end of the table. "Honey, have you been reading those crazy forensics journals again? I told you they'll give you nightmares."

Margot, Marianne, and Frankie froze while Duffy laughed into his plate.

Frankie pressed her lips together. "Yes, Daddy, I have been reading disturbing articles in forensics journals."

"You're lucky there's no lie jar," Marianne whispered.

THE TILT-A-WHIRL SPUN and she ended up smacking into Eric again.

Frankie yawned and leaned her head against the cool glass of his police vehicle. Eric had called her and Stan out of bed at 4 a.m. when a Jeep carrying a couple of tourists veered off the highway just across the county line and into a ditch, killing the driver. For once, Eric didn't suspect foul play, but he did need Frankie to declare the driver dead and sign off on the death certificate. Uncle Stan had transported the body back to McCready's, but Frankie had stayed at the scene to take some samples and pictures.

Frankie was rather proud that she and Eric had finally managed to get through a death scene without an argument. In fact, the whole process had been smooth as glass, right up until the moment when Herc the German shepherd started barking from the back of Eric's SUV.

"You brought your dog?" she'd said. "To an accident scene?"

"I wasn't payin' attention when I was stumblin' out of the house, half-asleep," Eric had said with a shrug. "He keeps jumpin' into my truck when I leave in the morning. I guess he rode in to work with his handler. He got past me when I was leavin' and jumped through the window. Nothing would get him out. I even Googled 'Get out of my truck' in German, in case there was some sort of training command for it. And he ignored me, other than giving me the shiniest, most pathetic puppy eyes I've ever seen. I figured it was better to bring him with me than to be late."

Once Herc had received some reassuring pats, he'd stayed quiet for the hour or so Frankie and Eric needed to document the scene. Now he was riding semi-shotgun, propping his paws on the console between them as the good sheriff gave her a ride home. While the canine former officer was generally aloof, he seemed to especially resent that Frankie had taken his seat, given the way he leaned all his weight against her. Every few miles, Herc would nuzzle Eric's arm and receive a scratch behind the ears.

"So you two seem to be gettin' along pretty well," Frankie noted.

The corner of Eric's mouth lifted. "Herc's a pretty low-key roommate. He doesn't chew or pee on things. He doesn't drink my beer. He doesn't try to control the TV."

"I had a college roommate who wouldn't stop doing any of those things," Frankie said to Herc, reaching out slowly so he could sniff her hand. "You are a very good dog."

Herc lolled his head onto Eric's shoulder and gave a repeat performance of the puppy eyes.

"You, you don't play fair," Eric said, pulling a dog biscuit out of his pocket. Herc snapped it up.

"Is there a reason you couldn't bring him in to work?"

Frankie asked, scratching the thick fur at Herc's neck. Herc leaned into the scratching but did not make eye contact, which she supposed was the doggy version of aloofness.

"Yeah, most of them having to do with liability insurance. He's not a police dog. The work is too different from airport security," he said. "It wouldn't be safe for him or the people he would interact with. Besides, he's worked long enough. He deserves a rest. He deserves to be a pet."

"That's sweet of you," Frankie told him. "To look out for him that way."

"Well, don't tell anybody."

"Not even Tootie?" Frankie asked. "She'd be real happy to know that the 'temporary' foster care thing is going to be permanent."

He arched his brows. "You assume a lot."

Frankie snorted as they turned onto the highway near the McCready compound. "You're never going to give this dog up, you giant man-shaped marshmallow."

Eric was about to deliver a no-doubt-scathing retort when he suddenly jammed his foot down on the brake.

Frankie shot him a severe look as the car shuddered to a halt. "What in the hell, Linden?"

"There!" Eric pointed a few feet down the highway, to where a little boy of two or three was toddling down the other side of the road in a red T-shirt and a pull-up diaper. Hercules sat up, ears perked, and started barking.

Slipping the truck into park, Eric jumped out, glancing back and forth for traffic as he ran across the road. He scooped the boy up into his arms. The toddler let out an alarmed squawk and struggled to get out of Eric's hold.

Frankie climbed out of her seat, opening the hatchback of the SUV and searching through her kit for first aid supplies. Herc huffed and leaped out of the truck. He followed Eric to the backseat, where Eric set the squirming boy on the upholstery.

Frankie looked the toddler over. He was a chubby little thing, a towhead with big brown eyes and a streak of some gummy red substance on one of his rounded cheeks. His bare legs were covered in bug bites and grass clippings, but his pull-up was dry and his Lightning McQueen shirt was relatively clean. He had to be at least three, but he'd yet to speak, other than fussing at Eric for picking him up. He eyed both of the strange adults warily.

"What is he doing out here alone?" Frankie asked as Eric opened a bottle of water and offered it to the boy. The toddler grabbed it and gulped it greedily, spilling a good part of it down his front. Frankie took a peanut-free granola bar from her kit and offered it to him.

"What's your name, sweetie?" Frankie asked.

The boy ducked his head against the truck seat. Eric frowned at her. "You don't know him? I thought you knew everybody."

"I've never seen him before, which in itself is weird. Unless he's a tourist's kid?" She didn't want to give voice to the even less preferable options roiling around in her head— abduction, incapacitated parents, or abandonment. Lake

Sackett was generally immune to bigger problems like those, but it couldn't stay insulated forever. Suddenly, she was glad it was Eric Linden by her side, handling this situation, and not Sheriff Rainey. It was possible Sheriff Rainey wouldn't have spotted the boy because he was playing with his radio, and would have driven right past him.

"Hey, buddy, can you tell me where you live?" Eric asked gently as the boy shook his head, grinding his face into the upholstery. "Can you tell me your name?"

The boy didn't answer. Herc whimpered and propped his feet on the lip of the door, nudging at the boy's bare leg with his nose. The boy jerked at the cold, wet contact. He stared at Herc for a long time, tiny eyebrows furrowed, and he reached out slowly.

"Wha's dis doggy's name?" he asked, not quite touching Herc's head.

Frankie wasn't sure why a simple question in that reedy voice was enough to bring tears to her eyes. But the fact that the boy was able to speak, that he was whole enough to ask about a dog, flooded her with relief.

"This is Herc. It's short for Hercules. He's a police dog, sort of," Eric said.

"Herca-lees, like the cartoon?" the boy asked.

"Yep, Hercules like the cartoon. Because Herc is so smart and strong. You want to pet him?"

Eric quietly gave the command for "still" and Herc was practically a statue. The boy ran his stubby fingers between Herc's ears, patting him gently. Herc looked to Eric, as if asking permission to touch the tiny human. Eric nodded ever so slightly and Herc pressed his head into the child's hand. The boy's tiny body seemed to relax and turned away from the seat.

"See? Hercules is a nice dog. He's my friend. He's big and brave, just like you. Can you be even braver for me and tell me your name?" Eric asked, in a tone so patient, Frankie could have mistaken him for a kindergarten teacher. What was worse, she couldn't think of anything to say to the boy after her rejected granola gambit. All she could do was uncap some gentle disinfectant for the boy's bug bites and dab at them while he was distracted.

"I'm Chase."

Eric nodded and smiled. "Do you know your last name?"

Chase shook his head.

"Do you know where you live?" Eric asked.

"'Tlanta," Chase said, grunting and shooting Frankie a nasty look when she cleaned a deeper scrape on his leg.

Eric stepped in front of Frankie and her evil bottle of antiseptic. His voice was bright and encouraging. "You live in Atlanta? That's awesome! Do you like it there?"

Chase nodded.

"How did you get all the way out here?"

Chase said solemnly, "Seein' Aunt Weeda."

"Weeda?" Eric turned to Frankie, who pursed her lips.

"Mommy's aunt. She's loud."

"Weeda. Weeda. Maybe he means Rita? Rita Carstairs?" Frankie looked to Chase. "Does that sound right? Rita Carstairs?"

Chase jerked his little shoulders. Frankie took out her phone and found Rita's Facebook profile. Shuddering, she scanned through several highly inappropriate bar photos before landing on a damn-near respectable selfie of Rita's face. She showed Chase her phone. He nodded vehemently and jabbed his grubby finger at the screen. "Aunt Weeda."

Frankie grinned. "Rita's place is over on Pecan Road. It's about half a mile that way."

"Got it. If you have her number, call it. If not, message her over Facebook." Eric buckled Chase into his car as best he could without a booster seat. Herc jumped in the backseat and put his head on Chase's leg. Chase patted the dog's head and began jabbering about something called *PAW Patrol*. Frankie reached over the seat, shrugging out of her coroner's jacket and tucking it around Chase's bare legs.

Frankie had assumed for years that her biological clock had never ticked. She liked Marianne's boys just fine, but she didn't look at Nate and Aiden as babies and think, *I need my own*. The moment they cried, she happily handed them right back to their parents and walked away to her diaper-free safe space. But now, with this poor sweet kid who had been lost and scared and probably just wanted his mama? She got it. She wanted to cuddle Chase close to her side and thought fighting bears made of lava would not be a step too far to keep him safe.

She blamed this shift in maternal instinct on Eric. Clearly his presence had scrambled her brain, and not in a fun, recreational way.

Frankie was reluctant to take her eyes off the baby, even

to dial Rita's home number. When she did, she got a busy signal. She'd never been so glad to see Rita's little cabin. So many things could have turned out differently in this scenario. What if she and Eric had taken a different route to her place? What if they'd been twenty minutes later or earlier? Chase could have been hit by a car. He could have fallen into a creek and drowned. He could have died of dehydration or exposure. He could have been hurt by an animal. She could have ended up with this boy on her table by the end of the day. She shuddered. She hated juvenile cases. She closed her eyes and gave thanks that she'd been spared that task.

They pulled into Rita Carstairs's driveway just in time to see a woman in pajama pants and sneakers scrambling like mad to open her car door as she struggled into a hoodie.

"Heads up," Frankie said quietly, putting her hand on Chase's leg.

"I see it," Eric murmured, slowing the SUV.

The younger woman turned to see the police car and her face crumpled, as if she was expecting the worst possible news. But the moment she spotted Chase in the window, she dropped her purse, shrieked, and ran at them. Frankie could see the tear streaks on the woman's cheeks from across the yard.

"Chase!" the woman screamed, slapping her hands against the back window before Eric could put the truck in park. Herc barked sharply, placing himself between the newcomer and Chase, as if he was warning her that he didn't quite trust her with his new human.

"Down, Herc," Eric said firmly.

Herc whuffed, but he settled down when Chase grabbed at the woman, happily shouting, "Mamamamamamama."

The woman was caught between giving the toddler kisses all over his face and checking him over for injuries. She unbuckled him and cradled him against her side. "Baby, oh, honey. Oh my God. Are you okay? What happened?"

Chase buried his face in his mother's neck and shook his head. She looked up at Frankie and Eric, eyes glassy. "Where did you find him? I just woke up a minute ago and he was gone!"

"What's your name, ma'am?" Eric asked.

"I'm Jenna Wollmack. I'm Chase's mom."

"Can I see some ID?"

Jenna nodded and retrieved her purse from Rita's lawn. Eric checked it against some scary police database for outstanding warrants and criminal history. Rita Carstairs came outside, bottle-blond hair askew, wearing sleep shorts and a Lynyrd Skynyrd T-shirt. An unlit cigarette dangled from her lips and she seemed absolutely unperturbed at the sight of a police car in her driveway at dawn. "Hey, Frankie. How's your mama?"

"Hey, Rita. Just fine, thanks."

Now that his mother had been located, Chase was way more interested in getting on the ground and playing with Herc. Eric slid out of his truck and gave Jenna her license back. "Ms. Wollmack, we found your son about half a mile from here, on the side of the highway, by himself."

Frankie was sure Eric didn't *mean* for the judgmental tone to taint his voice, but it hung there in the air, letting the woman know that her parenting skills were being scrutinized.

Jenna's eyes welled up with hot, shimmery tears. "Oh my God, honey, I'm so sorry."

"You're very lucky this didn't turn out some other way. You're very lucky we were the ones who found him," Eric said, the judgmental tone now in full force. Apparently he *did* mean for it to taint his voice.

"Do you know how he managed to get out of the house?" Frankie asked gently, shaking her head just the tiniest bit at her "partner."

Jenna wiped at her cheeks, balancing Chase's fidgeting form on her hip. "His preschool just had Fire Safety Week and they made sure the kids know how to work the locks on the doors to get out if they need to. We still have the child-proof lock at the top of our door at home, but my aunt Rita doesn't. I just didn't think he'd try it. His daddy's at home while we're here visitin', and I didn't think he'd try to go out without Daddy. He talked about going to see the goats at the Morrows' farm down the road before bed last night. Maybe that's where he was going?"

Chase's head popped up from his mother's throat and he nodded emphatically. "Like the goats. They run their heads into each other," he said. "Make a *big* noise."

"But you *have to wait* until Mommy goes with you before you can see the goats," Jenna told him, her voice getting shriller and shriller as she went on. "You can't leave the house alone. Do you know what could have happened! You could have been hit by a car! You could have stepped on glass! You could have fallen in a ditch. Someone could have picked you up and Mommy never would have seen you again!"

Eric placed a calming hand on Jenna's shoulder, interrupting her descent into a well-deserved panic attack. "Has he ever done anything like this before? If I call Child Protective Services in Atlanta, are there going to be any cases with your name on them?"

"Never," Jenna said, glancing toward her aunt. "He has everything I didn't have growin' up. My husband and I work a lot, but we're good parents. Call his preschool, his pediatrician, my neighbors, anybody. They'll tell you this kind of thing never happens. I haven't had a drink or a smoke since I found out he was comin' along. I breastfed him until he was a year old. He's at all the right percentiles, sees the doctor for every sniffle. He's had all of his shots. I take him to story time at the library. I buy freakin' organic food, even though it costs an arm and a leg. I'm a good mom."

"Okay, okay," Eric said, his shoulders relaxing as he held his hands up in what was maybe an *I don't think you're a completely terrible parent* gesture. "I'm sure you are. Just give me those phone numbers and I'll follow up with your pediatrician and the school. But for right now, I don't see any reason Chase can't stay with you."

"Thank you," she said, sniffing.

"Just be more careful with him, 'cause he was pretty determined about gettin' down the highway," Eric said, ruffling Chase's hair.

It took a little more paperwork, and Eric discreetly checking Jenna's criminal background, before they left Rita's driveway. Chase also had to be convinced to let go of Herc's collar, because he was pretty sure Herc needed to come home with him. Herc seemed half convinced himself, and was so pouty, he actually fell asleep in the backseat on the drive back to town.

"I would snark at you for bein' kind of rough on that poor mom, but I can see why you took the scared-straight route," Frankie said.

Eric hesitated before saying, "I know, I just—I thought about what could have gone wrong and I got a little loud. I am going to follow up with the school and the doctor. I want to make sure I did the right thing."

"I get it. You actually handled it pretty well, talkin' to Chase like that. I couldn't get him to open up, and I basically look like a cartoon character."

"You learn which questions to ask and how to ask them. I've had cases like that before, where I was out on patrol and found a little kid wandering alone down the street. But it was because Dad was passed out under a buncha beer cans. Or Mom was at work and the kid was bein' watched by siblings who were way too young for the job. Or no one was watchin' at all and no one cared. This was better. At least someone cared."

It was at moments like this that she was fully aware of how sheltered her childhood had been. She'd been fully supervised by a team of caring adults and medical professionals at all times. If she'd wandered any farther than her porch, there would have been a helicopter search.

Also, Eric's move to Lake Sackett was starting to make sense if working in Atlanta required a questioning strategy for wandering urban children.

Eric added, "And Chase's mom was so freaked out, that kid's going to be sleeping in a safety-deposit box for the rest of his life."

"So all's well that ends well," Frankie said brightly. "Except for Chase, who will be livin' in a steel bubble."

"I think I'm gonna go get some breakfast, try to earn some leeway from Ike. I've almost got him to the point where he doesn't glare at me when I walk through the door."

"Wow, you wore him down quicker than most." She pursed her lips. For a moment Frankie thought maybe he would ask her to join him, but he didn't. And that disappointed her more than she thought it would. She considered herself to be delightful morning company, once she was caffeinated, and sharing pancakes was something you did with a friend when you'd been through both the traumatic aftermath of a fatal wreck and finding a lost child. Okay, probably not in most friendships.

She let her head loll back on the headrest.

Fine, they were the type of acquaintances who merely informed each other of their breakfast plans but didn't extend invitations. Even after fatal wrecks and baby rescues.

FRANKIE CLOSED THE lower lid on Truman Waller's casket. She was proud of the picture she'd created for Mr. Truman, a man who'd been strong as an ox most of his life, only to have that strength sapped away by a stroke. With a padded suit and careful makeup, she'd managed to round his features and shoulders out to the shape he'd been in during his best years.

"Okay, Mr. Truman, I've done the best I can. I think your family will like seein' you just a little bit like the way they remember you." She gave the knot in his tie one last adjustment and rolled the casket over to the elevator. "I will miss your bad impersonation of Dale Earnhardt, which everybody thought was Jeff Foxworthy. No one really understood why you were impersonatin' either one, to be real honest about it. And I will miss the way that you always carried ladies' groceries to their cars, not because you thought they were weak, but because it was the nice thing to do."

Frankie rolled her shoulders and stretched her back. Mr. Truman was her third client of the day and she was feeling the hours on her feet. She had some closing paperwork for Mrs. Wannamaker's death certificate and then, if she was lucky and no one died, she might be able to sit for a while. She flopped into her chair and pored over the test results she'd printed that morning. "Jane Doe's" fasting blood glucose was damn near perfect. Her white blood cell counts were well within acceptable ranges. Her liver enzymes and kidney function were normal. Considering the amount of deep-fried foods she ate, her cholesterol levels were almost miraculous. She was the picture of health.

"Jane Doe, you are a persistently healthy basket case," she muttered, poring over the numbers again. She would enter them into a spreadsheet later, and use tracking software to determine any bothersome trends.

'Cause that was normal.

As county coroner, Frankie had access to medical testing equipment that—technically—was supposed to be used to determine cause of death in suspicious cases. And once a month, Frankie used that equipment to test her own blood chemistry and give her a week or two where she didn't worry about the possibility of adult-onset diabetes or organ failure. She wrote off the testing as "calibrating the machines," which was technically allowed, but honestly, the only thing that kept her from testing herself weekly was the threat of being accused of misuse of county equipment. Like Eric, she didn't want the words *gross incompetence* anywhere near her employment records.

Access to an i-STAT handheld blood analyzer wasn't the sole reason she took on the coroner's job. It was just a very important fringe benefit.

"Knock-knock!" Margot yelled from the stairs as Frankie jumped and shoved her test results into a drawer.

"Is this some new thing you're doing before you walk into rooms?" Frankie asked casually as Margot poked her head through the mortuary doors.

"No, I'm just giving you time to tell me whether there are any bodies being prepared before I walk in."

"Everybody is either covered or in a drawer," Frankie said.

Margot swallowed thickly. "You promise?"

"Yes," Frankie said. "I wouldn't expose you to anything that would scare you. That wouldn't exactly build a close cousinly relationship, now would it?"

"I don't think 'cousinly' is a word, but I'm touched by your thoughtfulness," Margot said, stepping carefully through the doors as if she was preparing for something to jump out at her at any moment. Margot looked considerably more composed today in a black suit that emphasized the curves she was developing thanks to Southern pork and carbs. Frankie guessed Kyle had done something to persuade Margot to stay in bed a couple of extra hours, but for the sake of her own mental health she did not picture what that "something" was.

"Why do you look like you're about to tell me that all of the abs in the Marvel Cinematic Universe are airbrushed on? Is something wrong or are you just that uncomfortable to be walking in here?" Frankie asked as Margot crossed her work space and headed for her computer.

"One, you should know that already. Hollywood airbrushing is real and rampant," Margot told her, pressing on Frankie's laptop touchpad, tapping in the password, and opening her own e-mail account. "And two, nothing's wrong, but I found out why Eric lost his job in Atlanta."

"How do you know my password?" Frankie asked.

"I know everybody's password," Margot said. "Uncle Bob had them written on the back of his blotter in his office, which I destroyed because if Jared Lewis or some other burglar broke in and found it, that could be a disaster."

"Good call," Frankie agreed as Margot opened an e-mail and clicked on a video attachment to one of her messages. Margot clicked PLAY and the screen showed a horde of zombies stumbling by what looked like the World of Coca-Cola in Atlanta. The sun was setting and the cameraman was cleverly backlighting his subjects against the eerie orange glow.

"What the . . . ?" Frankie scrunched up her face in confusion. "Why?"

"Just watch," Margot told her.

The cameraman, who appeared to be made up like Bub from *Day of the Dead*, turned the camera toward his face and gave a guttural zombie groan.

The camera panned over zombies in all shapes, sizes, and stages of decay. Some of the makeup was expertly applied, ready to shoot for any respectable horror movie. And some of the undead were very clearly covered in cheap store-bought prosthetics and food-dyed corn syrup. There were zombie doctors, zombie prom queens, zombie chefs, zombie marching-band nerds, and . . . a zombie nun? That was a little distasteful. Also nightmare fuel.

"It's a zombie walk?" Frankie said.

Margot nodded. "I looked it up. As far as zombie walks go, it's a big one and pretty well-regarded. The walkers stay respectful of the 'normies,' don't damage property or hold up traffic or try to intentionally scare people. From what I've seen, they actively avoid children unless the kids call them over and want to look at their makeup."

"Considerate zombies, who'da thunk it?" Frankie said. "And what does that have to do with anything?"

"Well, in any group, there are assholes."

Margot nodded toward the laptop screen. Bub the cameraman moved among the zombies and seemed to be zeroing in on three zombies dressed in tattered clown suits. They were stumbling in more of a "hundred proof" fashion than a walking-corpse style. And they were laughing. Zombies weren't supposed to laugh. It was decidedly creepy.

The rowdy zombies' aggression got worse the longer they walked. They dragged their fake-blood fingerprints over cars, knocked over garbage cans, and took swipes at tourists. Bub sighed heavily and finally moved toward the troublemakers with purpose, groaning, "Noooooo."

One of the zombies lurched toward a car parked near a

corner and raised what looked like a bloodstained juggling pin. Frankie heard Bub break character entirely and yell, "Hey, man, don't do that. Not cool."

The zombie smashed the pin through the car window. Before Bub could stop him, he started in on the windshield. The other zombies stopped in their tracks, breaking character and yelling for the clown to stop even as his friends egged him on. Suddenly, a cop on a Segway turned a corner and hopped off the machine.

"Atlanta PD! Stop!" Frankie instantly recognized Eric, even in the unfamiliar dark blue uniform. Eric's brow furrowed at the sight of a zombie herd ambling through Atlanta's museum district, but as the windshield broke, he shook it off and moved toward the destructive zombie trio.

The clowns seemed to think an armed man on a Segway was hilarious and staggered toward Eric, growling and swiping at him like they were going to punch him. Eric pulled his radio mic close to his face and seemed to be asking for backup.

"Guys, there are kids here. And lots of bystanders," Eric said. His voice rang with authority she'd never heard him use in Lake Sackett. This was a guy who was in charge, even when he had his palms raised as if he could calm them with the right hand gesture. "You seem to be intoxicated. You're in public. You just destroyed private property. That's a problem. You will sit on this curb and let everybody pass by. And then we're going to talk about this."

Hopped up on booze and undead confidence, the clowns

lunged for Eric. One of the zombies tried to grab Eric's arm, only to be thrown into his idiot friend. Another took advantage of Eric's distraction and punched him in the side of his head.

In a normal human voice, Bub said, "Oh, shit."

Eric told the puncher he was under arrest for assault and began to handcuff him. The guy's friend took great offense and rammed his fist into Eric's belly. Eric barely reacted beyond shoving the guy back. His face was set in harsh lines as he methodically kept the clowns away from him while attempting to handcuff the third. His adrenaline levels had to be sky high to take a hit like that and not even flinch.

Frankie noted that while he had one hand on his gun to keep it secured, Eric never pulled it. Even though it prevented him from being able to maneuver with his dominant hand, there were too many people around for him to risk it.

The zombie horde circled closer, yelling for the clowns to stop. Eric shoved them away and reached for the one weapon he had that wouldn't hurt a bystander. He picked up the Segway by the frame and threw it at them. It was an impressive feat of upper-body strength, heaving the machine at the three men hard enough to knock them to the ground.

And then the video ended.

Frankie sank back in her chair. "What in the hell did I just watch?"

"Apparently, he fractured that guy's arm," Margot said, pointing at the clown zombie frozen on the screen, pinned under the Segway's front wheel. "The other two suffered scrapes and bruises, and the misfortune of being jackasses, but that's it."

"Jar," Frankie said weakly, still trying to process what she'd seen on her screen. She recognized the expression on Eric's face, that abject fear and absolute certainty that life was about to end. How could someone feel that sort of fear and still manage to fight off three assailants and lift a Segway? The amount of adrenaline in his system must have been staggering.

"I only got it because I made friends with that tourism board bigwig in Atlanta during the festival planning. Kevin works in city hall and I thought maybe he might have heard something about Eric. The video was kept quiet and there wasn't any media coverage because of mutually assured destruction. The zombie jerks didn't want their event shut down and the police department clearly didn't want the bad press. The zombie assholes had enough to worry about with all the charges stacking up against them. And they were on very thin ice with the zombie walk coordinators. Apparently the threat of ostracism in the zombie community is a heavy one. Kevin only knew about it because the zombie group met with the tourism board to discuss PR for public events," Margot said.

"I wouldn't want that crowd turning on me," Frankie said. "So, that's Eric's big secret? That's why he ran to Lake Sackett? He got fired for throwing a Segway at people who were attacking him? Not to make light of the violence, but, honestly, this could have been much worse. No one was seriously injured. None of the other people in the crowd were hurt. By comparison to some other incidents over the last few years, this seems kind of minor."

"Officially, he resigned before the disciplinary process started," Margot said. "While throwing a Segway at people who are trying to hurt you may have been a reasonable human response, the police department didn't think this was an appropriate use of force. I imagine quitting was to keep his ability to get hired somewhere else."

"Well, still, it's not that . . . There are worse . . ." Frankie began. "Yeah, okay, fine, that's pretty awful all around. And it definitely explains why he reacts the way he does to dead bodies and the mortuary. He's probably having zombie PTSD flashbacks."

"Do you feel bad, having called him all those awful names, knowing that he had a humiliating public incident that pretty much ended his career?"

"No, I feel comfortable callin' an asshat an asshat, even when he has good reason for being an asshat."

"It's good that you're so flexible and considerate," Margot told her, shaking her golden head.

The intercom buzzed and her father's voice rang out of the speaker. "Frankie, honey, can you come upstairs?"

"Is there a problem with Mr. Truman?" Frankie asked.

"Just come on up," Bob told her.

Frankie looked to Margot, who shrugged. She slipped out of her lab coat and washed her hands. She hoped a customer wasn't upstairs complaining about a recent service, because that never went well, particularly if the customer had time to sit at home and stew over the grievance. She looked professional enough for a customer conversation, she supposed, a vibrant blue print dress over black tights and Mary Janes. It took a lot of close staring before an observer could see that the print was tiny *Harry Potter*–related constellations.

Frankie took time to straighten her side braid as she walked up the stairs, Margot close at her heels. "You were very brave to face down the big scary mortuary."

"It won't happen again for at least another year," Margot told her.

Frankie arrived upstairs to find Eric standing in the lobby with her father, E.J.J., and Stan. The wave of uncomfortable anxiety that washed over her caught her by surprise. How was she supposed to make eye contact with him after she'd seen that video? Also, why was he here? Had there been another suspicious death in town? Or had Jared Lewis faked his own murder and framed her for it? Her dad and uncles were all grinning, which pointed toward no. Then again, McCreadys were known for putting a pleasant face on sucky situations.

Eric took out his handcuffs and her heart dropped into her stomach and then to her knees. Because seeing Eric with handcuffs was doing destructive things to her common sense.

"Frances Ann McCready, I'm takin' you into custody."

"I didn't do it," she said quickly, and Eric frowned at her.

"You're this week's prisoner for Lock Down Hunger," he told her, carefully cuffing her hands in front of her body. His fingers were firm and warm around her wrists, sending a little shiver down her spine. "Why do you think I'm here?"

Frankie groaned and her head dropped, precariously close to resting on Eric's chest. She'd forgotten that she'd agreed to be McCready's representative at the annual Lock Down Hunger benefit. Throughout October, people from all over Lake Sackett would be "arrested" and their family and friends could bail them out by delivering a collection of groceries to the jail. The groceries would go to the local food bank, just in time for the poorer residents in Lake Sackett to stock their pantries for winter. The "prisoners" got their mug shot in the *Ledger* with a public thank-you for time served.

While that gave her a little bit of relief, she was still uncomfortable with how to act around Eric. It was like she'd seen him naked without him knowing, and now she couldn't make eye contact, which was a problem because her head was currently resting on his firm chest. Eventually she would have to lift her head. She also noted that Eric smelled pretty damn good: woodsy, with a smoky undertone of gunpowder.

"Wait," she cried, lifting her head and locking eyes with Eric. The space between them seemed to charge and contract all at once. Her cuffed hands came to rest against his stomach and his nose bumped precariously close to her hairline. She thanked good sense and Margot's influence that she'd taken to using a shampoo that was heavy on lavender oil. It was considerably more pleasant than the scent of formaldehyde.

She cleared her throat and Eric took a step back. Because they were in the same room as her family and that was not the place for surreptitious touching or hair sniffing. "I can't leave. I have work! Mr. Truman's service is in an hour. He might need a touch-up or something. And I still have Mrs. Wannamaker's paperwork to file and—"

Bob nudged her toward the door. "Sweet pea, we can handle it, and what we can't handle can wait until tomorrow. You've been workin' real hard lately and it won't hurt ya to enjoy a little time off."

"In jail?"

"Think of it as time in for good behavior," Bob suggested.

"Wait, we need to make the most of the handcuffs," Margot said, whipping out her phone and opening the camera app. "Okay, people, pretend that you're concerned and upset that your dearest undertaker is being hauled into the pokey. I can post it on the business's Facebook page to try to drive up bail donations. Couldn't hurt to mention the looming candy donation deadline for the Trunk-R-Treat, too. Double PR points score. Thanks, Frankie!" Margot dashed down the hall toward her office.

"She likes to find the bright side of things," Bob told a slightly befuddled Eric.

"Frankie, do you need your purse or anything?" Eric asked.

Her father, ever helpful, held out the shoulder bag he'd been hiding behind his back. "Here, hon, I picked it up for you. Mom says you get her special macaroni and cheese as a welcome-home dinner when you're sprung from the clink."

Frankie's cheeks flushed, because nothing makes you look like a mature, responsible adult like your mommy promising you mac 'n' cheese for dinner. "Thanks, Dad."

"Just remember, the first thing you have to do is find the biggest gal in the yard and then pick a fight with her so the other prisoners know you're not scared," Stan told her.

"Well, as of this afternoon, she's our only prisoner, so she should be okay," Eric said.

"No more Investigation Discovery for you," Frankie told him. "Turn off my computer, but don't touch anything on my desk!" she called as Eric pushed her outside and toward the police SUV.

"Your family is . . . not like other families," Eric told her, opening the front passenger door.

"Don't I know it," she muttered. She appreciated that he was letting her sit in the front. She'd seen what drunks were capable of doing to the backseat and she really liked this dress.

The drive to the county courthouse/jail was quiet and awkward. After establishing that Eric had followed up on Chase Wollmack and the little boy was just fine, they couldn't seem to find anything to talk about. Frankie realized that they'd never been alone in a space this small without some other person (or body or dog) as a buffer. She felt like she couldn't say anything without blurting out, "I know your zombie secret!" And Eric pretended to be busy, playing with the buttons on the radio and asking Landry if he'd completed various tasks around town.

Frankie realized that she didn't really know what happened to the "prisoner" during Lock Down Hunger. Uncle Junior had done this duty when she was a kid, and then E.J.J., who was giving it up only because the conditions were a little extreme for a man in his advanced years. Stan never took it on because he'd spent some time in Lake Sackett's cells during his drunker years and didn't want a return visit, even for charity. The handcuffs were for show and photo opportunities, but would she actually be kept in a cell? Or would they let her play with some of the equipment? She'd always wanted to know how a beanbag gun worked. And now that Eric had supposedly cleaned out the hoarder's rat's nest that had led to Sheriff Rainey's early "retirement," maybe she would be able to find some of that equipment without digging.

Janey, the sheriff's department dispatcher and desk clerk, greeted her at the jail door with a big hug, which Frankie didn't think was part of the usual incarceration protocol.

"We're so excited you're being arrested this year!" Janey cried, her rounded cheeks flushed with excitement. "Last week, Chuck Smiley came in and he just napped the whole time. It was so borin'!"

Eric cleared his throat and raised his eyebrows. "Entertainin' us isn't really the point of the fund-raiser, Janey."

Janey's flush turned to an all-out blush and she grabbed

Frankie by the wrist and dragged her to the mug shot area. Frankie only had time to refresh her bright red lipstick before she was handed her LOCK DOWN HUNGER placard. She struck a pinup pose with an exaggerated wink. Because why not?

Eric's lips twitched. "Well, that's gonna go over well in the *Ledger.*"

"I make it a point to needle the masses," Frankie told him as Landry uncuffed her. Tall, perpetually pale, and lanky, despite his mother's earnest efforts to fatten him up, Landry grinned as he led the way to the three cells lined up against the back wall. The institutional gray space was open to the office, *Mayberry* style. Each cell contained a toilet and a cot spread with a log cabin quilt hand-stitched by Landry's mama. The bars were ancient, but the county's crime rate didn't merit anything more and the county commission was loath to spend money on unnecessary upgrades in an economic slump.

There were also several bottles of water on the cot, courtesy of Janey. But considering the open plan bathroom facilities, Frankie was going to pass.

"My mama thinks it's real nice of you to take over the Lock Down duty," Landry said, his cheeks flushing as he closed her cell door and turned the key. Frankie smiled at him. Landry had always been a sweet guy. He was one of the few boys who'd invited her to dances in high school. Unfortunately, he was so dim that he posed a danger to himself and others. He'd gotten the job as a deputy only because Sheriff Rainey was his uncle.

"Thank you, Landry. How's your mama?"

"Oh, she's doin' real well. Recovering from her elbow surgery just fine," he said. "Never did figure out how that shelf collapsed on her. I fixed it myself."

"Yeah . . . it's a mystery," Frankie said.

Eager to change the subject, Janey asked, "You know you're the first lady we've had in the cells all year?"

"Not even Sara Lee Bolton?" Frankie asked, her brows furrowed.

"Sara Lee raised such a ruckus when she was taken into custody, we had to send her to a more secure facility two counties over," Landry said.

"Now, that I believe," Frankie said. She noticed that Eric had appeared behind Landry and seemed none too pleased that his two employees were loitering outside her cell.

Eric cleared his throat. "Are you on a break, Deputy Mitchell?"

Landry's mouth dropped open. "Ah, no, sir, I'm not."

"Maybe it would be a better use of your time to go fill out the rest of your paperwork," Eric said, tilting his chin down so it almost looked like he was peering over a pair of invisible glasses. He reminded Frankie eerily of her eighth-grade math teacher, Mr. Stewart. Come to think of it, Mr. Stewart had featured heavily in her first sex dream.

She needed to change the subject of her internal monologue. Now.

Landry's ruddy cheeks flushed even darker. "Yes, sir."

"Talk to you later, Landry," Frankie said as Landry scurried off.

"You don't have to fuss at him," Frankie whispered harshly to Eric. "You know he damn near idolizes you."

"He needs to focus on his work instead of goofin' off," Eric told her. "Now, you get comfortable and wait for your family to come bail you out. Just sit down and relax and . . . don't touch anything. Your uncle Stan said you'd been workin' too hard. Several times."

Frankie sat down on the cot, grumbling, "Why does everybody keep trying to sentence me to vacation time?"

FRANKIE WAS ON the verge of dozing off on her cot when Stan and Margot rolled into the sheriff's office with one of those flatbed carts stacked with cases of oatmeal, dried beans, pasta—any staple that had a long shelf life.

The flat cart also happened to be the same one Stan used to dolly new caskets into the funeral home, but no one needed to know that.

"Yes!" Frankie cried, popping up from the cot. "Release me from this hellish prison!"

"Janey put potpourri and fresh pillows in there for you," Eric said, nodding to the little blown-glass bowl near the cot. "Your hell smells like apple-cinnamon."

"You do realize that in most places, the jail, the sheriff's office, the courthouse, and the sanitation department are not all in one building, right?" Margot asked, glancing around the office. "I mean, this is super convenient, but it feels sort of crowded."

Janey told her, "We didn't have a lot of municipal money to throw around."

Stan beamed at his daughter and put his arm around her shoulders. Frankie's mouth fell open. For all his affection for Frankie, Stan had never beamed in her presence, not once. And to Frankie's greater surprise, Margot smiled right back and sort of dipped her head toward Stan. It wasn't a huge gesture of father-daughter affection, but it still put a lump in Frankie's throat. She was ridiculously and unabashedly happy for her sad-sack uncle. Maybe they'd be hugging by Christmas.

"She's been a model prisoner," Janey told Stan. "No biting or gouging."

"Doin' the family proud," Stan said with a snort.

"I got the key right here," Landry said, turning to the three key rings on hooks on the wall, marked 1, 2, and 3. Each old-fashioned iron key was paired with a small handcuff key. In his enthusiasm, Landry yanked a little too hard on the 2 key ring. And Landry, being Landry, lost his grip and let the ring slip from his fingers. It flew across the room, sliding over the waxed floor and straight toward the heating grate. Landry scrambled to the grate, where the ring hung through the quarter-size vent holes. The tiny, precariously balanced handcuff key was the only thing keeping it from falling all the way into the ventilation system.

"No, Landry, don't!" Frankie cried, just as Landry slid toward the grate on his knees, jostling the weight of the keys. The ring slipped through the grate and dropped into the vent with a distant *clang*. And then another *clang*, which, frankly, sounded like it was mocking her.

"Son, tell me you didn't." Stan marveled while the reality of the situation slowly dawned on Margot's face.

Frankie let her forehead thunk against the bars. "He did."

Margot simply watched in mute horror, her eyes darting from the grate to Frankie and back.

"It went straight on down the vent," Landry said, peering through the grate.

"It's okay," Eric assured Frankie, his hands raised. "It's okay. We have backup keys for all the cells. Right, Landry?"

"Right." Landry smiled in relief for a moment and then his face fell. "Oh . . . shoot."

Frankie turned to Landry. "What do you mean, 'oh shoot'?"

"Well, the backup key isn't here," Landry said. "It's at my house. I took it there when the office started gettin' real messy under Sheriff Rainey. I was afraid we'd lose it."

"Well, then just go home and get it!" Frankie exclaimed, her voice cracking like ice under a school bus.

"That's the problem," Landry said. "I can't. I don't know where it is."

Frankie closed her eyes and pinched her lips shut before she could say something in the "terroristic threatening" category. Her anxiety clawed through her chest like a living thing, shredding everything it touched. Her fingers went cold and numb and she tried to shake the blood flow back into them. Her stomach seemed to be turning itself inside out and crawling up her throat. Was she having a stroke? Was this what massive cardiac failure felt like?

"What about a locksmith?" Eric asked.

Janey shrugged. "Closest one's in Hollman, which is about an hour away. But that lock's about a hundred years old, so old I'm not sure his equipment would work anyway."

"Can we cut the bars?" Margot asked.

"The jail's on the historical registry, so we'd have to get permission from a circuit judge to make any alterations," Eric said. "Which isn't likely this late on a Friday. Also, we've only got the three cells. I know I'm the only candidate running for the job, but it doesn't exactly speak well for me as the interim sheriff that I'm cuttin' apart what little equipment we have because my deputy took home the keys and lost them."

Frankie raised her eyebrows and gave Eric a look that *definitely* fell into the category of terroristic.

"That was the wrong thing to say," Eric admitted, turning to his deputy. "Landry, go home and find that key."

"Sure. It's gotta be in my bedroom somewhere," Landry said, giving a little salute.

Frankie flopped onto the cot. "My freedom depends on Landry. I'm going to die in here."

"You're going to be fine," Stan promised. "Worse comes to worst, you can tunnel your way out."

"Not the time for humor," Margot told him, shaking her head.

"What if Landry can't find the key?" Frankie whispered. "He couldn't find his ass with both hands and a map."

"Then we explore our locksmith and injunction options," Eric promised, walking into the adjoining cell. He was right behind her, his voice low and reassuring in her ear. "You're not stuck here. This is a temporary situation, a few hours, tops. Take deep breaths, Frankie, come on."

Frankie took three very large, gulping breaths. Eric reached through the bars and put his hand on her spine, a warm, comforting weight right between her shoulder blades. She knew she was being ridiculous. She knew she wasn't in any *real* danger. But the idea of not being able to leave this space, of having no control over food, showering, clothes— the weight of it all crowded the breath from her lungs. She had to stop joking around about going to jail. She clearly wasn't built for it.

"All right," Frankie said, nodding. She looked up to see Stan giving Eric the eyeball. Eric slowly withdrew his hand and backed away from the bars. "I'm all right."

"We'll get you out of here before you know it, Frankie," Janey promised. "And in a few weeks, you'll forget how pissed off you are at Landry and you'll turn it into one of your funny stories. You'll get free beers out of it for months."

"Thanks, Janey," Frankie grumbled.

"But you're okay for now, right?" Margot asked. "You have food and water and a bathroom . . . ish."

"Why does your voice sound so weird right now?" Frankie asked.

"It's just that Friday night is pizza night with Kyle and the girls," Margot said. "And they're waiting on me. And if you're okay and there's no chance of getting you out anytime soon . . . and Dad's my ride home . . ."

"You're abandoning me?"

"'Abandoning' is such an ugly word," Margot protested.

"I will remember this the next time you're in jail," Frankie promised.

"Well, I've never been to jail, so that's an empty threat," Margot told her.

"You're a McCready. Your time will come!" Frankie shot back. When Margot made a confused-pouty face, Frankie sighed. "You can go. I'll be fine. I'll just stay here, alone, behind bars, with only a quilt for company."

"Great," Margot said, grabbing Stan's hand and dragging him out of the office. "Text me if Landry finds the keys."

"I was bein' sarcastic," Frankie called as they cleared the door. "You should recognize it, by now! Stan! Don't tell my mama about this, she'll freak out! Stan!"

Stan raised his hand as he walked out the door. "Got it!"

"I can't believe they left me," Frankie said.

"You told them to leave," Janey said.

"Yeah, *once*. I figured it would take a few more times. Whatever happened to family loyalty?"

"Well, what were they supposed to do, spend the next few hours staring at you in captivity?"

"No," Frankie grumbled.

"And on that note," Janey said, "please don't take it personal, Frankie, but I've got to head home, too. I'm supposed to meet my sister for fish fry and bingo."

Frankie moaned. She'd forgotten that the sheriff's office closed at nine. After that, all 911 calls were routed through the nearest state police post. Eric got a call in case of a serious incident like a drowning or a shooting, but anything else was handled by the state troopers. So the office was about to close, with her inside. It was like those nightmares she used to have about being trapped in a Kmart overnight and being chased by headless mannequins.

"Sounds like a scintillatin' evening," Frankie said. "Go on."

Janey grabbed her purse and keys and waggled her fingers as she ran out of the room.

"Frankie, don't panic. Everything's going to be fine," Eric told her.

"What about this situation strikes you as fine, Eric?"

"Well . . . You . . . I . . ." Eric tried to keep the laugh in, but it bubbled up as a guffaw that had him bending at the waist.

"It's not funny," she exclaimed. She wanted to swat at him, but there were bars in the way and her arms were only so long.

"I'm sorry," he said, wiping at his eyes. It occurred to Frankie that she'd never heard Eric laugh like that. And while she was pissed that it was at her expense, it did a lot to ease that cold ache in her middle. It was a really nice laugh.

"I shouldn't have laughed. And I shouldn't have made that crack about not lookin' good if I cut the bars. It's just, who else would this happen to?"

"No one," Frankie said, rolling her eyes.

"It will be a few hours, tops, maybe overnight," Eric said. "I mean, Landry's gotta find the key, right? Even he's not dumb enough to throw something like that away."

Frankie deadpanned, "Landry, the guy who damn near smothered himself because he put a plastic poncho on wrong?"

"I didn't know about that one," Eric said, pursing his lips as his hands slipped around the bars of her cell. "It's kind of a miracle he's survived this long, especially carryin' around a handgun."

"It really is," she said. "What about Hercules? Is he going to be okay while you stay late?"

"Yeah, I dropped by the house this afternoon, fed him, let him out to run in the yard. He likes sleepin' on the back porch better anyway. Are you hungry?" he asked. "I could run down to the Rise and Shine and grab somethin' to eat."

"No, don't leave," she said, and without intending to, she grabbed at his hands. He stared down at their joined hands for a second and she jerked away. Or at least, she tried to. Eric caught her hand and held it firm, rubbing her cold fingers with his warm ones.

"I won't," he promised. "I can call. I bet Ike Grandy would hand-deliver it for you."

She nodded. "Probably."

"A double bacon cheeseburger, onion rings, and a strawberry shake. Your usual, right?"

She nodded, slowly drawing her hands out of Eric's as he pulled his cell phone out of his pocket. She sat back on her cot while he ordered the food. She kicked off her shoes. How was she going to sleep in here? And even if Eric had a T-shirt she could use for pajamas—she drew the line at prisoner orange, thank you very much—how was she going to change clothes? Would Eric leave her here when his shift was over and tell her he'd see her in the morning? She would be stuck. She pulled at the collar of her dress, a cold flush of dread running from her stomach through her legs. The little choices she had that let her pretend she had control over her life—her food, her clothes, the ability to walk out of a room if she wanted to—they were all gone. She was that scared kid in the hospital again, helpless. She was trapped, alone, unable to tell her family how unhappy she was or how scared, because she didn't want them to worry. She could choke on the words trapped in her throat. She bent over on the cot, drawing a deep breath through her nose. She was losing it, and she'd only been trapped in here for twenty minutes.

The claustrophobia that had gnawed at her insides just a few moments before returned, but as a dull throb. She heard metal scraping against the floor in the next cell. She turned to see Eric sliding that cell's cot toward the bars closest to her.

"You know, Janey told me that the original builders claimed that the constant supervision of an open plan kept the prisoners from being able to escape. But I think they just wanted easier paperwork." His tone was conversational, as if she weren't stuck in a century-old jail cell, waiting for an idiot to free her with a spare key. He was trying to soothe her. She'd spent enough time being placated to know what it sounded like. But she appreciated the gesture all the same. He could have just left her there while he went home to his considerably more adorable dog.

"I don't see the connection," Frankie said, turning and facing him.

"Well." He kicked off his boots and unbuckled his gun belt. His whole body seemed to relax without its weight. He sat cross-legged on the cot, facing her cell. "They didn't have to take their prisoners into interrogation rooms or mess with securin' doors. The deputies could just shout to the prisoners in their cells when they wanted to know how to spell their names."

"Are you trying to distract me with inane details?" she asked, narrowing her eyes at him.

The corners of his mouth lifted and he spread his palms. "It's either that or I show you card tricks."

"I'll pass," she said, shaking her head. "I don't like magicians. You can never keep track of their hands."

"Eh, it's a good way to pass the time when you're stuck in a squad car for hours at a stretch, waitin' for a call. It encourages dexterity. Plus, kids always think they're funny. It's a good way to distract 'em when they're upset or scared over some trouble their parents have gotten themselves into. I didn't break them out with Chase because, well, there just wasn't time."

"Uncle Junior used to make little cranes out of Double-mint wrappers," she said.

"Origami?" he asked, his eyebrows raised.

She nodded. "The redneck version, I guess. He learned it from some library book. Working in the mortuary, he didn't deal with mourners at McCready's very often, but when he did see kids, it was usually when they were upset or scared. He liked being able to give them something pretty out of nothin', something they could put in their pocket and take with them."

"You have a nice smile when you talk about your family," he said, gesturing to her face. "I mean, you have a lot of different types of smiles, some of them sickly sweet and some of them scary as hell. But the nicest one is when you talk about your family."

She raised an eyebrow. "Thank . . . you?"

"Delivery!" Ike walked into the office with a heavy hunter's jacket over his apron. If he found it at all odd to be delivering a bag full of sandwiches to a jail cell, he didn't let on.

"Hey, Frankie," he said, handing the grease-spotted bag to Eric. He jerked his head toward the towering pile of groceries. "I heard you got a pretty good haul for your bail. That'll help a lot of people. Good for you."

"Thanks, Ike."

Ike eyed the bars. "Don't the Lock Down prisoners get sprung before dinner? How much longer are you stickin' around?"

Frankie frowned.

"Sore subject," Eric said, shaking his head and making a *cut it out* gesture at his throat.

Ike shrugged. "Okay, then. I put a little horseradish in the ground beef mix this time. Tell me what you think."

Frankie grinned. "Sure thing. Put the bill on my tab."

"Eh, consider it part of your bail donation," Ike said. "Well, I gotta be gettin' back to the diner."

"Thanks, Ike," Eric said as the short-order cook ambled out of the office.

"G'night!" Frankie called as Eric slid her to-go cup through the bars of her cell. He laid out their greasy diner fare like it was a royal feast, folding her napkin in half and fluffing the wax paper around her onion rings before handing them to her.

Frankie's cell buzzed from inside her purse. She checked the screen and winced. Her mama was texting, asking why she wasn't home from being "arrested" yet. Grimacing, Frankie texted back a flimsy excuse about meeting Marianne for drinks at the Dirty Deer, and then, of course, had to text Marianne to apprise her of the alibi. And then Frankie's dad texted, and the cycle started all over again.

"Your burger is going to get cold," Eric said around a mouthful of turkey melt. He'd already dug into his sandwich and was halfway through his side salad—a side salad Eric had to beg Ike to assemble out of burger toppings under great protest. Even in a jail sleepover, his choices were distressingly adult.

Frankie put her phone aside with a groan. She shoved her burger into her mouth and chewed glumly. "I know. My parents are just worried and I can't tell them where I am, because if I did, you'd have three McCreadys in here freakin' out instead of just me."

"You lie to your parents? I'm oddly disappointed by that. You seem so close."

"We are close. We are. I just need to protect them from certain information because otherwise they get sent into this weird panic spiral where they smother me with their love and I end up filled with frustrated rage-slash-guilt."

"Have you ever tried telling them to back off?"

"Yes, in many ways, and they always have some very reasonable excuse as to why it's okay to stomp all over my life because they worry so much."

"So you stay frustrated and guilty because it's easier?"

"Says the guy who knows exactly jack squat about my life."

He waved in the general direction of her head with his fork. "I'm just sayin' that most parents would be a little put off by the rainbow hair and the clothes and the mortician thing, but yours? I'm thinking if I went into your parents' house right now, they would have some sort of sculpture made out of your eyelashes."

She pulled a horrified face, almost revealing a mouthful of onion ring. She clapped a hand over her lips and swallowed. "First of all, having your child work with dead bodies isn't all that shocking in a family that runs a funeral home. In fact, it's sort of a chosen-one-in-every-generation thing, if you want that funeral home to continue running."

"Is there a 'second'? How do you explain your parents' bizarre devotion?" he asked.

"You gotta understand, my mom and dad planned on having a house full, but it just didn't work out for them. I was my parents' miracle baby after years of trying, so they were already prone to thinking I was the greatest thing ever. And when you have what you consider to be a miracle baby, and then that baby gets sick and ends up hospitalized for most of her childhood, it's pretty easy to find the bright side to every day she's breathing."

"You were sick?"

She nodded. "You could say that I was very closely supervised when I was a kid. They had a tendency to freak out when I got the tiniest little fever, and I didn't like upsetting them, so when I started feeling tired all the time and getting bruises in weird places, I didn't say anything. I was only eight and I didn't understand those were early warning signs for leukemia."

"What?"

"Yeah, a really nasty rare form of it. I had this cold that wouldn't go away. It just lingered on for weeks. When I finally got sick enough that I couldn't hide it and Mama took me to the doctor, well, he got a little pissy with them for not noticing earlier. I don't think either parent ever really recovered from that. They spent years driving me back and forth to St. Jude, sitting with me through chemo, making little hats to cover my bald head. There were days they said good-bye to me and weren't sure if they'd come back to find me breathing."

"You were bald?"

"As an egg," she said, nodding. "The chemo did a number on me. Took years for my hair to grow back, and when it did, I swore the first thing I would do when it was long enough was dye it purple, bright, bright purple. So everybody would know that I had hair again."

"Reasonable."

"I thought so. And I never really stopped," she said, waving at her hair with its purple and blue highlights. "Whenever I get too wound up, my mama blames it on my 'triple dose' of McCready—Uncle Stan was able to donate bone marrow when I was strong enough, and then Duffy a while later. But Mama always forgives me, no matter what I do. It's possible that the rainbow hair and the weird clothes may have sprung from a pathological need to see how far I could push my parents before they got angry with me. The answer was 'pretty dang far.' And then it was more about me being a grown-ass woman in a small town. And if I want purple and blue hair, I should have purple and blue hair, no matter what anyone else thinks. That's more of that triple dose of McCready stubbornness; try not to be terrified."

"Too late," he muttered around his last bite of sandwich. "But you're okay now?"

"Sure, my doctors say I'm healthy as a horse. Very little chance of recurrence," she said, avoiding eye contact. He didn't need to know that she was a self-obsessed hypochondriac who saw cancer in every twinge. She slid her onion rings closer to the bars, within his reach. "But it led to my current career, so it wasn't all bad."

"This time you're going to have to explain the connection to me," he said. She smiled as he took an onion ring and bit into it.

She sipped a long draw from her milkshake. "Well, I spent a good chunk of my childhood knowing that I could die at any time. That my cancer could get worse. That a cold could take me out. I came dangerously close to becoming an agoraphobic tween. I decided that I had to stop being scared of death, because otherwise I was going to spend my life too scared to live it. I forced myself to go into the mortuary and spent time with Uncle Junior. At first, it was scary and gross and I had nightmares like you wouldn't believe. Mostly about my own funeral. But eventually, it wasn't so scary. It was just science. And I'd always been really good with science. Uncle Junior taught me everything I know about takin' care of the bodies while givin' them dignity. He taught me all of the tricks to make them look like themselves, so their loved ones have something to comfort them before the burial. He helped me see the beauty in death alongside the inescapable finality. Also, he taught me that when somethin' scares you, you pull your bootstraps up and give it the finger, so it knows who it's messin' with."

"You were a child when he taught you this?" he asked, balling up their food wrappers and tossing them in Ike's paper bag.

Frankie explained, "He was trying to help me. I am blessed with multiple father figures, but Junior probably had the biggest impact on me. Please don't ever tell my daddy that." She frowned, her bottom lip trembling a little. "His was the only funeral preparation I've ever bowed out on. I just couldn't bring myself to do it. I had to call in a pathologist friend in Atlanta."

"That's . . . pretty normal, I would say. I could barely bring myself to go to my dad's funeral, and I didn't have to touch the body."

"I'm sorry. I didn't realize your dad had passed."

"Just a few years ago. He was a cop."

"Really?" Frankie's brows rose. "Wow, that's a big can of psychological implications poppin' open."

"I know, I'm a cliché," he said. "My whole family was. Mom couldn't take the stress of wonderin' whether he would come home at night, so she left. I was eleven or so. I didn't want to leave my friends or my school and she said fine. She kept in touch, called every week. She's livin' in Florida now, married to a nice accountant. We just . . . don't talk much. Dad worked his ass off, got his twenty years in, stayed smart and safe. Never had so much as a scratch, which made Mom's leavin' seem that much more pointless. And then he had a heart attack about a year into his retirement, dropped dead face-first into his tomato plants."

"I'm sorry."

"He would have preferred it to a lot of other ways to go out. But it was just me plannin' the funeral, and I barely got through it. I wish I'd had someone like E.J.J. helpin' me, because by the time I was done makin' decisions, I didn't even want to come to the service."

"What, you didn't have any aunts and uncles? Cousins?" He shook his head.

"What's that like?" she marveled. "What do you do over holidays? Or Sundays? Or breakfast? Or beers?"

"I usually picked up the holiday shifts so the guys with families could take the day off. The shift captain's wife would bring in a spread for us, which was always nice."

"So you were eating reheated turkey off of a paper plate in a station house? That's the saddest thing I've ever heard. This entire conversation has gotten entirely too serious. We need to go back to snipin' at each other like a couple of jerks."

"Right, the emotional wounds have just scabbed over, really," he said, gathering their dinner trash together and throwing it in the garbage. "Too soon."

"So, we'll play *I Never*."

He shook his head vehemently. "No, no, nothing good has ever followed that sentence. No. RaeAnn Jenkins cried and then threw up in my lap in tenth grade during a round of *I Never*. I haven't been right since."

"Come on. It's a jail sleepover. What's a sleepover without stupid, embarrassing games? I'll finally get some background information on you without the upsetting emotional baggage."

"That's not really helpin' your case."

"Surely you've got a bottle stashed somewhere in the office. What self-respectin' cop doesn't have whiskey stashed in his desk drawer?"

"I'm technically on duty. I'm not going to drink on duty in the office. I might as well just lock myself in with key ring number three over there."

"Fine," she said. "It doesn't have to be a drinkin' game. Go get Janey's chocolate stash."

Eric went to Janey's desk and retrieved the jar of Hershey's Kisses she kept next to her phone. "I'm not sure about this. I know better than to get between a woman and chocolate."

"I'll replace them in the morning." Frankie snaked her hand through the bars and into the jar and grabbed a handful of kisses. She put five in a row in front of her on the cot and then reached through the bars and set up a little line of kisses on the cot in front of Eric.

"You know the rules. One of us makes a statement about something we haven't done. If either of us have, in fact, done that thing, we eat the chocolate. Or if we get to the point that we get sick, we just take the chocolate and add it to our stash."

"Still don't think this is a good idea," he told her.

"Man up, Linden."

"Fine," he said, adding several more kisses to the lines in front of them. "I never walked out of a movie because it was too awful to stay in the theater."

"Lame," she said, rolling her eyes. Though she did take a kiss. Eric laughed but refrained from his chocolate.

"I never cheated in school," she said. Her eyes went wide when his hand reached for a kiss.

"Really!" she exclaimed.

"I peered at a neighbor's spelling test in fourth grade," he insisted. "It's not like I hired someone to take the SATs for me."

"I'm just sayin' it's nice to see a tiny crack in that ethical armor of yours."

"I never got a tattoo I regret," he said, watching her carefully.

She smiled blithely but didn't take the chocolate. Neither did Eric.

Frankie smirked. "I never got a tattoo."

Eric rolled his eyes and unwrapped a kiss. Frankie was already chewing on hers.

"Really?" he exclaimed. "It was so dark that night, I didn't see it. Where is it?"

"There are no follow-up questions in *I Never*," she informed him primly. "Unless you want to play *You Show Me Yours and I'll Show You Mine*, which is another kinda game altogether."

Eric's cheeks flushed delightfully and Frankie cackled.

"I never snuck out after a one-night stand, leaving the other person wondering what the hell had gone wrong."

Frankie sagged against the cot. "So we're talking about this now?"

"You told me about having cancer. How much harder can it be to talk about this?"

"But we've been doing such a good job of ignoring the tension and pretending it didn't happen!"

"Have we?" Eric asked, squinting at her.

Grabbing for more candy, she said, "I didn't mean to hurt your feelings. I don't think this will make it sound better, but it didn't occur to me that your feelings would be hurt. Most of my . . . partners appreciate the fact that I leave without being asked, that I don't linger and ask awkward questions about getting breakfast."

"Is this something that you do very often?"

"I definitely wouldn't use the word 'often.' It has nothing to do with me 'not being that type of girl.' I just don't have that sort of time in my schedule. I enjoy sex. I'm not going to apologize for that. I'm safe and responsible and I happen to think I'm pretty good at it. You certainly didn't have any complaints."

He raised his hands in a surrender position. "Wasn't gonna say anything . . . and no, I did not."

She snorted. "But sometimes, all that information I mentioned, the stuff I can't tell my parents? The pressure builds up and I take a night or two for myself away from everybody else, where I just do what I want without thinking about what anyone else feels about it. I am sorry that I made you feel bad. That was not my intention. I was trying to keep things simple."

"Well, I was probably a little more vulnerable about it than I normally would be, what with my whole life getting uprooted."

"I never got tossed out of a bar," Frankie said.

They both took a piece of chocolate. Frankie held up a hand. "It was Duffy's fault."

"I never lost a fight."

Eric sighed and ate a piece of chocolate.

Frankie winced. "You don't mean the zombies, do you? Because I think throwing a Segway counts as a win."

Eric's mouth fell open. "You know?"

She cringed. "I'm so sorry. Margot found the video through one of her contacts in Atlanta. She has contacts everywhere. She's like Olivia Pope, but meaner."

"You've seen the video?" He groaned, grinding the heels of his hands into his eyes.

"You looked really good in those uniform shorts, if it makes you feel any better."

He threw his arms up. "How is that supposed to make me feel better?"

"Do you want to talk about it?" she asked.

"Not really, no."

"But now I feel bad!" she cried.

"Well, I'm so sorry you're feelin' the consequences of your actions. I know it's a rare moment for you."

"Easy," she warned him. "I'm sorry you had a bad experience, but there's no reason to throw shade at my whole upbringin'."

"It wasn't just the zombies. I wish it was that simple, that I was scared of a stupid TV monster." He sighed. "Look, I've been a cop for ten years. I've seen bodies after they've been hit by trains. I've seen them when they've been in their apartment for a week, until someone notices the smell. I've even seen a few pulled out of rivers. And it only got worse when I started working as an accident reconstructionist and got called to scenes before the paramedics were done. Seeing people who haven't passed on yet, but they're moments away from it. You know it and they know it, and sometimes, there's this look in their eyes, like they just fucking refuse to accept that they're going to die, they're just going to keep on going no matter what their body tells them. They just keep *going*. That leaves a mark on you. There's some things you can never unsee."

She nodded, mentally blocking out a series of images that would just not be helpful right now. "Yeah."

"So, no, I'm not a big fan of zombie movies or TV shows. The idea of the things I've seen coming to life and following me around, not exactly entertainment," he said.

"I'm not much on those movies, either. I see enough of it at work. And the wacky ways they dispose of the zombies are, in my opinion, kind of mean-spirited," she said.

"Well, of course the girl who holds polite conversation with dead bodies is going to side with the zombies," he said, chuckling. "Last year, I started developing some . . . tics. Got jumpy at noises. My mouth would go all dry and my palms would get sweaty when I'd get called out to an accident. Couldn't concentrate long enough to write a ticket. All classic PTSD symptoms, only I didn't realize that because as far as I was concerned, I didn't have any trauma. It certainly wasn't as bad as some of the people I worked with who were veterans, guys who had seen actual combat. One of them pointed out that I was having problems. I was lucky my shift supervisor liked me enough to get me transferred from traffic to a Segway assignment in the tourist district, instead of forcing me on leave.

"Well, we have what I guess you'd call a strong 'zombie culture.' Movie nights at parks, dances and conventions where everybody dresses up as a zombie. Or sometimes groups of people just show up to a movie theater in full makeup to watch a zombie movie. But the worst are the zombie walks. Even if you know they're coming, it still looks like hell on earth, the beginning of the apocalypse in all of those movies, herds of them ambling down the street, groaning. And their makeup is so realistic. Even when you *know* it's not real, it's just unnerving.

"Most of the zombie walkers are real polite about it. They don't want to scare anybody or cause problems, they're just out havin' fun, like trick-or-treating for adults. But that night, I got a bad batch. They came at me and it was like every nightmare I've ever had. That look in the eye, that 'just going to keep going' look, that's what I saw in their eyes. And I just panicked." He shook his head, swallowing thickly. "I'll be honest, I can't remember a lot of what happened."

"I saw the video. You tried to reason with them. You gave them fair warning . . . and then you threw a Segway at them, which I did not expect."

"That part I remember."

"Those things are heavy."

"You know those stories about mothers who lift cars off of their children?" he said. "Same principle, only with a panicked full-grown man and a Segway."

"Why didn't you pull your gun or your Taser or something?" she asked.

He shook his head. "Too many people. I could have hit a bystander. I didn't want to hurt anybody."

"They started it," Frankie noted.

"Yeah, the higher-ups didn't see it that way. They were pretty humorless about the whole thing. The lead clown ended up with a fractured arm. I got to resign before they fired me so I could keep part of my pension."

"I'm so sorry," she said. "By comparison, I guess our little town seems like a big vacation."

"I'm not going to lie. I moved to Lake Sackett because the murder rate was pretty much nothing. I didn't want to have to deal with bodies again."

"So why were you pushing the murder agenda so hard every time someone died of non-natural causes?" she exclaimed.

"Because I wanted to be thorough. I wanted to do a good job, no matter what. I screwed up my last job so bad, I have to prove to myself that I'm not a chronic dumbass. And I don't want to use the term 'interim sheriff' with you again, but with Sheriff Rainey's legacy of hoardin', I already had the cards stacked against me."

"We would have had a way less antagonistic beginnin' to our relationship if you'd just said so," she told him, lying on her side and facing him.

"Yeah, well, I wasn't exactly ready to lay myself bare to the sharp-tongued girl with the neon hair and friends in the morgue. I don't know if you're aware of this, but you can be pretty damn intimidatin' when you want to be."

"Thank you," she said, yawning. Between the belly full of Ike's comfort food and the drain of panic adrenaline from her system, she was getting pretty tired.

He lay down on his side, too, facing her. "This is the weirdest conversation I've ever had with a woman."

"Well, consider the source." She snorted, rubbing her face into the way-higher-than-standard-prison-quality pillow.

It was odd, being this close to Eric but having the bars between them. And yet, in a way, Frankie was grateful for the bars. They protected her from false hope. *Well, he would reach out and touch me, but the bars are in the way.* They protected her from potential rejection. *Well, I would reach out and touch* him, *but the darn bars are in the way.* She stayed in her space and he stayed in his, and there was some comfort in knowing that's the way things were going to stay for at least the night.

"I'm kind of glad this happened," he said, folding his own pillow in half under his head. "I mean, I'm sorry you were locked up and scared and everything. But I think it's good, us talkin' like this. Before, I thought you were this manic nightmare person. But now I know you have reasons for being completely crazy."

"You say the sweetest things," she murmured, her eyelids fluttering closed. It would just be for a second. Surely Landry would show up at any moment, keys in hand. She was just going to rest her eyes for a minute.

SHE WOKE TO sunlight streaming through the sheriff's office window. Her face was pressed against the bars, her forehead lodged in the hollow of Eric's throat. That spicy-smoky smell of him had leached into her own clothes and she found she didn't mind so much. Eric's arm had snaked through the bars overnight, his hand curled around her back. His fingers were flexed around the ridges of her spine. And he was breathing really heavily.

No, wait.

Frankie lifted her head to see Hercules standing on the other side of her bars, staring at her.

On her top ten list of weird dates, this ranked near number one.

A cold weight settled over Frankie's chest, to the point that she couldn't bear to stay still. She slid out from under Eric's arm. She'd slept with Eric Linden, but not. She'd actually *slept* with the man. She couldn't remember the last time she'd spent the night with someone, other than that one time she'd dozed off immediately after sex and woke to find her partner playing *Halo* with his roommates while she slept on his couch. But somehow, this seemed worse. That claustrophobic feeling squeezed at her belly again, and she didn't think it had anything to do with the close confines of her cell.

She jerked back, throwing her elbow and knocking her bowl of potpourri to the floor with a crash.

"What? Frankie?" Eric jerked awake with a gasp at the sound of shattering glass. He glanced around the cells. "Why?"

She nodded toward the German shepherd. "Your dog is here."

"Herc?" Eric said, lifting his head from the pillow. "Hey, boy, what are you doin' here?"

Herc snapped to attention and trotted into the cell, nudging at Eric's hand with his nose.

"How did he get in?" she asked, sitting up and straightening her clothes. In the night, she'd obviously drooled down her chin. She wiped at it furiously while Eric fussed with the dog. Also, it tasted like a squirrel had built a nest of Funyuns in her mouth while she slept. She pinched her lips together, lest the smell of her morning breath escape.

"He's smarter than most people," Eric told her, scratching behind Herc's ears. "Either he found an open window or Landry left a door open."

"I feel a lot less secure about the county's tax records now," she muttered.

"He must have jumped the fence and come lookin' for me when I didn't come home last night." Eric rubbed his hands around Herc's muzzle, making it look like he was stretching the dog's cheeks to and fro. "I'm sorry, buddy. I didn't mean to worry you. Frankie just ran into a little bit of trouble and I had to stick around to help her."

Herc made a disgruntled whining noise and whuffed at Frankie.

"So that's how it is?" Frankie said, raising her eyebrows at the dog. "I thought we were friends."

"I'll make coffee," Eric said.

"Good, that means *we* can stay friends." Frankie groaned. She was not a morning person. Eric didn't need full exposure to uncaffeinated Frankie.

"Frankie!" Landry came charging into the jail. "I found it!"

Frankie turned to find Landry standing at the bars, wearing a fresh uniform and jangling the spare key. "My mama remembered as she was making breakfast. She put it in the urn with my daddy's ashes because she figured we'd never throw that out. She just forgot till now."

"Well, that was very helpful of her," Frankie said, sliding out of bed. She had to pee so bad her eyes were floating, and the sooner Landry opened the door, the better.

Landry nodded toward the mussed bed in the next cell.

"Hey, did the sheriff keep you company last night? That was real nice of him."

"Landry, would you please let me out?" Frankie said through gritted teeth.

"Oh, sure thing," he said, unlocking the door.

"Don't take this personal," she told him. He yelped as she shoved him aside, out of the cell doorway, and ran down the hall to the (not quite as) public ladies' room.

As she yanked the bathroom door open, she heard Landry moan, "I think she cracked my ribs."

FRANKIE'S HOMECOMING FROM jail was not exactly triumphant.

After showering and changing, Frankie drove her uncle's truck to work to find Duffy and her father standing at the open side entrance. She slid out of the truck, approaching them from behind. She could see large gouges in the metal door frame from across the parking lot, not to mention hear the increasingly annoying *whoop* of an alarm inside the building. As she approached, she noticed that the hallway lights were on and several of the paint-by-number Jesuses were strewn across the floor. Bob's own office door was still closed. Frankie hoped that meant that the office records and all the customers' payment information were safe.

It was rare to see Duffy with anything less than a jovial facial expression. But the frown didn't leave his face as he said, "I'm starting to dislike Jared Lewis as much as you do."

Frankie asked him, "What's happened here?"

"Someone pried the office door open," Bob said. "We didn't want to disturb anything before the sheriff got here, so we haven't gone in yet."

"What about the security camera?" she asked. "Do you think it caught anything this time?"

"Took it out with a brick," Duffy said, nodding toward the broken remnants of a camera, dangling by electrical cords.

"What about the trail cam?" She pointed toward the trees near the shoreline, where she and Duffy had installed a motion-activated camera of the type typically used by wildlife photographers and hunters.

"Apparently he brought two bricks."

"What in the fu—?"

"Swear jar," Bob reminded her.

"Fuuuuuudge," she grumbled. "He's a teenager. How in the hell is he able to get away with this stuff? Did he know where all the cameras were? Did he find a map of them or something?"

"He does seem to have a talent for it," Bob said.

"From now until Halloween, we have someone sitting in the parking lot and watching the doors. With a shotgun. I'll even take a shift myself."

"No," Bob said, shaking his head.

Duffy added, "No, no. No guns. We will not arm you. No one wins in a situation where you are armed."

Bob tilted his head. "Sorry, honey, the whole family voted and agreed that you don't get a gun. Besides, I'm sure one of the cameras got a picture of . . . whoever this was."

"Daddy, please."

"Your mama said we should keep an open mind," Bob told her. "It's not that we don't believe you, doodle bug. We just need to consider the possibility it's someone else causin' the trouble."

"Have you checked the other doors?" she asked.

"They're all just fine," Duffy said. "And the outbuildings, the Snack Shack, the bait shop, the dock, everything. It's all fine."

"Any way to shut off the alarm?" she asked, tapping at her ear.

Bob frowned. "Nope, it's not really an alarm, just one of those cheap babyproofing motion sensor things you can put on doors when you're afraid your kiddo's going to bolt for the front yard. Margot's taken to hangin' it from the office door."

"I happen to know a toddler who could use one of those," Frankie muttered.

Frankie couldn't help but feel guilty that on the one night she was locked in a jail cell and unable to defend her territory, Jared had actually broken into the building. He'd never managed to open a door before. And it was killing her, not knowing what he had touched and broken or whether he'd gotten into the mortuary. She had a pretty considerable lock on the interior morgue door. She couldn't even imagine how awful and guilty she would feel if Jared had done something to one of her clients. Then again, maybe Jared had finally managed to see a dead body and was lying in a puddle of his own urine on her office floor.

It was probably wrong how much that thought cheered her up.

Eric pulled his police vehicle into the parking lot with his blue lights flashing. The fact that he considered this situation an actual emergency was also surprisingly cheering.

Eric cut the lights and parked. He smiled as he crossed the lot. She realized that she was standing next to her father while making eye contact with the man she'd just slept next to, and that was seriously awkward.

"Hey, folks, everybody okay?"

Frankie nodded, praying that her face wasn't completely weird at the moment. "Just fine."

"Yeah, but we're not real sure what's goin' on in there," Bob said. "We didn't want to go in and disturb anything you needed to document."

"Smart," Eric affirmed. "How long have you been here?"

"About twenty minutes. Nobody's come out and we haven't heard anything except the damn alarm."

"Jar," Duffy muttered.

"I need y'all to stand over there and call the state police if you hear anything," Eric said, carefully drawing his gun from his side holster. He walked toward the door, gun pointed at the ground, then stopped to add, "Do not call Landry."

"Understood, do not make the situation worse," Frankie agreed. "Please be careful."

"Don't worry. This is a situation I'm actually trained for."

Eric walked down the hall, reached into the babyproofing monitor, and yanked out the batteries.

"Thank you," Bob said, his shoulders relaxing under the lack of whooping noise.

Frankie gnawed her lip as she watched Eric disappear down the hall.

"Aw, you're worried about your boyfriend," Duffy cooed. "That's so cute."

Frankie smiled sharply at him. "I will burn everything you love."

Duffy snorted.

After a tense few minutes, Eric was walking down the hall with his gun holstered. "It's clear. Y'all can't come in yet, but whoever was here is gone."

"Did he get into the morgue?" Frankie asked.

"Nope, no damage to the door and it was still locked."

"Oh, thank Drogon." She sighed.

"What about the showroom?" Bob asked.

"No, that looked okay, too. But your hallway is pretty wrecked," he said, pulling out his phone and taking pictures of the damage. "I think he got this far, set off the alarm, and ran out."

"Are you going to take fingerprints?" Frankie asked. "Swab for DNA? I have the kits in my office."

"Frankie, you've seen our budget. I have about enough in my forensics fund to run DNA once a year. Do you think I should spend that money on a break-in where there was no significant damage, as opposed to, say, saving it in case one of our citizens gets murdered?"

"Probably the murder," she admitted. "But fingerprints?"

"I can dust for them," he said. "But considerin' that the person who you think is responsible for this doesn't have a criminal record, that probably won't do you a lot of good."

"But he can be charged for this, right?" she asked. "And for the damage to our door and the cameras?"

"If I can prove he did it, yes."

"I'll be right back." She bolted around Eric, holding her hands in an upright surrender position so she didn't touch anything.

"Frankie, what are you doing?" Eric asked, following her down the stairs.

"When we added new cameras, I asked the tech to route the signal to my computer, because I'm not eighty years old and I understand that you occasionally have to check the feed," she said, using her key to unlock the morgue doors.

"Mornin', everybody, sorry to run in all abrupt like this, I've just got something I need to do," she called to the occupants of the drawers as she fired up the overhead lights. "I'll make polite chitchat later."

"Still weird that you talk to them."

She turned to see Eric hovering near the entrance of her office, not quite willing to step inside. "Really? Everybody's in storage. You're not going to see anything."

Eric shuddered and grumbled simultaneously as he walked to her desk. Frankie pulled up the feeds from the trail cam and the office entrance camera. The trail cam was activated by motion around 1:30 a.m. A dark figure wearing a hoodie and a ski mask stepped into frame from the dock area. Frankie couldn't help but note that he was wearing gloves when he tossed the brick at the camera, ending the feed. She pulled up the office door feed from around 1:30 and watched the dark figure toss a brick at the camera. He never quite got close enough for the camera to pick up on any distinguishing features.

"Crap," she grumbled.

"Well, I will be sure to put an APB out for all local ninjas," Eric said.

She glared at him.

"Too soon to joke," he agreed.

"He walked into frame from the dock area, so he must have used a canoe or kayak or something to get across the lake. Jared has this obnoxious orange kayak that he actually named. *The Velociraptor.*"

"I don't like to call children foul names, but that kid's a real douche," Eric said.

"Agreed."

"Can you e-mail me a copy of the footage?" he asked. "I'll be back in my office in an hour or so."

"Where are you goin?" she asked.

"I'm going to go to the Lewis residence and imply none too subtly that a vehicle matching Jared's SUV's description was spotted near the funeral home last night and considering the break-in, it's quite reasonable to question his whereabouts."

"But I just told you, he probably took a kayak," she said, jerking her thumb toward the screen.

"Yeah, but I doubt his mother knows that," Eric told her. "And maybe we'll get lucky and he'll say something dumb like, 'I didn't drive to vandalize the funeral home, I took my kayak.'"

"I know I'm the one who normally escalates these situations beyond all reason, but is it really a good idea to question Jared's parents when you can't prove anything?"

He shrugged. "Sometimes if you apply the right amount of social pressure, the problem can resolve itself. Even if we can't prove this was Jared, maybe if we scare Jared's mom without doing anything permanent, she can stop Jared from escalatin'."

"It's cute that you think that would work." She stood and he took a step back. Suddenly, his posture became rigid again, as if moving reminded him of where he was, and he backed toward the door. "There is no reasoning with Marnette Lewis. There's only dodging passive-aggressive barbs and trying not to get hit in the face with her fake designer purse."

"Well, I'm gonna try anyway," he said. "It's time to get this matter officially on the record."

"You have no idea how much I've wanted a man to say those words to me."

IT TOOK DUFFY, Frankie, and her father more than an hour to clean up the broken Jesus frames. Gravity plus thirty-year-old cheap craft canvas meant very few of them were salvageable.

"Aw, this was Mom's favorite," Bob said, holding up a

busted painting depicting Jesus holding a rainbow that arched between his palms. "She really liked all the purple in this one."

"I'm sorry, Daddy. It feels like this is my fault, with this whole weird rivalry with Jared Lewis."

"Oh, doodle bug, you know that's not true. You can't be responsible for the actions of a teenage jack . . . rabbit."

"That one didn't even make sense; you're payin' for it anyway," Duffy told him.

"He's gone too far this time," Frankie said, gesturing to the paint-by-number carnage thrown around the hallway. "This isn't funny anymore."

"Wasn't all that funny to begin with," Duffy noted.

"What if he'd gotten into the morgue? How would I explain that to the families who trust their loved ones to us?" she exclaimed. "'I'm sorry that I provoked a local kid into desecrating your relative's corpse'?"

"But he didn't get that far, Frankie, and I'll bet that bein' chased off by an alarm and questioned by the police is probably going to make him think twice before—"

Margot came through the door. Her hair and makeup were magazine perfect as usual, but her dark blue designer suit seemed to be splattered with big dots of blue and green paint.

"Hi, everybody, I realize I just got here, but I'm going to need to go home to change," she said. "I'll be back in thirty minutes."

"Margot, honey, why do you have paint all over your pretty suit?" Bob asked.

Margot sighed. "I may have suggested that Aunt Donna ask Fred Dodge out on a date."

Duffy's expression was horrified. "Oh, Margot, no."

"And then?" Frankie asked.

"I said that their constant arguing was basically extended foreplay," Margot said, her lips pulled back in a grimace. "And then she pulled a paintball gun from behind the bait shop counter and went Tony Montana on me."

Frankie winced. "Woman, have you been drinkin' at nine in the mornin'?"

"I was overconfident," Margot admitted.

"We warned you," Duffy said.

"I'll go talk to her," Bob said, shaking his head as he walked outside toward the bait shop.

"Hey, did y'all sign the report paperwork I left?" Eric ducked around Bob and knocked on the door frame. He frowned at the state of Margot's suit. "Is this related to the break-in or an issue I'm going to have to handle separately?"

"Separate issue, but it was friendly fire." Margot sighed.

"One day, I will understand the things that this family says, and on that day I will be . . . so scared," Eric said.

"How was questioning at the Lewis residence?" Duffy asked.

"I couldn't get Jared to crack," Eric said, frowning. "He is immune to most interrogation techniques, also the application of guilt and shame. And the reasonable doubt that I might have spotted his car on the surveillance video."

"I told you," Frankie retorted.

"Also, his mother insists that Jared was home all night, watchin' TV with her. And that he went to bed at ten sharp," Eric said.

"What did she say they were watching?" Margot asked.

"The Real Housewives of New York City."

"I know it's a lie, but it would serve him right if it was true," Frankie said.

"And she claims that Jared is such a heavy sleeper that there's no way he woke up in the middle of the night and left the house without her knowin'."

"Marnette Lewis takes an elephant-level dose of Ambien every night," Frankie said. "She wouldn't know if the Hulk smashed her nightstand. So we're basically at a dead end."

"I'm sorry, but yes," Eric said.

"I'll get your paperwork for you, Sheriff, it's in my office," Margot told him.

"Thank you, Margot."

Eric turned to Frankie and stepped closer, so she could hear a little better. She shut down the involuntary shiver with iron will. "So I was thinking that I might take you out to dinner, a proper dinner to make up for the whole 'my deputy accidentally and illegally incarcerated you overnight' thing."

Frankie moved back, ever so slightly, just as Margot walked back into the hallway, paperwork in hand. "Oh, no, I couldn't."

Eric, clearly caught off guard by her refusal, frowned. "Why? Because I couldn't get the Lewis kid to confess to breaking in?"

"What? No, that would be crazy," Frankie scoffed. "I just have plans, with my cousins, tonight. And I can't break them."

"We do?" Margot asked, arching her eyebrow. And when she saw the look on Frankie's face, she said, "We do. We do. We do." In such different tones with each repetition that it was obviously a lie.

Honestly, it was as if Frankie had taught her nothing.

"I, too, remember those plans and will pick you up at six," Duffy said, just a little less awkwardly. "Which we have already agreed to."

"Well, I guess I'll catch up with you some other time," Eric said.

"Okay," Frankie assured him. "When I haven't made plans with my cousins."

"Which we all knew about," Margot added.

"All right, then," Eric said, holding up his paperwork. "I'll get back to you if I have any more information."

"Bye!" Frankie said, waving her hand just a little too hard as Eric walked out. She turned to Margot. "Don't help me anymore."

DUFFY DIDN'T LIKE the idea of lying to law enforcement officials, since that was technically a crime, so he insisted on actually picking Margot and Frankie up at six and driving them to the Dirty Deer. The bar was the hottest (read: only)

night spot in town, serving beer and moonshine-based cock-tails through a haze of barbecue smoke and neon light. Carl and Marianne, who had managed to convince Tootie to take the boys for the evening, were waiting in a coveted circular booth with a pitcher of beer between them. They were actually cuddled together, close talking and smiling silly secret smiles, despite the fact that they'd been married for more than ten years. Carl even turned his ever-present Braves cap around so Marianne wouldn't get smacked with the bill.

Frankie still didn't understand how her perfect, professional cousin had ended up with a scruffy redneck like Carl, but they'd been completely, disgustingly in love with each other since high school. They made their differences work and were raising their two sons to be intelligent little goobers, who just happened to be very good at shooting and cooking their own squirrels.

There were times when Frankie saw the ridiculous, calf-eyed love that her cousin and Carl had for each other and honestly thought it was sort of gross.

"Hey, there," Carl called, unfurling himself from around Marianne to scoot even closer and make room on the bench seat. "Not that we mind an excuse for a night out, but what was the sudden urgent need to see us?"

"Frankie lied to a cop," Duffy said, pouring himself a beer from the pitcher.

Carl's tone was injured. "Why can't you ever just say 'I missed you,' man?"

"Frankie turned down an invitation from a perfectly nice

law enforcement official and made up a cousin hootenanny to justify her no," Margot said.

"That's a blatant misuse of the word 'hootenanny,'" Frankie told her.

"It's not Landry, right?" Carl asked Duffy, who shook his head.

"Well, I appreciate the invitation anyway," Marianne said. "When you start to think of pizza rolls and Cartoon Network as a quality evening, it's time to get out of the house."

"So, why did we reject the perfectly nice law enforcement official with the bitable bottom lip and the ridiculous—and I mean, ri-dic-u-lous—body?" Margot asked.

"Easy, girl," Marianne said, patting Margot's arm.

"I'm in a relationship, I'm not dead from the waist down," Margot shot back.

"I don't do relationships," Frankie said, taking her own beer.

"That's it?"

Frankie insisted, "I don't do relationships."

Margot patted her hand. "Look, I get it. You know how much I struggled even starting a relationship with Kyle. The fact that he had kids scared me so badly, I didn't even consider a relationship with him at first. Dirty, bendy, mind-blowing sex, yes, but not a relationship."

Duffy shuddered. "I'm just going to turn this way," he said, angling his body toward Carl and Marianne, who were rubbing noses. "Oh, come on, guys."

Duffy stalked away from the booth, toward the pool table.

Frankie took a long sip of her beer. "But then after the world-rockin' sex, you had your big Oprah moment of clarity and now you and Kyle and the kids are basically an Honest commercial come to life."

Margot told her, "That was unnecessarily harsh."

"Sorry," Frankie muttered. "That *was* harsh. Look, my biggest goal as a kid was living long enough to get a driver's license. I never even considered that I could find someone I love, get married."

"But you're not sick anymore, Frankie. You've been in remission for years."

"Spoken like someone who's never been sick. My rational brain knows that, but the rest of my body hasn't gotten the memo. Even after you're better, it changes the way you think about the future, what you want in life, what could happen next year. Every ache, every twinge is cancer. And you're scared to talk to the doctor about it, because you don't really want to hear one telling you again that you're sick and you might not get better."

"And you haven't talked to anybody about this?" Margot asked.

"My doctor knows, but only because I call in every little ache and pain."

Margot shook her head. "But you're always so upbeat . . ."

"You've never heard of faking it till you make it?" She gestured to her recently rehighlighted hair.

"I thought the hair and the clothes were an eff-you to the neighbors."

Frankie waggled her hand. "Sixty-forty. Besides, none of this really matters. I'm not exactly in the right place in my life that I could even have a real relationship, so I'm just going to let this thing with Eric fizzle away and go back to my weekends in Atlanta whenever I need an outlet."

"Not in a place where you can have a relationship? What do you mean by that?" Marianne asked.

"I live in my parents' house in my childhood bedroom. That doesn't exactly scream 'ready for commitment.'"

"So change that, if it's what you want," Margot said, shrugging while Marianne made subtle *cut it out* gestures with her hands. "Move out. You can always stay in the apprentice apartment for a while until you figure things out long term." She paused to watch Marianne's hand motions. "What?"

"Every time I try to bring up moving out, I chicken out because I don't want to hurt my parents," Frankie said, slumping back in her seat.

Margot frowned. "Aw, that sucks."

"How did you two do it?"

"My mother didn't care how quickly I moved out, as long as I was moving into the right neighborhood," Margot said.

"I didn't give my parents the opportunity to argue because I pretty much ran away," Marianne said. "And then, when I came back, I basically just told them how things were going to work, because allowing my mama any room to argue would have led to disaster."

"I don't think I can do that," Frankie said. "It just seems ungrateful, after everything they've done for me."

Marianne put her arm around Frankie. "Well, it sucks, but you're going to have to decide whether their feelings are more important than you being happy. Nobody is going to be able to do it for you. This is definitely one of those solo quest things."

"I could come up with a list of talking points for you, help you put the best spin on it," Margot said with a shrug. Marianne lifted a brow, making Margot add, "But I won't. Because that wouldn't help you grow as a person."

"I appreciate the thought," Frankie told her.

"Wait, what are we talkin' about?" Carl asked.

Frankie hesitated, not wanting Carl to know exactly how much she was struggling with relatively simple adulting.

"Frankie and the sheriff have crazy sexual chemistry, but when he asked her on a real date—as opposed to spending the night in the jail together, don't think we're not going to talk about that," Margot noted quickly, smirking at her cousin, "she lied and said she had plans with us."

"You're datin' the sheriff?" Carl exclaimed. "Do you think he can get me out of a speedin' ticket? It's from a state trooper, but all cops are friends, right?"

"Why is that the first question out of your mouth?" Frankie asked. "Also, Margot just said I turned the sheriff down."

"When did you get another speedin' ticket?" Marianne asked.

Carl told her, "I've been waitin' my whole life to know someone married to a cop."

"We're not *married*. We're not even dating!"

Carl smirked at her as Duffy returned to the table to refresh his beer. "We'll see. You don't get this stirred up over somebody you don't want to pair up with for life."

Margot sighed. "Dear God."

"His redneck Yoda routine shouldn't be hot, but somehow, it is," Marianne said, shrugging.

"I don't have the stomach for beer now," Duffy told his sister. "I hope you're happy."

FRANKIE STUMBLED INTO the kitchen, thinking of the box of special-edition vanilla latte Pop-Tarts in the cupboard. She'd mostly restrained herself the night before, so while she was suffering from a mild headache and a distinct case of squirrel mouth, she was relatively unscathed. A couple of Pop-Tarts and some Tylenol and she'd be right as rain.

Tootie swore by a big greasy breakfast biscuit and her Devil's Due, a disgusting concoction of herbs, eggs, and mystery substances, but for Frankie, the best cure for a hangover was a buttload of sugar and questionable food dyes. She would probably be driving Duffy into work, though, because witnessing his best friend and his sister canoodling all night had sent him toward the moonshine side of the drink menu. Margot hadn't really drunk anything, because Duffy's faces were enough to keep her entertained.

But alas, Frankie's rendezvous with her beloved toaster pastries was not to be, because her mama was at the stove, laying fat strips of bacon in a pan. Mama's frizzled strawberry-blond hair was tied up in a bun on top of her head, which she did only when she was planning some serious feeding. Frankie's daddy was sitting at the table, drinking some of her mother's high-octane coffee and reading the *Ledger*.

"Hey, doodle bug!" he chirped, adjusting the napkin tucked into his shirt collar. "How's the head? You were at the Dirty Deer pretty late."

"Did Stan or Carl talk to you or something?"

"Nah, I looked up that 'find your friends' thing on my phone. You showed up at the Dirty Deer until almost closing time."

"That is not okay. And I'm turning off my location services," Frankie told him, thanking her lucky stars that he hadn't been tracking her like wildlife while she was technically in "captivity."

"No!" Bob exclaimed. "I like being able to find where you are, no matter what time it is! It's for my peace of mind."

"Tracking your child like wildlife is not acceptable parenting, even if they're underage. All you're telling me is that you can't trust me."

"I trust you! I just don't trust anybody else," Bob insisted. "Can we just think about it for a while before you do anything drastic?"

"Drastic would be me attaching my phone to one of Tootie's dogs and sending you on a wild dachshund chase."

"Please, doodle bug, just give me some time to adjust," he begged her.

She pursed her lips as his look of panicked discomfort pricked at her conscience. She knew, better than anyone, how quickly an everyday situation could turn tragic. And she'd seen enough anguished loved ones in that final moment when they lost all hope that everything would be okay that she wanted to prevent her father from going through anything similar. Even though she felt the opportunity for a first step toward independence slipping through her fingers, she said, "Fine."

"Thank you. Now, how's the head?"

"I'm not too bad off," she said. "I actually didn't drink as much as Duffy, who still likes to pretend Carl and Marianne sleep in bunk beds."

"I'm making you breakfast. An egg in a nest with some bacon," her mama said, pushing Frankie into one of the old-school aluminum kitchenette chairs the family had been using for years. Bob poured Frankie a glass of juice.

"I'm not that hungry," Frankie said. "I was just going to have some Pop-Tarts."

"Nonsense!" Mama insisted. "Pop-Tarts are just empty calories and carbs. No nutritional value at all."

Frankie muttered into her juice, "Yeah, that's what makes them awesome."

"Well, I threw them out. They're terrible for you."

Frankie spat orange juice onto her Pusheen T-shirt. "You did what?"

"I threw them out! You don't need all those chemicals and preservatives in your body, honey."

First the phone tracking and now this? How could so much be going wrong in one morning? She was handling this all so badly and she didn't know how to stop the downward slide. Maybe if she'd had more practice talking about this sort of thing with her parents, it wouldn't feel like she was so out of control.

Resentment boiled through Frankie's gut and rose through her throat as seething words. "So Pop-Tarts are bad, but the sheer amount of deep-fried carbs you ply me with on a daily basis is okay?" she shot back.

Mama's blue eyes went wide. She'd never heard that tone from her daughter before.

Bob frowned at her. "Frankie, your mama's only trying to make sure you stay healthy."

"Which would be understandable if I was five, but I'm a grown woman who used her hard-earned paycheck to purchase a rare, limited-run version of her favorite treat, only for her mother to toss it in the garbage. That's not okay, Mama; you could have at least talked to me about it before you threw them out. Why would you not ask me?"

"Well, honey, I didn't do it to hurt your feelings. I just, I worry about you and whether you get the right kind of food to keep you strong and healthy. I just thought it would be better if you weren't tempted."

"Because you're the parent and I'm the child and you know better."

"Yes," Leslie said, and suddenly her brow furrowed and

she shook her head. "No, that's not what I meant. You are an adult and I respect you. I just worry, that's all."

"So your worrying—both of you worrying—is more important than me being able to choose my own food or go where I want without being tracked like a parolee. How long is that going to last? Do I get to choose my own food when I'm thirty? When I'm forty?"

"That's enough, Frances Ann," her father told her. "We can hash out our situation later. But your mama didn't do it to hurt you. She may have messed up, but she did it because she loves you."

Frankie's head whipped toward her father, and when she saw the rare look of disappointment on his face, all the fire in her belly was doused by shame. Her resolve crumbled and her head dropped into her hands. Her parents weren't doing this for the sake of controlling her. The babying, the breakfasts, the tracking, they were coming from a place of love. Good intentions didn't make their efforts any less annoying, but at least she could say they meant well. How many people did she know who couldn't say the same of their parents?

"I'm sorry," she said, sighing. "I'm just grumpy and tired from last night. I shouldn't have snapped at you, Mama."

Mama smiled and patted her shoulder. "It's all right, honey. I know you didn't mean it."

The peace in the kitchen restored, Frankie said, "I thought you were scheduled to go in early this morning, Daddy."

Bob waved his hand dismissively. "Eh, Margot's takin' my meeting with the Portenoys so I could drive you into work. I figured you'd be feelin' rough."

Frankie frowned. She knew her parents were indulgent, but this seemed like an underwhelming response to one's adult daughter going out to tie one on. Also, her father was reading the sports page. Bob McCready was enthusiastic about a lot of things in life, but sports was not one of them. He knew enough about the Dawgs and the Braves to keep up polite, surface conversation, but he never read the sports section.

"What's goin' on?" Frankie asked.

"Nothin'," Bob said, putting the paper in front of his face so he wasn't making eye contact.

"Why are you readin' the sports section?"

"Because I want to see whether . . . Scooter McCluskey's on the injured list."

"Did you just make that name up?" Frankie asked.

Bob cleared his throat. "No."

"Daddy, what's in the paper that you don't want me to see?"

"Nothing!" Bob squeaked.

"No, I'd like to see the front page of the *Ledger*, please."

"I lost it," Leslie said, clearing her throat.

"You lost it?" Frankie deadpanned. "In the ten-step walk from the front porch?"

"One of Tootie's dogs must have eaten it."

Frankie rolled her eyes and bounced out of the chair.

She opened the door to the stainless steel freezer, digging under Mama's bags of frozen hash browns. She pulled out a neatly folded section of newspaper. "Really, Mama? The freezer? It doesn't work with the Halloween candy. Why would it work now?"

"Frankie, honey, now don't get upset," Bob cautioned.

"What in the hell?" Frankie gasped.

Featured prominently on the front page of the *Ledger*, above the fold, was one of the pictures Margot had taken of Frankie getting "arrested." But the headline mentioned nothing about Lock Down Hunger or the fact that the arrest was fake. It just said LOCAL CORONER TAKEN INTO CUSTODY BY SHERIFF ERIC LINDEN and mentioned an "In Other News" story on an interior page. And because it was the picture where Margot had suggested that everybody pretend they were deeply concerned that their undertaker/relative was being hauled away, E.J.J., Stan, Bob, and Frankie all looked appropriately grim.

"How did they even get Margot's picture?" Frankie cried, leafing through the paper.

"Facebook," Leslie said.

"But Margot only put it up yesterday!"

"It's the information age, Frankie," Leslie said.

Grunting, Frankie found the "In Other News" story by Gary Thrope: SHERIFF'S DEPARTMENT INVESTIGATING A BREAK-IN AT MCCREADY'S FAMILY FUNERAL HOME. Gary, the paper's chief news reporter, livestock reporter, and copy editor, used careful wording and omissions to imply that while the door to the funeral home was most certainly pried open, the sheriff hadn't found any evidence of someone from *outside* the family breaking in. The story didn't mention the surveillance footage or the broken Jesus paintings, but it did mention that Frankie was questioned for quite some time. All in all, between the story and picture, the implication was that Frankie had staged the break-in and Eric was charging her for it.

"Oh, come on!" she cried, slapping the paper on the table. "Has E.J.J. seen this?"

"First thing this morning," Bob said. "He's not upset. He knows you didn't do anything and Gary is bein' a jackass. E.J.J.'s going down to talk to him first thing this morning. He does *not* want you talking to anyone at the paper. He wants you to have breakfast and go in to work as usual."

"What in the hell did I do to Gary Thrope?" Frankie huffed. "I haven't even spoken to him in weeks, not since the Huffman drowning."

"Honey, think about it, real hard," Leslie told her, frowning as she slid a plate full of bacon and egg-fried-bread in front of her. The frown was off-putting. Her mama was a relentlessly positive person, particularly in the morning. But her mother looked almost . . . frustrated with her? This expression was so foreign to Frankie that she wasn't quite sure how to identify it.

Frankie groaned, scrubbing her hands over her face. Gary Thrope was married to Lynnie Thrope, one of Marnette Lewis's multitude of cousins. There was no free press in Lake Sackett when in-laws were involved.

Leslie forced a breath out of her nose and then smiled tightly. "It's a really good picture of you."

"Mama, no."

IT TOOK ALL of Frankie's self-control, which was not legendary, to force herself to go to work, do her job, and not make multiple phone calls to the newspaper, the national guard, and Oprah to vent her anger. She tried not to take it personally that E.J.J. had taken her cell phone before she'd gone down to the mortuary. And taken the line out of the back of her office phone. And had Margot change the password to the business's Wi-Fi.

The only positive in the situation was that Eric couldn't call her, either. Given the multiple waves of conflicting feelings she had about that particular law enforcement official, she thought that was for the best.

By three, she'd processed four clients, reorganized all of her supplies, and caught up on all of her paperwork. She was actually considering cleaning out her filing cabinet when Margot knocked on the mortuary door.

"Everybody covered?" she asked.

"Yep, come on in." Frankie stripped off her rubber cleaning gloves and shoved them behind her back, as if she weren't just about to spray bleach into her filing drawer.

"Were you about to Clorox your filing cabinet?" Margot asked.

"No comment."

"You know what you need?" Margot said.

"A crossbow and about three pounds of saltwater taffy?"

"No," Margot said. "For so many reasons, no."

"Dang it," Frankie muttered.

"You need a distraction," Margot told her.

"I won't argue with you there."

"So, come with me to the Trunk-R-Treat meeting at the elementary school. You can help me fend off the craziest of the moms. It will be fun!" Margot exclaimed, smiling and doing the whole jazz-hands maneuver.

Frankie closed her hands over Margot's fingers and held them together. "I know we were raised differently, but that's no excuse for your flawed definition of fun."

"Come on!" Margot said. "It will get you out of the mortuary, and you'll have the chance to show your friends and neighbors that you are not, in fact, in jail right now for faking a break-in!"

"I hate it when you make a good point." Frankie sighed, shrugging out of her lab coat. "I thought the PTA wasn't running the Trunk-R-Treat. Why is the meeting being held at the school?"

Margot waited by the exit bay while Frankie shut down her computer. "It was the only place other than the Baptist church that was big enough for the crowd. I've found that holding meetings in a nondenominational building results in fewer comparisons between reading *Harry Potter* and devil worship."

"How does that even come up in conversation?"

Margot's expression became alarmingly cheerful. "You'd be amazed."

THE MEETING TURNED out to be more fun than Frankie expected. She felt like Margot's enforcer, sitting at the front of the school library, glaring at the moms when they got unruly.

And unruly they were.

First, there came Margot's big announcement of the evening, which was that she'd signed up so many people to run trunks that the event would have to move to the elementary school, which had a perfect circular drop-off lot to host the cars, while the food booths could be set up at the teachers' parking spaces. All hell broke loose. Women started yelling about tradition and "community values." Frankie was completely confused, because as far as she was concerned, having so many cars involved that the event had to be moved to a larger space was a good thing. And it took Margot several explanations, a few mild threats, and an insinuation that maybe the objecting moms didn't *want* the event to go well before they accepted that the festivities had a new home.

Then came the special requests. Laurie Huff, the mother of two of the meanest girls in the third grade, wanted to make a rule that if one child showed up in the same costume as another child, the latecomer had to go home and change.

Lizzie Withnall wanted to propose that all the participating trunks give away plain M&M's because otherwise, the kids might be overwhelmed with choices. Charlene Hall wanted to change the name of the event entirely, because she felt the Trunk-R-Treat was too closely related to Halloween and, therefore, evil.

Charlene didn't have kids. She just really hated Halloween.

If not for Frankie and Sweet Johnnie Reed, who was a vocal supporter of Margot, the meeting might have fallen into chaos. When Laurie said that her daughters' Halloween would be ruined if someone else wore *their* costumes, Sweet Johnnie said, "Oh, shug, surely your daughters have more generosity of spirit than to send some other child home and make them miss out on treats, just because they have the same outfit?"

When Annabeth Blackwell suggested no candy be distributed, only dried fruit, Frankie told her, "Get out." And then stared at her until Annabeth felt so uncomfortable that she walked out.

Eventually the troublemakers quieted down and Margot was able to establish a list of trunk volunteers, the placement of cars, how much candy still needed to be purchased, and so forth. A few hours later, they had a respectable plan of operations and had whittled away most of the ridiculous rules through the sheer force of Margot's will. The only decision left was to determine the prizes for the best trunk decorations, but Margot insisted that she would choose them so they would remain a surprise. And then she dismissed the Trunk-R-Treat moms with a cheerful "Everything is well in hand, ladies. Now get out."

And to Frankie's surprise, they got out.

"You are really growing into your role as a small-town mover and shaker,"

"Believe it or not, Marianne says this is nothing compared to the meetings they have to plan the school holiday pageant—"

Suddenly, Margot bent over the wastebasket and threw up copious amounts of, well, everything.

"Holy crap, Margot, are you okay?" Frankie said, grabbing a bottle of water from the refreshment table and forcing Margot—and the wastebasket she was clutching to her chest—into a nearby chair. Before Frankie could bring the bottle to Margot's lips, she threw up again.

"Phew." Frankie blew out a breath and held her face away from Margot's misery.

"Oh, please, you deal with dead bodies all day," Margot croaked.

"The dead don't puke," Frankie told her. "Are you okay? Is this regular sick or food poisoning sick? Did you eat something Aunt Donna made? We've warned you over and over."

"No, I haven't been food-poisoned by Aunt Donna," Margot told her, rolling her eyes and then vomiting again.

"But what else could it be?" Frankie thought back to their night at the Dirty Deer. Margot hadn't actually had any beer, now that she thought about it. Every time Frankie had poured one for her, Margot had passed it along to Duffy. She'd had water with her possum eggs. Come to think of it, she'd eaten a crazy amount of possum eggs.

Frankie gasped. "Margot, are you pregnant?"

"I haven't had the nerve to take a test yet, but yeah, I'm pretty sure I am," Margot said, wiping at her watery eyes.

"How?"

Margot glared at Frankie. "The usual way."

"I know 'how,' I'm just askin' how a modern, worldly girl like yourself managed to get knocked up. Don't you know about birth control? Keepin' a dime between your knees and all that?"

Margot snickered, grabbing a tissue from the librarian's desk and blowing her nose. "The dime thing is one we didn't try. We've been really careful, but nothing's one hundred percent effective. Especially when you're under stress, which, let's face it—as nice as everything has been since I've moved back, gettin' to know my dad, gettin' to know the family, organizin' the Founders' Festival, adjustin' to a life that in- volves dogs and children and school schedules . . . yeah, it's all been stressful."

"Are you happy?"

"I don't know!" Margot sobbed. "First of all, 'morning sickness' is bullshit. I've been throwing up round the clock, which was my first clue that something was wrong. And I'm tired and my boobs hurt and I'm eating everything in sight. I tried to ignore the symptoms, thinking maybe I just had the flu or something, but here we are. And second, I just don't know. It's not that I'm scared. I mean, sure, Kyle and I have only been dating for a couple of months. I have eyeliners older than our relationship. It must have happened one of the first times we were together. And he's got the girls, and I don't want him to think I'm trapping him, and I definitely don't want the girls to think I'm trying to replace them with another baby. And I have no idea whether I'm ready for this, because I just got to the point where spending time with kids didn't make me want to break out in hives. But when I think about having a baby with Kyle and raising it with all of the family nearby, it's almost enough to make me forget how badly this messes up my life plan. I wouldn't want anybody else's baby, but I would want Kyle's baby. He makes really nice babies."

Frankie felt so bad for Margot, she wouldn't even mention the swear jar. She knelt next to her, squeezing Margot's hand. "Well, first, we're going to go to the drugstore two towns over so no one sees you buying a pregnancy test, and you're going to woman up and pee on a stick so we get an answer one way or another. And then you're going to see a doctor, and then you're going to tell Kyle. And then you're going to tell Stan, but you have to promise to wait until I'm there so I can see his face."

"My dad!" Margot cried, burying her face in her tissue. "How am I supposed to tell my dad?"

Frankie patted her shoulder. "Well, he wasn't around for any of your teenage crises, so this is his chance to make up for his absence."

"Thank you, Frankie." Margot sniffed as Frankie hugged her. "I really appreciate your help."

"Well, you wanted to distract me from my problems. Mission accomplished."

FRANKIE DROPPED MARGOT at home with the pregnancy tests she'd bought at a Walgreens fifty miles away. Margot insisted that she didn't want to take a pregnancy test in a gas station bathroom, and promised to let Frankie know the results, after talking to a doctor and Kyle.

Once again, Frankie was struck by the huge difference between her cousin's life and her own. Margot suspecting that she was pregnant had stirred something wholly new in Frankie. Margot was only a few years older, but here she was, in a mostly functional relationship, living on her own, and starting a family. Frankie couldn't even imagine having a child right now. She couldn't imagine having a child in the next five years, not stuck in this weird delayed adolescent limbo. And she didn't know how to start fighting her way out of it and keep her resolve in the face of hurting her parents. She couldn't even fight for her right to Pop-Tarts.

When she thought about Margot's life, Frankie was . . . envious. She'd never begrudged someone their story. She loved her own life. She had a loving family, a great job, plus enthusiastic and athletic sex with an interesting array of partners. But seeing Margot moving into a new stage like pregnancy, Frankie was jealous of her cousin. And she was ashamed of that jealousy. And even more ashamed of how she'd been dodging Eric since that morning in the jail cell.

The upside to Margot's situation was that she hadn't thought about Gary Thrope or his abuse of the First Amendment for hours. Not until she walked onto her parents' porch and found E.J.J. sitting on the swing. It was like being stalked by Andy Griffith, if Andy Griffith spent less time on his guitar and more time making his own beef jerky.

"So, you've had an interestin' day."

"It's safe to say that I hate everybody and everything," Frankie told him, sliding next to him on the swing. E.J.J. handed her a beer. "Except you."

"The paper has agreed to print a 'clarification' denotin' that you were not, in fact, charged with anything during your arrest for charity," E.J.J. said. "Technically, nothing in the article was false, it was all implication, so they wouldn't print a retraction."

Frankie frowned. "And what page will that clarification run on?"

"Page seven. Next to the public notice about predatory zebra mussels."

Frankie moaned and flopped her head back. "No . . ."

"You shouldn't underestimate the draw of zebra mussels. They're scary."

"So that's it?" she asked. "Marnette Lewis gets her cousin's husband to run an article that makes me look like an unstable criminal and I get a 'Sorry, I did a half-ass job' clarification next to the mussel warning?"

"No, the only way to really hurt Gary is to cancel Mc-Cready's advertisements in the paper for the next three months and to tell his boss that the reason I'm cancelin' them is because of Gary's 'creativity.'"

"Won't that hurt the business, too?"

"Honey, we're the only funeral home in town," he told her. "We buy ads in the *Ledger* because we want the *Ledger* to stay in business. Small local papers are the heart of towns like ours. But if they bite the hand that supports them, they deserve to feel the sting."

"Damn, Uncle E.J.J., that's downright Machiavellian of you."

"The business has weathered worse storms than this, Frankie. In the 1940s, there were rumors that we buried somebody alive. In 1962, your grandpa tripped at the county fair, split his pants, and mooned the mayor's wife. In 1979, your aunt Tootie played the wrong song for a funeral, which caused a fight and someone ended up getting thrown through the stained-glass window. And now, you're in a battle of wits with a teenager, and losin'."

"Hey!"

"The amazin' thing about small towns is that, eventually, someone else will come along and do something dumber and get people's attention, and they'll forget all about you."

"We didn't really bury someone alive, did we?" Frankie asked. "Because you were a little vague with the details there."

"Not that we know of."

"Not reassuring."

He snickered, wrapping his arm around her shoulders and kissing her temple. "I think maybe you should talk to your sheriff friend. He was trying to get a hold of you and was pretty worried when you didn't pick up."

"Well, I would, but someone took my cell phone."

He chuckled and dropped the phone into her hand. "Good night, honey."

As he shuffled toward his front door, Frankie unlocked her phone and scrolled through the messages and missed calls. Her thumb hovered over the settings icon. Thinking of Margot and the huge steps she was taking, Frankie opened the privacy settings and flicked her thumb over LOCATION SERVICES. Taking a deep breath, she turned it off.

Her dad would just have to learn to live with it.

10

DESPITE THE FACT that she'd had a very long day, Frankie took Duffy's truck and drove to the old Pickney place. Frankie McCready might be stuck in emotional limbo and have medical anxieties out the wazoo, but she was not a coward when it came to men. If Margot could face her unexpected bun in the oven, Frankie could talk to Eric and have a grown-up discussion about boundaries and sex and intimacy. And if it turned out he didn't like her that way after all and she had completely misinterpreted every gesture he'd made, she would just use the funeral home's backhoe to dig her own grave and hide out there for a few months.

The Pickney place was one of the cheaper vacation cabins in town, having been rented out by Roseann Pickney's children when Roseann went to assisted living. It had gotten pretty run-down after the water dump. With so many options available, the tourists went after the nicer places at discounted prices available during an economic crisis.

Still, the Pickney place had a beautiful view of the lake and the hills, far away from the town proper so there was no light pollution, noise, or . . . people to ruin it. Frankie approached the chain-link fence, where Herc met her at the gate. She felt like she was being approved by the dog before being allowed to visit his master.

Herc sat back on his haunches, which she interpreted as doggy-speak for *You may pass.*

"Eric?" she called. "It's Frankie."

Herc trotted alongside as she circled the cabin. Eric wasn't on the back deck, with its mismatched chairs and Herc's chewed-up hanks of rope. Through the back door's window, she spied a big blue dog cushion by Eric's couch, with *HERC* embroidered on it in gold letters. She smirked.

"You've pretty much got him wrapped around your little paw, don't you?"

Herc yowled and nudged her leg. He seemed to be herding her toward the water, so she carefully picked her way down a sloping hill. She heard splashing and peered through the fading light to see a man-type shape slipping through the water.

Eric was swimming, without a shirt. And she didn't see any trunks, either.

Oh, praise Legolas.

Even though it was blurred by the water, she was seeing a lot of Eric.

A *lot* of Eric.

It was like watching a dirty merman fantasy come to life. He was diving through the water, turning, barreling, stroking around the dock. There was no rhyme or reason to it. He was just having *fun*. Frankie didn't think she'd ever seen him having fun. His whole body shape was different, relaxed and loose . . . and so naked.

Now Eric was looking back at her. Frankie was ogling him pretty openly. And somehow, she'd moved much closer to the dock than she realized.

"Shit!" he yelped, ducking deeper under the water.

"Yipe!" she yelled back, clapping her hands over her eyes.

Herc barked from the back porch, because he apparently didn't want to be left out of the conversation.

"I'm sorry, Frankie! I didn't know you were comin' over!" he shouted, treading water and moving behind the dock, where she could see less.

"I would have called, but I didn't think you would be super-thrilled to have me come over. What are you doing?" she said.

"I'm swimming," he said. "I think that's fairly obvious."

"Are you aware that indecent exposure is a crime in this state?" she asked, nodding toward the discarded towel on the dock.

"Yeah, well, you're the only person that's come out here since I moved in, so I figured I was safe. Why are you out here, anyway?"

"My uncle thought I should probably check in with you.

He said you were worried when you couldn't get a hold of me." She smirked.

"I wasn't worried," he scoffed. "I was interested in knowin' where you were, because I couldn't reach you. And that's . . . important, because . . . there could be an accident and I would need you. Because . . . dead people."

"Smooth," she told him.

He laughed and slapped a bit of water at her. She shrieked as it splattered across her cheek. "Yikes! Aren't you freezing?"

"Not really," he said. "It's not any worse than a swimmin' pool. You coming in?"

Frankie grinned and dropped to a sitting position on the dock. "Nope."

"Why not?" Eric edged closer around the dock, keeping his waistline well below the water.

"Because swimming in the lake at night—naked—is how horror movies start."

He grinned, slicking his hair back from his face. "First, don't knock naked swimmin' until you've tried it. And second, come on, hundreds of people swim in this lake every day over the summer."

"Yeah, in the deeper parts of the lake. Not in the shallows, where there are hundreds of turtles, including snappin' turtles, who are more than willin' to take a bite out of your bits when you step on them."

Eric was about to scoff, but his face went slack as he jerked left, as if something had touched him under the water. "Shit!"

Frankie cackled as he scrambled toward the ladder and leaped out of the water. Her laughter died on her lips as full-frontal Eric came into view: long, muscled legs; rangy arms; slender, high-arched feet that were directly proportional to, well—she tried not to look, honestly, but it was right there at eye level. The water, clearly, had not been that cold. On the other hand, if it *had* been cold and he was still in that range? Damn.

His proportions—his *other* proportions—didn't seem quite human, either. How was it possible to have hips that narrow with shoulders that wide? How did the little droplets of water manage to cling to every dip and outline like that?

Frankie opened her mouth to say something, anything, that would somehow make this moment less awkward, but nothing could possibly accomplish it. There was a long silence while they stared at each other and then Eric smoothly dropped to his knees and slid his mouth against Frankie's. The shock of the cold flesh against hers was enough to make her gasp. His tongue tentatively reached out for her parted lips and she welcomed it. Whatever uncertainty he had about his job and his home, Eric was sure of himself here; tasting and taking and nipping at her lips until she felt disconnected from everything but his mouth.

The kiss became soft and lazy. She felt enclosed as he crouched over her, like he was protecting her from the wind and the potential angry woodland creatures. She slid her hands over his bare wet shoulders and into his thick hair. Her fingers worked down his body, exploring those ridges and dips of muscle. She liked this thing where the guy started off naked. It meant less work for her.

"I just want to point out this is exactly how people die in horror movies," she whispered as Eric nipped little kisses along her throat.

"Worth the risk," he murmured against her shoulder.

Eric sat back on his haunches to pull her shirt off. She sat up a bit, wriggling out of her Survey Corps T-shirt. He took in the sight of her bright yellow bra with the little winky-face emojis and grinned. He yanked at one tightly laced purple sneaker.

"Wait, I'm a double-knotter." But as soon as she said it, the shoe came loose and went flying over his shoulder and into the lake with a *plop*. She burst out laughing. "What are you doing?"

"I'll get you other shoes," he swore, swooping in for another kiss that was half laughter, half breathless antici-pation of *more nakedness*. He peeled her leggings away and knelt between her thighs like a man at prayer. She slid her hands down his back, relishing the outline of every muscle, before squeezing his round cheeks. Yep, just as firm as she suspected.

He settled between her thighs, bracing his hands under her legs, and suddenly looked up. "You sure about this?" he asked. "You sure you're okay?"

"You may recall I've done this before. Not on a dock, of

course, but then again, I'm not the one throwing their partner's shoe in the lake, rookie."

"Point taken." Eric laughed, kissing her jaw as he began the long, slow slide inside her.

FRANKIE WOKE FROM a deep and dreamless sleep and felt a breeze on her face. She was cold and could feel splinters in her butt. This was uncomfortable, but she definitely appreciated the techniques Eric had used to give her what amounted to sex Ambien. The man was good with his hands, and his tongue. And the other parts weren't too shabby, either.

She lifted her head from the piled clothes supporting it. The moon was still rising over the water lapping at the dock. Eric was stretched out next to her, his arm thrown across her waist.

She really had to stop waking up in such odd situations with Eric. She reached into her purse and checked her phone. It was after midnight. She had three missed calls from her parents, who were clearly panicking that she was out so late. This was what she got for turning off location services.

She heard the *click-clack* of toenails across the wooden boards. She yanked her shirt over her chest and turned to see Herc's long snout hovering near her face. He did not seem pleased to find his master in this position. If Herc had resented Frankie before, this would not improve things between them.

"Hey, Herc," Eric mumbled, reaching up and patting the dog's head.

"I don't think Herc should see this. This is like your toddler walking in on you naked," Frankie said with a yawn. "This could be traumatic for all of us."

Eric took Frankie's jacket and covered himself. "You're probably right. Herc, go on up to the house."

Herc whined, but trotted to the back porch.

"By the way, I saw the embroidered dog bed." She picked up her panties and leggings and rolled them back on in one smooth motion.

Eric cleared his throat. "They were practically givin' 'em away at PetSmart."

"Mm-hmm." She snickered. "I need to head home."

He frowned. "Because your parents are expecting you?"

"There's no official curfew. But the disappointed looks over the breakfast table are punishment enough."

"Which you wouldn't have to put up with if you moved out."

"One step at a time," she told him.

"What was the first step?" he asked.

"Turning off the location services on my phone so they can't use nanny software to find me."

"Wow, how did your parents respond to that?"

"I don't know yet."

An expression of disappointment crossed his face. "You didn't tell them?"

"One. Step. At. A. Time."

He sighed. "I'll drive you home. The deer are out like crazy right now. And I wouldn't feel right lettin' you drive home all alone."

"I've been drivin' these roads since I was sixteen," she said.

"How many fatal deer-versus-vehicle collisions have you handled since you became coroner?"

"This is going to be a very awkward arrangement if you're going to insist on using logic." It was no accident that she'd used the word *arrangement* instead of *relationship*. She'd enjoyed sex with Eric, but she wasn't naive enough to believe that meant they were going steady. If he wanted to have sex again, she would be more than happy to throw herself right in, but all those old doubts about anything else were rising right back to the surface. She regretted nothing, but she wasn't quite ready for more.

"Please, for the sake of my patriarchal and overprotective heart, let me drive you home? I'll pick you up in the morning in Duffy's truck."

"Fine." She slid back into her shirt. "Because that means I get to watch you run naked back to your cabin."

"But I have my towel."

"No, you don't!" She grabbed the towel from the dock

and ran toward the house in her bare feet. She yelped as he picked her up and threw her over his shoulder in a fireman's carry. The position put her up close and personal with one of her favorite body parts, which she liberally smacked as he carried her onto his porch.

"I would feel bad, but you did throw away my shoes."

ERIC AGREED TO stop by the funeral home on the way to the family compound, just to make sure the newly rein-stalled cameras were still intact. She was pleased to find that all was quiet when they rolled onto the gravel parking lot. But she noted that Eric cut his headlights the moment they turned off the highway, and he parked the squad car in a shaded area near the dock, away from the floodlights.

"I'm just going to get out and check the doors," Eric told her, getting his holster and flashlight out of the glove com-partment.

"Okay," she said, hopping out of the truck.

"What do you think you're doin'?"

"I'm goin' with you."

"No, you're not."

"I'm going to be able to spot problems way easier than you could."

Eric scrunched up his face. "Logic."

She snickered and followed him, picking her way care-fully across the gravel in a pair of Eric's old rubber boots.

"Just stay behind me," he told her.

They checked the perimeter of the building and found nothing out of place. The cameras were running. The doors were secured. They were about to walk around the office building to Eric's vehicle when a black SUV rolled into the parking lot on idle.

"What the shit?" Eric gasped, shoving Frankie behind the corner of the building, out of sight.

Eric's whole body changed shape. His back was straighter, his shoulders wider. Frankie peeked around the corner and saw Jared Lewis's lanky form climb out of his SUV. He was dressed in all black, but hadn't bothered to pull his ski mask over his face yet.

Frankie hissed angrily, rage burning up her throat to form some very foul words. Eric pushed her back again and shushed her. *Shushed* her!

Jared pulled his ski mask over his face and took a large crowbar out of the passenger seat. Frankie glanced toward the security camera, recently placed in a recessed eave of the roofline. Jared was right in view. With a grin that felt downright evil, Frankie pushed at Eric's shoulders, but Eric shook his head. They watched as Jared approached the mortuary bay doors and slipped the crowbar into the doorjamb.

"Stop him!" Frankie whispered.

"I have to wait," he whispered back. But the second Jared pulled on the crowbar, attempting to open the door, Eric rounded the corner, shining the flashlight in Jared's face. "Sheriff's department!"

Frankie was so caught off guard by the authoritative tone that for a second, she held up her hands. Jared, however, looked ready to bolt.

"Don't do it, son," Eric barked. "Now, drop the crowbar."

Jared flung the crowbar on the ground, nearly to Frankie's feet. Eric frowned at him. "Really?"

"You have to call my parents!" Jared squeaked. "You can't arrest me without my parents' permission."

Frankie frowned. What legal shows had this kid been watching?

Eric responded, "I don't have to do anything yet. Put your hands up and keep them there."

Eric walked forward and carefully removed Jared's mask. Frankie rounded the corner just as his face was revealed. She smirked even as he scowled at her. It was like the best episode of *Scooby-Doo* ever.

"What are you doing here, Mr. Lewis?" Eric demanded.

Jared widened his eyes, as if he could somehow channel the guilelessness of cute Internet kittens. "Well, Sheriff, I heard about all the trouble the McCreadys have been havin' and I thought I should stop by to make sure the building's locked up tight."

"With a crowbar?"

Jared shrugged. "Sure, how else do ya check if a door is locked?"

"What in the hell?" Frankie cried. "Please tell me you don't believe this shit."

"Frankie, please."

Frankie stomped over to the back of Jared's SUV and opened the hatch door. Inside was a mannequin in a cardboard box, splashed all over with fake blood with stitches drawn on it in Sharpie. The fake "cadaver" had a sign around its neck that read STITCH ME UP, DR. FRANKENSTEIN.

Frankie practically snarled at Jared. He was reducing Frankie's work to a cliché horror movie trope. He was disrespecting her, her family, and worse, the people inside her morgue.

"Right, and I guess this was just a Halloween decoration you're drivin' to some late-night charity function?" Frankie asked, her jaw clenched so tight it ached.

She'd tried being mature. She'd tried turning the other cheek. She'd tried ignoring it. Clearly none of these things were working. It was time for some justice.

"She's not allowed to search my car!" Jared howled, stepping toward Frankie. "I didn't give permission for that!"

"It would be best if you just shut up and stayed still, Mr. Lewis," Eric told him. "I don't want to cuff you, but I will. Even without that creepy mannequin setup, I saw you with my own eyes, attempting to pry open the door to the McCready's mortuary. That is a punishable offense and you will be charged for it."

"What! No!" Jared yelled. "You can't prove anything!"

Frankie, meanwhile, had stomped toward Jared, scooping up the crowbar from where he had thrown it.

"Frankie," Eric said, watching warily as she pointed the crowbar at Jared.

"That's it, Jared Lewis. I'm sick of this stupid game. I'm sick of your bullshit," she said. "You've gone too far. Don't you see that? It's one thing to mess with me, but you've messed with my family. You've disrespected the people who trusted us to take care of their loved ones. Hell, you're disrespecting the dead!" She swung the crowbar toward the SUV to point at the mannequin.

Eric stepped between Jared and the blunt object. "Whoa, Frankie, just calm down, put down the crowbar. I've got this handled."

"Oh, you mean the crowbar that this kid brought to my place of business to pry open a door and illegally enter? Sure." Frankie flung her arm to the side and let go of the crowbar. She'd only meant to throw it to the ground, but instead she was watching it in slow motion as it twirled toward the SUV. It was headed straight for the not-exactly-cheap halogen headlight, and there was nothing she could do to stop it. She winced as the glass shattered in a glittering shower on the ground.

"Frankie." Eric sighed, dropping his head.

"She can't do that!" Jared yelled, his face mottling red under his acne scars. "She can't bust up my car!"

"No, she can't," Eric said. "And you will be able to file a report when I take you to the sheriff's office to call your parents." He leveled a distinctly annoyed glare at Frankie. "Because destroying someone's headlight, even if he's really annoying, is still a crime. In fact, waving a heavy object at a minor isn't a great idea. And if the Lewises want to press charges, I'm going to have to file them!"

Now that Frankie wasn't armed, Jared's bravado was back. "That's right, Sheriff. I want her charged with destruction of private property. Call my parents. I'm sure my mama will say the same thing."

"Crap." Frankie grumbled as Eric maneuvered Jared into the backseat of the squad car. He raised the metal grate between the two rows of seats, so there was no doubt Jared was being taken into custody. Frankie, at least, was allowed to sit in the front seat. Dread filled her belly as Eric silently drove into town. She'd never been in this much trouble. Then again, she'd never broken the law before. She couldn't believe she'd actually busted the headlight. Usually when she did something stupid and destructive, she was the only one who got hurt. She did feel pretty awful that she'd messed up Jared's car, but she felt equally angry that the little bastard had been about to vandalize her domain *again*.

She glanced back at him, sitting behind the cage in a *squad car*, and he didn't even seem fazed. He was just glaring out the window, as if being caught burglarizing a building was so horribly inconvenient for him. She didn't understand it. She was the product of indulgent parents, and she didn't behave this way. It was like seeing the Mirror Universe version of herself, without the beard.

Speaking of her parents, she texted them to say she was

fine and was spending the night at the apprentice apartment. It was a blatant lie, but there was still some chance she could keep them from finding out about this.

She crossed her arms over her chest and wondered how the hell things had gone so wrong so quickly. Just a few hours ago, she had been cooling in the sweat of good sex, and now she was possibly being arrested by said sex partner. This was not the sort of thing that happened to responsible adults with decent karma.

The Lewises met them at the sheriff's office, and it turned out that they did indeed want to press charges. In fact, Frankie was pretty glad there was a cop present because Marnette Lewis looked ready to tear her face off with those acrylic nails.

"I want her charged!" Marnette yelled as Frankie sat in an uncomfortable chair near Janey's desk. Marnette cradled Jared's head to her bosom. She was dressed in a twinset and pearls, even at two in the morning. Her face was streaked with tears and eyeliner, as apparently she'd given herself a full smoky eye before arriving to pick up her "poor, sweet boy."

Jared was shrinking into Marnette's side, clutching at her like it was the great "Jared didn't really shoot out the high school gym windows with a potato gun" debacle all over again. "I want her put away! She's a menace! Everybody knows she's insane, but no one wants to say anything because she's been 'sick.'"

Vern Lewis was also very clearly wearing his county manager hat instead of his parent hat as he loomed over her. A jowly man with prematurely graying hair, Vern had basically inherited the job from his father, running for the position when Vern Sr. died in the early aughts. Vern wasn't terribly interested in local politics and moved to correct Jared or use his influence only when Marnette pried him out of his Barcalounger.

"Ms. McCready, I can't tell you how disappointed I am in you as a county employee, damaging my son's car like that. I've tolerated your bad attitude toward him because everybody seems to tolerate your, what'dya call 'em, 'eccentricities,' around here, and I figure a single woman at your age deserves a little pity."

"Pity!"

He continued as if she hadn't spoken. "But this is goin' too far. You broke my son's headlight with a crowbar."

"Putting him in danger!" Marnette cried.

"Putting him in danger," Vern repeated. "He can't drive his car to school now, which means he can't drive his friends, either. He can't drive his grandma to the grocery store. He can't do any of his service projects. You've really hurt him."

Frankie snorted. "Okay, first of all, your poor, sweet boy brought the crowbar with him. We saw him take it out of his car and then try to pry the back door of the funeral home open. So let's stop pretendin' that I stopped him in the act of rescuing a kitten from quicksand. Your son is a criminal. And by the way, everybody in town knows he charges his grandma gas money when he drives her to the grocery, because she complains to the other ladies at bingo about it. And his service project for church? There's no such thing as the Institute for Blind Orphan Squirrels."

"You dirty lyin' bitch!" Marnette cried.

"Easy," Eric warned her.

"My boy doesn't lie! You're just obsessed with him—it's sick! Stalking a teenage boy this way."

"The teenage boy who was caught red-handed breaking into my office. Right." Frankie looked to Eric.

"And you!" Marnette whirled on Eric, jabbing her finger into his face. "You're lettin' her drag you right into her insanity. Comin' to my house and questioning my boy like he's some sort of common criminal. Shame on you for taking that circus freak's side when we're the *real* victims here."

"Hey!" Eric shouted.

"You are just ten pounds of crazy in a five-pound sack, aren't you?" Frankie rolled her eyes. "Can I go to jail now? I'm sure the company will be better, if not smarter."

Eric nodded. "I'm going to need you folks to sign some paperwork."

"We'll sign anything you want!" Marnette exclaimed. "Just as long as she goes to jail where she belongs!"

"Actually, the paperwork is related to the charges against Jared."

Marnette cried, "But he's just a baby! He didn't mean any harm."

"Trespassing on private property after the owners have

specifically and repeatedly told him not to cross the property line is illegal, Mrs. Lewis. As is attempting to enter the building by breaking in. I don't care what his intentions were. And there will be additional charges if I can prove that it was his crowbar that pried open the office door last week."

"Even if it was his crowbar, that doesn't mean that he pried open the door. It could have been anyone who got into our garage!" Marnette insisted.

"Really, you're suggesting that someone else used the same crowbar to break into the same building on a different night? Kind of pushing plausible deniability to its breaking point, aren't you?" Frankie asked.

"My son will not be charged in my county," Vern shouted.

"Good thing it's not an election year for your position, huh, Vern?"

Vern scowled at Frankie. "I've had enough of your lip, young lady."

Frankie smiled ever so sweetly. "Which is too bad, really, since I've got so much of it to spare."

"Your parents should have tanned your hide every chance they got; maybe you woulda turned out normal," he told her.

"Enough!" Eric shouted. "Look, Jared's a minor and he can be released into your custody, but he will still be charged *as a minor* with trespassing and attempted break-in, which is what he was doin' when we found him," he told the Lewises.

"And how, exactly, Sheriff, did you just happen to be in the funeral home parking lot with Ms. McCready?" Vern asked.

"With your son," Frankie noted.

"After midnight," Vern added.

"With. Your. Son," Frankie growled.

"That's none of your business," Eric told him. "The court will contact you about arraignments and such. Please answer all correspondence in a timely manner."

"I don't think so." Vern shrugged.

"You won't respond to the court papers in a timely manner?"

"No, I don't think we need to file any papers. I think, what with the circumstances and the stress Jared's been through, we can agree that he deserves a little extra consideration, don't you?"

Eric took a deep breath and stared Vern down. "No, sir, I don't believe that's the case."

"As your supervisor, I'd say it is."

"As much as I appreciate my job, Vern, I don't believe it's in the best interest of the county to let Jared go without consequences. Especially when I just talked to Mrs. Lewis about Jared's behavior this week and that only seemed to make him escalate. He needs consequences now, so he can figure out a better way to behave."

"Don't you tell me how to parent my child!" Marnette seethed.

Eric said, "You appointed me to uphold the law. That applies to everybody, even your family. You wouldn't want me as your sheriff, otherwise."

Vern's graying brows met in the middle of his forehead.

"Well, your being sheriff can be a temporary situation, if you keep this up."

Marnette smirked. "Real temporary."

Eric's lips disappeared into a thin line. "I guess that's just a chance I'll have to take."

Vern stared at Eric, attempting to loom over him, too, despite being two inches shorter. Eric just stared right back.

"If you don't sign the paperwork, Jared stays in my custody and I call the district judge." There was that voice of authority again. Frankie felt a flash of guilt and irritation over the little shiver it sent down her spine. Later, she was going to have to sit down and closely examine the motivations that fueled her kinks.

Vern and Eric continued to stare at each other. Eric stared harder, so Vern backed down and signed the papers. "This isn't the last time we'll talk about this."

"I'm sure it won't be."

Marnette ushered Jared out of the room like she was pulling him out of a fire. Jared smirked over his shoulder at Frankie. She managed not to make an obscene gesture at him; that was the limit of her maturity.

The minute the Lewises were out the door, Eric turned on Frankie, threw up his arms, and said, "What the hell?"

"I'm so sorry," Frankie said.

"Just, don't." He sighed. "And I feel really weird sayin' this, but get in the cell, Frankie."

"Are you kidding?"

"I just told Vern Lewis that the law applies to everybody.

You're being charged with a crime," he told her, motioning toward the cell.

"It's a misdemeanor."

"It's a crime; that means you get in the jail cell until someone can come and bail you out."

"I thought I was allowed to bail myself out if I have enough cash on me."

"Do you have enough cash on you?"

"No."

"So what's your point?" he asked.

"Do you usually arrest the girls you sleep with? Because that's some creepy *Dateline* shit," she grumbled as she pushed past him into the third cell—one she *hadn't* been locked in.

"No, and I'm not exactly happy with the position you're putting me in, either. Nobody told you to pick up a crowbar and start swinging it at a minor."

"I wasn't swinging it *at* a minor. I was swinging it 'minor adjacent.' And the headlight was an accident," she insisted. "A reaction fueled by heightened emotions. You know, like picking up a Segway and throwing it at somebody."

Hurt rippled across Eric's face and she wished she could suck the words back into her mouth. But since that was impossible, she was going to just have to commit and lean into it.

"That's not okay," he told her.

"I know," she said.

"Look, this is clearly not how I wanted the evening to

end, either. We can plead the charge down. When I give my report, I'll make it clear to the judge that you didn't intend to break the headlight. Between that, the video from the security cameras that show you flailing instead of actually aiming at the headlight, and your years of service to the county, surely she'll let you off."

"Yeah, Caroline Moultry's usually pretty reasonable. On the bright side, now you see that I'm not a crazy person."

"Maybe not the best time to make that argument," he told her.

"I'm sayin', there's finally concrete proof of Jared breaking into the funeral home. We saw it with our own eyes, and it was caught on the cameras. His mom can't deny it happened. I consider that a win," she said.

"Just call somebody to come bail you out. I'm sure your parents are waiting by the phone, wondering where you are," Eric said, walking away from her. She double-checked to make sure the key was on the hook, but she was still relieved when Eric didn't shut the door behind her. She pulled out her phone and scrolled through the contacts, stopping on M, and internally winced at calling Marianne after two in the morning.

"Someone better be dead," Marianne mumbled into the phone.

Frankie sighed. "No more dead people than usual. But, um, I might need you to come by the jail."

"Again?"

"Please, just come pick me up."

In the background, Frankie could hear Carl's muffled voice ask, "Baby, who died?"

Marianne whispered for Carl to go back to sleep and said, "I'll be right there."

Frankie slipped off Eric's boots and flopped on the cot. The quilts were still on the cots, but the potpourri and homey touches from Frankie's charity arrest were missing. She yawned, but there was no way she was going to sleep in a jail cell *again*.

Though her evening had started off pretty nicely, this was an awful end. On the other hand, her arrest did resolve a lot of Frankie's current internal struggles. If nothing else, the guy literally putting you in a cage was a pretty good reason not to be in a relationship with him.

Forty-five minutes later, Marianne marched into the jail with Duffy at her heels. They'd both changed out of pajamas, which Frankie appreciated. Nothing said "classy" like being bailed out by someone wearing Tweety Bird lounge pants.

"Aw, you brought Duffy, too?" she called, sitting up.

"Well, he didn't get to participate the last time you were in jail," Marianne yelled back. Then she turned to Eric and glared at him the whole time she was signing the paperwork for Frankie's bail. Duffy, however, was standing on the other side of the bars, trying to snap a picture with his phone. "You know, when I imagined this moment . . . this is pretty much how I thought it would go."

"Shut it, Duffy," she said, walking out of the cell in bare feet.

"Whoa, whoa, whoa, are you allowed to do that?" Duffy asked, an exaggerated expression of shock on his face. "I don't want to be part of a jailbreak."

"I will hurt you," she growled.

"How was prison?"

"Changes a woman. *Orange Is the New Black* was very misleading," she told him.

"Did you lift weights while you were on the inside?" he asked. "If not, I'm not worried."

"Frankie will be represented by George Pritchett," Marianne was telling Eric as Frankie approached the main desk. "And by the time he's done with the charge, the department will be issuing a formal apology to Frankie, with flowers. It's completely ridiculous that she was charged at all, when that little snot was the one trespassing and breaking into a private building."

"Look, I didn't want to charge her, either, but I didn't have a choice."

"If he'd actually made it into the building and she pulled him out, would you have charged her with assault, too?" Marianne demanded crisply.

"Marianne, I appreciate the loyalty, but let's just go."

Eric nodded toward her feet. "Frankie, you're barefoot."

"I left your boots in the cell."

"What happened to your shoes?" Duffy asked, glancing between Frankie and Eric, a suspicious expression taking shape on his face. "Why were you wearin' his boots? What's goin' on?"

"You can't walk around barefoot," Eric told her. "Just take the boots."

"I'm good. You keep them," she told him. "That way we don't have to meet up to exchange them or anything. Let's just agree not to talk for a few days."

"There's a lot of gravel between here and your cousins' car," Eric noted.

Frankie lifted her brows and climbed onto the counter. "Duffy?"

Duffy angled his body so Frankie could wrap her arms around his neck. He pulled her up into a piggyback position, settling her relatively slight weight against his back. Frankie nodded to Eric, as if this were a totally normal way for one to leave the jail. "Sheriff."

"So what happened to your shoes?" Duffy asked.

"Just keep walkin'," Frankie told him.

11

FRANKIE LIFTED HER head from her pillow and found Deputy Landry Mitchell over her, smiling.

"What in the living fuck!" she shouted, thinking she was somehow back in the jail cell. She scrambled back across her twin mattress and fell into the crack between her bed and the wall. "Ow."

"Jar!" Tootie crowed, moving the poster she was holding over Frankie's bed. It seemed to be an election poster that showed Landry smirking with a waving American flag and a bald eagle posed in flight behind him. Frankie groaned and dropped her head against her mattress. It was way too early and Frankie had gotten way too little sleep to deal with Tootie's special brand of morning humor. Or her dog pack, which was currently milling around Frankie's childhood bedroom, sniffing at her old stuffed animals.

"What is that?" Frankie yelled. "Also, why are you standing over me? Also, can I take away your key to the front door? When will my voice return to its normal volume?"

"Don't be silly." Tootie sniffed. "Your parents don't ever lock the door."

"What is that?" Frankie hissed. She pushed herself up using the cheerfully painted yellow wall until she was standing and snatched the poster from Tootie.

"Landry Mitchell is running for sheriff," Tootie said. "As a write-in candidate."

"How?" Frankie marveled, staring at Landry's aggressively patriotic pose. "He is an irony-free zone."

A new addition to the pack, a young lab mix named Rocky, was chewing on her Captain America–themed platform heels.

"Out, dogs!" Frankie yelled. "Go downstairs."

Lulu the pit bull sniffed indignantly and led the charge into the hallway.

"These posters sprang up in every business window in town this mornin'," Tootie said. "He's got a billboard near the Dirty Deer. And Ed Hotchkiss said they're puttin' in one of those bench ads on Main Street tomorrow."

Frankie climbed back over her bed. "Wait, Landry's mama balances his checkbook for him because he still owes money to the Columbia Record Club. How did he pay for billboards and posters? And a bench?"

Tootie shrugged, sitting down on the bed. "I suspect he is not bankrollin' his own campaign. And I doubt it was his idea to run in the first place. I'm sure he thought about it once or twice, but someone probably had to fill out the paperwork for him at the courthouse. Who in town has that sort of money and an ax to grind against anyone who shows you loyalty?"

Frankie yawned. "The Lewises?"

"You'll notice that Vern Lewis used the same eagle in the background of his campaign posters last time he ran." Tootie tapped the clip art in question with her finger.

"But Eric only arrested Jared last night," Frankie said.

"Yes, and trust me, that tidbit has made the rounds, which Marnette is plenty upset about. But honey, your sheriff *questioned* Jared a few days ago, and that gave Marnette all the time she needed to have these tasteful posters rush-ordered at her cousin's print shop in Athens."

"How many cousins does Marnette have?" Frankie groaned. Suddenly Vern Lewis's comment about Eric being sheriff "temporarily" made a lot more sense. "So, they're gettin' revenge on Eric for darin' to question Jared, by tryin' to put an idiot in office?" She stumbled around the foot of her bed, tripping over a pair of mermaid-print leggings. "That's just wrong."

"Welcome to small-town politics. And regular-size-town politics."

Frankie threw her closet door open and pulled out a pair of jeans and a T-shirt with the "Can't Hear You" door knocker from *Labyrinth* on it. Tootie had the grace to look the other way while Frankie struggled into her clothes.

"I'm going to go talk to my dad," Frankie said. "Maybe he can talk some sense into Vern Lewis."

"When has that ever worked?" Tootie called after her.

"It's worth a shot!"

Frankie ran outside to find that while her dad's truck was gone, Margot was climbing into the funeral home's van. "Hey, pukey, can I ride in to work with you?"

"If I say no, are you going to smash my headlights?" Margot shot back.

Frankie nodded. "Well played."

Margot was getting pretty good at driving the large van over the county's bumpy roads. Frankie settled into the passenger seat and pondered how smart it was to have run out of her house without her cell phone. Margot was still looking a bit peaky, but she was wearing office clothes that matched and full makeup, which was a step up from vomity Margot.

"So how are you feelin'?" Frankie asked carefully.

"Fine," Margot said. "A little less pukey, but still super tired and I have to pee every five seconds. Aunt Donna actually brought me a bottle of cranberry juice, which means she could actually be worried about me. Or that she is annoyed by me."

"It could be either one," Frankie admitted. "Have you talked to Kyle yet?"

Margot's mouth pulled back at the corners. "No."

"Margot!"

"I have an appointment at an OB's office in Atlanta the day after tomorrow. I don't want to talk to him until I have all the information."

"You don't think Kyle would like to go to the appointment?"

"I'm not going to take shit from someone who spent last night in jail for vandalizing a teenager's bro-mobile. You're not exactly cornering the market on emotional maturity."

"Point taken."

"The Trunk-R-Treat is tomorrow. I just have to white-knuckle my way through that, and stay as far away from the chili as I possibly can, because all tomato-based products make me throw up now. Go to the appointment, eat my weight in cheesecake, as there seems to be a Cheesecake Factory down the street from my doctor's office, and then figure out how I'm going to tell Kyle that when I say 'I'm covered,' what it actually means is 'I'm the point-zero-zero-zero-one percent of the population that ruins the birth control curve for everybody.'"

"I don't know if I would open with that," Frankie said. "According to the Internet, all the cool girls are presenting their partners with pee-soaked positive pregnancy tests."

"Hard pass."

"Also, I'm assuming it was a positive test. You never said."

Margot shook her head. "Yeah, I haven't really wanted to tell anybody until I talked to Kyle. It feels like a weird betrayal to discuss it with other people, and yet I don't have the balls to talk to him about it. I am a conundrum of dysfunctional personality traits."

"Please, don't say you don't have the balls. Let's respect your apparently fruitful lady bits. You don't have the *ovaries*."

"Rude," Margot muttered. "So, change of subject, how much trouble are *you* in?"

"I don't know. It sounds like my trouble is negotiable, but Eric's is just getting started."

Margot winced. "The election posters?"

"How late did I sleep? How does everybody know about that already?"

Margot shrugged. "Small town."

FRANKIE FOLLOWED MARGOT right into her father's office. Bob was sitting at his desk with his tie thrown over his shoulder, eating a vanilla latte Pop-Tart and dunking it into his coffee.

Frankie gasped. "Daddy, are those my Pop-Tarts?"

Bob dropped the purloined pastry into the wastebasket. "No."

"Did you dig my Pop-Tarts out of the trash?"

"I'm out," Margot said, raising her hands and marching back out to the hallway. "I'm going to go have Breakfast Sticks with my dad!"

"I may have dug your Pop-Tarts out of the trash," Bob said.

"Oh, Daddy, no."

"They were wrapped," he told her, sliding a package her way. "And you made such a big deal out of your mama throwing them away, I thought I should get them back for you."

A cold flash of guilt swept through her middle. "Thank you. So I'm guessin' that you heard about my trouble last night."

"Did you really break the boy's headlight?"

"Not intentionally."

"That only counts in horseshoes."

She shook her head. "I don't think that's the expression."

"I'll talk to his daddy, see if we can get somethin' worked out, pay to have the headlight fixed."

"Actually, no, Marianne's handlin' the legal stuff. And I'd rather go through the right channels, that way Eric doesn't suffer for it later."

Her dad smirked. "Eric, huh?"

"Not even remotely the right time to tease about the sheriff," she said. "But that is what I came to talk to you about."

"You didn't just come by to talk to your father because you love him?"

"The same father who just stole my Pop-Tarts?"

"Reclaimed!" Bob protested.

"I need you to talk to Vern Lewis about Eric. He's putting up Landry Mitchell as some sort of straw man candidate to get Eric voted out."

"Why would he do that?"

"Because Eric dared to question Jared a few days ago and Marnette is freaking out. Of course, she's freaking out worse now that Eric took Jared into custody last night."

Bob grinned. "So he really took Jared into custody? Good for him."

"Yeah, except for the part about Vern trying to get Eric fired now. Or unelected. I'm not really sure what the word would be. Do you think you can talk to him, local politician to local politician? Make him see how insane it is to try to replace an effective sheriff who keeps us safe with Landry? I mean, of all people, *Landry*."

"Well, honey, I don't know if I'll be able to talk any sense into Vern. You know it's not really him that's the problem, it's Marnette pullin' the strings. And she's not going to take well to the embarrassment of her son bein' arrested."

"Nope."

"Because this is a very small town and it's only been about seven hours and everybody knows."

"I'm aware."

Bob sat back in his chair, sipping his coffee. "So when you were in jail—for real this time—you didn't call your mama and me? You called your cousins instead?"

Frankie pinched her lips together. "I didn't want to worry you."

"Honey, of course a man is going to worry when his daughter goes missin' in the middle of the night. And don't think I didn't notice that you turned off the 'find my friends' thing, because I did. You said we could trust you. How can I trust you if you do things like that without talking to us? You can't lie to us and tell us you're okay when you're not. And you can't lie to us and tell us that you're at work when you're in jail."

"Actually, I was with a friend at the time I sent that text. The jail thing happened later."

"Which friend?" Bob asked.

"Not important."

"Which friend?" he asked again.

Frankie's cheeks flushed.

"Was it—you were with the sheriff when you texted?" he asked, his eyes wide. "But that was after midnight."

"Yes, it was," Frankie said, not quite able to look her father in the eye.

"Wait, and then he arrested you?"

"Actually, he arrested me before I texted you."

"Well, that's not right. I mean, I know times have changed, but surely the right thing to do at the end of the night is to drive your date home, not lock her up."

"Technically, he was trying to drive me home when we stopped at the funeral home to check on everything," she said. "Also, technically, he didn't lock the cell door."

"What a gentleman," Bob drawled.

Frankie sighed. She appreciated her father's tendency to be indignant on her behalf, but she was really trying to be emotionally mature and pragmatic about this whole arrest thing. She needed a little less indignant support.

"Don't go gettin' mad at Eric. I broke the headlight and I had to answer for it."

"Still seems wrong to me."

"Well, you're an old-fashioned guy."

FRANKIE WASN'T SURE how she felt about returning to the sheriff's office. Good things did not happen for her when she walked through that door.

Janey was sitting at her desk and made grabby hands when she saw that Frankie was carrying a bag from the Snack Shack. Frankie had expected some admonishment from her mama about her arrest or at least the fact that she'd been so rude as to damage Jared's car. But Mama just kissed her on the cheek, told her to make sure she didn't work too hard after her ordeal, and gave Frankie her breakfast order.

Frankie dropped the Breakfast Stick on Janey's desk with a flourish. Breakfast Sticks were Leslie's original breakfast creation involving bacon wrapped around a sausage, stuffed with cheese, dipped in egg batter, and, of course, deep-fried.

"So I had a lot of interestin' paperwork to process this morning," Janey said.

"I brought you breakfast, so teasin' me would be bad manners."

Janey pouted. "You ruin all of my fun."

"What if I told you there were hash browns in that bag?"

Janey peeked into the white bag and squealed. "You're forgiven! The sheriff is in his office. But I'm going to warn ya, he's in a mood."

"Not exactly a surprise," Frankie muttered.

"Good luck," Janey told her around a mouthful of deep-fried egg and sausage.

Frankie inhaled deeply and knocked on the frame of his office door. "Permission to enter?"

"Come in," he said with a deep breath. "You know, no matter what your mama tells you, you don't have to send us a thank-you note after we arrest you."

"Ha," she shot back, sliding into the seat across from his desk. She glanced around his office. While his degree from UGA was hanging on the wall, along with a picture of a preteen Eric and a handsome man in a police uniform, she noticed that there were no relics of his own time with the Atlanta Police Department. That made her a bit sad. No matter how it had ended, Eric shouldn't just pretend that part of his life had never happened.

"So how are you?"

"I'm not going to lie. I'm a damn sight far away from okay."

Eric nodded. "I can respect the honesty."

"It's pretty quiet around here," she noted.

"Yeah, well, Deputy Mitchell has taken a leave of absence to focus on his campaign," Eric said, blowing out a breath.

"The election's only a week away. Does he—or Marnette Lewis, for that matter, because that's who's fundin' his campaign—really expect to launch a write-in campaign in a week?"

Eric looked oddly affronted. "Marnette Lewis is fundin' his campaign? Because of last night?"

"No, if I was going to guess, I would say that Marnette Lewis is fundin' his campaign because you had the nerve to come to her house and question her about the last break-in at McCready's."

He rocked back in his chair. "That woman is evil in a twinset."

"Mean as a snake in an outhouse," Frankie agreed. "Look,

tomorrow night is Halloween. Everybody is going to be distracted by the Trunk-R-Treat and the festivities and such. There's no way Jared's going to tolerate being thwarted quite so publicly, letting all his little skeevy high school friends laugh at him for getting busted by the sheriff and the town crazy smashin' his headlight in. He's going to go big and he's going to use Halloween as a cover."

"Really?" Eric scoffed. "Surely to heaven, he'll know that we'll be watchin' the place. He's not going to risk getting caught *again*. His parents aren't going to let him out of their sight."

"I don't know if you've noticed this, but logic and Jared Lewis parted company a while ago," Frankie retorted. "Just wait a little while, long enough for his parents to fall asleep, and he'll be there."

"He just got arrested. He goes to court next week!"

"Clearly you overestimate the amount of self-preservation contained in a juvenile male douche brain."

"Frankie, I can't get caught up in your . . . situation again," he said. "There are other people and businesses in this town that deserve my attention. Not to mention, I've got to actually campaign for my job, now that there's another candidate. I mean, sure, that candidate is an idiot, but he's got some really nice posters."

"Look, just come out to the funeral home after dark for a little while, and keep watch. I'll bring some of my mama's fried chicken. It will be like a picnic, in a parkin' lot, in the dark."

"Well, as romantic as that sounds and as much as I love your mama's fried chicken, there's no freakin' way I'm hangin' out in a parkin' lot with you again. Not after what happened last time. You are going to go to that Trunk-R-Treat. You are going to pass out candy and smile at small children and you are going to stay within sight of the Lewises, so they can't accuse you of doin' anything stupid and/or terrible."

"Fine," she said. "But just so you know, twenty-four hours only gives me like six or seven costume options, all of them the sexy version of somethin'."

"I would really love to sit here and listen to you list each and every one of those costumes."

"Too soon," she told him, shaking her head.

Eric snorted, and continued, "But I just want to be clear, in order to ensure that the Lewises won't accuse you of doin' something stupid and/or terrible, you can't do anything stupid and/or terrible."

"I won't do anything stupid or terrible," she promised in a dead, disinterested tone.

"You're going to have to practice it a few more times before I believe it."

"Will you at least stop by the funeral home to check on things at some point during the night? Even if Jared appears to be holding a Bible study in a very public place with witnesses?"

"Frankie."

"He has minions who could carry out his evil bidding for him!"

"Has anyone ever told you that your persistence borders on a serious character flaw?"

Frankie grinned. "Every damn day."

"All right, all right." He sighed. "To make you happy, I will stop by the funeral home tomorrow night. But only after I see you spend a good portion of the evening at the Trunk-R-Treat."

"Fine."

"And maybe later, you can try on some of those costume options for me."

"Still a little too soon," she told him.

"But we're okay, right?" he asked, nodding in the direction of the jail cells. "With everything?"

"I'm not sure. Last night was pretty unprecedented in terms of, well, everything. I will let you know when I'm ready to talk about it or anything else related to last night."

"Fair enough," he said as she stood. He escorted her to the main office and spotted Janey's bag from the Snack Shack. "Hey, why does Janey get breakfast?"

"She didn't arrest me last night."

"I knew you weren't going to let that go."

"Yeah, I'm funny that way."

"Will you at least share the hash browns?" Eric asked Janey.

"Hell no!"

12

FRANKIE DROPPED TUBES of Life Savers into the bags of a Hulk, a (nonbloody) vampire, and a knight.

"Thank you!" they cried before darting to the next car. Frankie grinned, the fluffy tulle skirt of her costume billowing in the cool autumn breeze. The sun had set and the air smelled of spicy chili and novelty glitter hairspray. The Trunk-R-Treat was in full swing, and the McCready family was involved like a house on fire. Tootie was dressed as a fire hydrant and had five dogs on leashes, because she found that sort of thing funny. Stan, Frankie, and Bob were handing out candy to children from their trunk "stall." Leslie was running the fireside chili station, scooping up her secret five-alarm recipe for the masses, straight from the family's cast-iron pot. In some sort of All Hallows' Eve miracle, Tootie and Leslie managed to bake twenty catering pans full of cornbread without fighting over adding sugar. (Because Leslie added the sugar when Tootie wasn't looking.)

Margot was dressed as the Scarecrow from *The Wizard of Oz*, to match Kyle's Cowardly Lion costume and the girls' Dorothy and Glinda costumes. She flitted from one place to another like a hyper hummingbird, trying to make sure everything ran smoothly, but mostly she looked like she was running herself ragged. Every once in a while, a gust of wind would blow the scent of the chili station her way and she would stop, swallow heavily, and then shake it off and keep running.

Carl and Marianne skipped costumes because they might hinder their ability to chase down a sugared-up Nate, who was dressed as the Flash. Aiden was dressed as Where's Waldo, but in a camouflage print, because "only dummies try to hide while dressed as a peppermint stick."

More than three dozen cars were arranged in a semicircle in the elementary school drop-off lot. Each was parked with its trunk pointed toward the interior of the circle, with the trunks propped open and decorated to the nines. The Murrays had done their trunk in a "lab-created candy gone mad" theme with beakers and dry ice bubbling in colored water and fake "evil" candy made out of Styrofoam. The Grandys had gone classic with spiderwebs, Ike's grandma's big iron kettle filled with popcorn balls, and a "scary sounds" soundtrack CD. Others went for family-friendly versions of ghost cowboys, ghost pirates, and ghost doctors. Frankie's own family stuck with what they had, a readily available hearse and an old pine coffin that they'd filled to the brim with Tootsie Pops, Life Savers, and Nerds.

The PTA had dragged out some of the games from the spring carnival and set them up in the center of the circle so the kids who'd already made the rounds for treats could toss rings around two-liter bottles or bean bags through the mouth of a giant Sasquatch. It made Frankie a little sad that the trick-or-treaters were missing out on the fun of going door to door for their treats, like youngsters in suburbs did. But she knew this was considerably safer than wandering the roads in the dark, especially in an area where your nearest neighbor could live a mile away.

Eric, who had stuck with his usual costume of "sexy law enforcement officer," had put in an appearance as the festivities opened. He'd kept his distance, though he'd waggled his eyebrows when he saw her costume. She was taking that as a win. The Lewises were present, of course. They were dressed as Mary and Joseph. They were dressed as the parents of Jesus Christ, while handing out little boxes of raisins. Frankie wasn't sure whether she was more offended by the implication that their son was the Messiah or the fact that they were handing out health food and pretending that it was candy. Six of one, half a dozen of the other, really.

Jared had the good taste not to dress to match his parents. He was dressed as Frankenstein. Hilarious. Any time Frankie made eye contact with him, he smirked and lumbered toward the McCready booth, only to change direction just before he reached it. It was the Halloween version of "I'm not touching you, I'm not touching you!" Fortunately, Frankie had plenty of distractions to keep her from doing anything ugly in public.

Religious objections aside, no one had complained about anyone else's costume. No one had gone home in a huff to change. No one's treats were turned away. And most importantly, no one had gone into anaphylaxis, so at least the "no peanut treat" rule had been respected. For just a moment, she could pretend she lived in a normal town with normal people in it.

And then she heard a woman say, "Uh, no, honey, let's skip this one."

She turned to see Hailey McIver, whom Frankie had known since first grade, steering her five-year-old Power Ranger away from the McCready's trunk, glancing over her shoulder like Frankie was handing out poisoned apples.

Frankie glanced down at her costume. She wasn't even going for scary this year. She was flippin' adorable. She looked up to see Marnette Lewis smirking at her, which was a pretty shocking expression coming from the Virgin Mary.

"Don't pay them any mind," Stan told her. "People have been steerin' their kids away from me for years. I haven't had a sniffle since the seventies."

"Yeah, but you're cantankerous and grumpy. I'm delightful. Look at me, I'm practically a cartoon character."

He glanced down at her costume. "I've been meaning to ask. What are you supposed to be?"

"I'm a peach!" she said, twirling around so the layers of gradient-peach tulle that made up her skirt belled around her sparkly peach leggings and bright pink Converse. A fluffy dark peach sweater topped the outfit, along with a green leaf-shaped beret.

"You don't look like any peach I've ever seen," he grumbled.

"Well, I tried building a fruit-shaped costume, but the papier-mâché was taking too long to dry," she said. "At least I didn't say I was a *sexy* peach."

Stan grimaced. "Yeah, thanks for that."

"Is it cheatin' that we serve our candy out of a hearse? I mean, it kind of gives us an unfair advantage over the other cars, in terms of theme."

"I think this is one of the few times where we should just roll with the advantage of our job," he told her.

"So, the Lewis boy seems to be enjoying himself," Stan noted as Jared used his Frankenstein walk to herd Birdie Sherman, a smaller classmate of his, until she was cornered against a truck. Before she could raise her arms to push him, Birdie's older brother, Billy, wedged himself between them and shoved Jared away.

Jared just shrugged and went to find a new target. Marnette made an ugly hissing noise, but Billy wasn't as easily pushed around as the adults of Lake Sackett. Billy escorted his sister to a group of her friends, which would be more difficult for Jared to herd.

"Yes, he's makin' a real spectacle of himself, makin' sure everybody sees him yuckin' it up, so when he slips away to break into the funeral home, there's reasonable doubt."

"Are you trying his case already?" Stan asked as Frankie dropped more candy into the bags of a fairy and a Mario.

"I've been trying his case in my head since he turned thirteen," she muttered.

She glanced around the lot and realized that she didn't see Eric anywhere. Maybe he'd already left to check on Mc-Cready's while things were running smoothly at the Trunk-R-Treat? It meant a lot to her that, even after everything they'd been through, he still took her seriously enough to check the place. It was almost enough to make her forget the whole jail thing.

There was a very good chance she would be givin' him a treat later.

Kyle led his daughters to the car. "Girls, please climb in the back of the hearse and find three pieces of candy you want to eat."

"Yay!" The girls crowed and scrambled through the car door.

"Interesting approach to parentin'," Stan said.

Kyle dragged off the yarn lion mane and propped himself against the hearse, trying to catch his breath. "I hate Halloween."

"It could be worse," Frankie told him, just as Nate ran by screaming like a British police siren.

"Son, slow down!" Carl cried as he ran after Nate.

"I told you not to let him eat that Laffy Taffy!" Frankie yelled after him. She turned to Kyle. "See?"

Kyle shuddered. "There but for the grace of God."

Inside the hearse, the girls were chowing down on chocolate but getting restless. Juniper swiped at sticky streaks on her cheeks. "Daddy, can we go play *Toss Across?*"

"Sure, girls, I'll take you," Stan said, holding his hands out. The girls scrambled out of the car.

"Thank you." Kyle sighed. "I would say that's not necessary, but I'm fadin' fast, here."

"You okay?"

"Do you have any idea what's up with your cousin?" he asked. "She's been so wound up about the Trunk-R-Treat, she hasn't been sleeping. She just tosses and turns, which means I haven't been sleeping. And when I don't sleep, the kids can smell it on me, like bees can smell fear. And that's when an elementary school becomes the Thunderdome, where chaos is the rule of law."

Frankie froze. Oh, man. She was a lot of things, but she was not a good liar. And she was pretty sure Margot didn't want Kyle to find out about the arrival of his future child while wearing a Cowardly Lion costume, propped up on a hearse. And Margot probably didn't want him to hear it from Frankie.

"You don't think maybe you're bein' a little overdramatic?" Frankie asked, her voice cracking slightly.

"She woke me up around three this morning to ask me if I thought we had enough hay bales set around for the proper fall aesthetic. And I didn't get back to sleep, ever. I've been up since three, Frankie, on Halloween, with two girls under ten. I love the woman, but if she doesn't sleep soon, I may take her down with a tranq dart. I mean, I'll do it gently, but she will sleep."

"I'm sure it's just the stress of plannin' all this," she assured him.

"It had better be . . ." Kyle's voice trailed off as he stared at something over Frankie's shoulder. She turned to see two dads shoving each other.

"Dammit." Frankie groaned. Corey Dahl and David Paulson had been engaged in a long-term pissing match ever since senior year, when David replaced Corey on the first string of the football team *and* impregnated Corey's aunt. They couldn't seem to see each other without some sort of shoving or name-calling. The aunt's baby's baptism had been a disaster.

The crowd around Corey and David parted and the shoving progressed to an all-out fight. Carnival games were knocked over. Candy bags were dropped and abandoned as people rushed their kids out of harm's way. Families started dashing toward their cars. A few more ambitious teenagers used the distraction to load their bags up with candy.

Frankie tossed her cell phone to her mother, who was holding Tootie and the pack in place behind the chili station. "Mama, call Eric's number and tell him to get here now!"

"Where the hell is he?" Kyle asked as they rushed toward the commotion.

Frankie shook her head. "He said he had a couple of places he needed to patrol tonight with Landry out of commission."

"What's happening?" Leslie asked, pulling at Frankie's arms to guide her away from the tensions. "Honey, did you have anything to do with this?"

"What do you mean by that?"

Leslie shrugged, looking ill at ease. "Well, sometimes you speak before you think—even though I know you don't mean to—and things like this happen."

"I didn't start this!" she exclaimed. "They didn't need me to start this. Corey and David are always looking for reasons to fight."

"I'm just saying, you should be more careful."

"Boys, boys!" Bob yelled as Corey punched David in the mouth. "Just stop this now. There's kids here and we don't want anybody to get hurt!"

Frankie grabbed her father by the back of his Colonel Sanders costume and pulled him away from the fray. "Daddy, you will not put yourself between those two idiots!"

"I'm fine," Bob insisted, just as David dodged a swing from Corey and almost head-butted him. Unfortunately, when David moved to return the punch, he hit Mike Carp, who got pissed, handed his wife their kids' treat bags, and punched David in the forehead. David's cousin Donnie took exception to this and tried to hit Mike with a plastic pumpkin full of Jujubes. And it was all chaos from there.

By the time Kyle used his scary principal voice to make the fighting stop, there were multiple black eyes, a broken nose, and a dislocated thumb. Eric rolled onto the scene, lights flashing, as the crowd was dispersing. David, Corey, and several of their cousins were sitting on the curb, held in place by the authority in Kyle's voice.

Eric's face was grim as he approached. Vern Lewis was glaring at Eric as he crossed the lot, and Frankie couldn't help but feel a flutter of dread in her belly. He didn't even look at her, but she didn't mind. Eric was in sheriff mode. He did not have time to smile at her, no matter how cute her costume was.

"What seems to be the problem here, guys?" Eric asked. Several people piped up from the surrounding crowd, volunteering their versions of the tale, but they quieted down as Eric raised his hands. Frankie's head tilted. Interesting.

Families dispersed, trunks were closed, and the Mc-Creadys helped pack up the games and food. Eric collected the statements of all the idiots involved, and none of them were inclined to press charges. He let them off with citations for causing a public disturbance and warned them to go straight home.

"I'm checkin' the Dirty Deer later. If any of you are there, you're goin' to jail," he told them as they walked away.

Frankie slid the casket full of candy into the hearse and closed the back hatch. She tapped the top twice and Bob drove carefully through the traffic of the crowded parking lot. Leslie was riding up front with an industrial vat of chili balanced in her lap.

Margot was oddly weepy as she checked close-down tasks on her clipboard. She was good at keeping a stoic face, but she couldn't hide the tear streaks through the yellow scarecrow face paint.

"I'm sorry, Margot. Except for the fisticuffs from a couple of idiots, it was a really nice evening," Frankie told her. "Lots of kids got their candy. No one was traumatized by a costume. The Crider family won the trunk decorating contest with a rather ingenious and nonviolent Aliens Attack a Pumpkin Farm theme."

"Yeah, but the fisticuffs are all that people will remember," Margot said, wiping at her cheeks. "I just—everybody worked really hard on this, and I can't believe those guys thought it would be okay to fight at what is basically a children's party."

At this, Margot broke into full-on sobbing and Frankie froze. As far as she knew, Margot hadn't cried when flamingos went berserk at a fancy gala she'd thrown in Chicago and tanked her event planning career. And now she was crying because a fistfight broke out in public, in Lake Sackett, on a holiday. Pregnancy hormones were a sonofabitch.

Stan patted Margot's shoulder. "Aw, Sweet Tea, they fight everywhere. They knocked over the baptismal during a christening. They've taken out the town Christmas tree during the community lightin' ceremony. Everybody knows you can't control those two. It's not your fault."

Margot sniffled and threw her arms around her dad's neck, smashing her face into his shirt. Stan's eyes widened in shock, but he very carefully put his arms around her and began patting her back as she cried. Frankie gave him an enthusiastic thumbs-up behind Margot's back. He shook his head at her.

"Y'all all right?" Eric asked, frowning at the sobbing scarecrow.

Frankie jerked her head away from Stan and Margot's moment. Eric followed her to the opposite side of the parking lot. "Margot's fine. She just worked really hard on tonight and she took David and Corey's fighting a little personally."

"So how far along is she?"

Frankie's mouth dropped open. "How did you . . . ?"

"She's crying over a Halloween party. She picked a baggy costume. And the last time I saw her at your office, she was drinking ginger tea instead of your mom's battery acid–flavored coffee."

"You should have made detective," she told him. "She hasn't told Kyle yet. Or anybody, really, so mum's the word, okay?"

"Exactly," he said. "So, I like this costume."

"Thank you," she said, twirling for him. "Of all my options, this one was the fruitiest."

"Well, I was thinkin' that you could bring the other, less fruity options to my place and maybe try them on for me."

"I don't know."

"I've checked out McCready's. All of the cameras are intact. The doors are locked up. It's all secured. And Jared Lewis just got into his parents' car with them. I think you can rest easy for the night."

"It's Halloween night. He always strikes on Halloween. He won't break his pattern."

"He's a teenage boy, not a serial killer," Eric retorted. "You're like Linus waiting for the Great Pumpkin. You're obsessed! He's not going to show up to the place where he just got arrested."

"But he didn't suffer any consequences, which will make him that much bolder."

He pulled a sour face. "Hey."

"I'm just sayin' he was witnessed by the sheriff breakin' into a buildin' and nothin' happened to him yet. That's the kind of thing that builds a criminal ego."

"You seem to be 'just sayin'' quite a bit!"

Across the lot, she saw Stan hand Margot off to Kyle. With Hazel and June tugging at her sleeves, Margot immediately stopped crying and began questioning the girls about their night and how much candy they'd snagged. Kyle put his arm around her while the girls dragged her toward his car.

"Maybe we should stop talkin' now."

"Maybe we should," he said. "Look, you don't have to come over to my place, but please promise me that you won't go stake out your family's funeral home for the night. Just go home. I don't want to hear about you goin' to the Lewis house and tryin' to shut Jared's bedroom window with a nail gun."

"That's not a terrible idea," she said.

"Frankie, please, for the sake of my job, just go home."

Frankie nodded and headed toward her uncle, who was climbing into the funeral home van. She didn't feel bad for not offering some sort of PDA before she walked off.

They didn't seem to be in the right place for it, literally or figuratively.

"Margot okay?" Frankie asked Stan.

"Yeah, I think she just kind of hit her limit for the day," Stan said. "Poor thing. Kyle will take good care of her. He's a good guy."

Frankie smiled, but she wondered how Stan was going to feel about that "good guy" when he found out Kyle had knocked up his little girl. The mix of elation at finally becoming a grandparent and horror at realizing his Margot was not just playing tiddlywinks when she spent the night at Kyle's was going to produce the most complicated expression ever to cross his leathery face.

"So, you want me to drop you at home?" Stan asked.

She pressed her lips together in a contemplative expression. "No."

SITTING AT HER desk in the mortuary, Frankie poured milk and chocolate syrup into an oversize Ravenclaw mug of her mama's high-test coffee. After her uncle had dropped her off at the funeral home, she'd changed into some comfortable clothes and spent a very long evening sitting in her morgue, eating mini candy bars, watching the security feeds, and waiting for Jared to try to open the back door.

At 6 a.m., she finally figured out that he wasn't coming and nodded off at her desk with her face smashed against her keyboard. And now she had three bodies to prep. She'd had maybe an hour of sleep. And she had nougat in her hair with no way of getting it out.

Why hadn't Jared shown up? He always made some attempt on Halloween. Had she really misread him so much? Or maybe he didn't feel the need to break in again, when he had already humiliated her with an arrest and potential lawsuit over his headlight? Maybe that was better than whatever he had planned in the morgue? Maybe the real prize for him wasn't seeing a body in the morgue, but torturing Frankie.

Was Eric right? Was she obsessed?

She startled fully awake when a fist hammered at the back door. She glanced at her phone. It was only 8 a.m. With the late night at the Trunk-R-Treat, no one else in the family was planning to come in before ten. Maybe Naomi was bringing her another client? Surely she would have gotten a call if there'd been some sort of fatality. She opened the door to find Eric in plain clothes, holding a sheaf of papers in his hand.

And he was not happy to see her.

"I thought I asked you, very reasonably, to go home last night," he said, sounding very tired and very angry as he cautiously entered the room. He glanced around, but relaxed after seeing that the only body on the tables was covered with a sheet. "But you came here anyway, and you *slept here*?"

"You don't know that I spent the night here."

Eric glanced down at her legs pointedly.

Oh, right. She'd forgotten that she was wearing her Pac-Man pajama pants under her lab coat.

"It's casual Friday," she insisted.

"It's Wednesday."

"Which makes it even more unexpected and special," she said, fanning her fingers into jazz hands. And when his expression didn't change, she threw her head back. "Okay, so I came here after the Trunk-R-Treat. And I sat at my desk, completely safe, watching the security feeds."

He groaned, dropping his face into his hands. "Frankie!"

"I had to make sure my clients were okay!"

"So your dead people are more important to you than your safety or my career?"

"Yes." She gently tugged the sheet off of the body on the table. "This is Horace Lowell. He was a nice old man who sat in the corner booth of the diner every single morning, sipping coffee and smiling at everybody while he read his paper. You know how people realized something had happened to him over the weekend? Because he didn't show up in his corner booth. So Ike sent one of his line cooks to check on him."

She crossed the room to pull open a morgue drawer.

"Frankie, don't!" Eric said, wincing.

She gently pulled the sheet away from the body of an elderly woman. "This is Beulah Lawrence. She was eighty-five and died in her sleep on Sunday. She's the mother of four, the grandmother of nine. She taught me piano when I was a kid and she always told me I did a good job, even when I played terribly."

She reached for another drawer. "This is—"

"Okay, stop, I get it."

"Do you?" she asked. "These are people I've known my whole life. That's why I get so nuts at the idea of someone coming in here and disturbing them. Not because it's my domain or because I don't want to be embarrassed, but because I don't want them to be taken advantage of by some entitled teenage jackass who's got an ax to grind with me. I won't be the reason their families are put through hell, on top of grieving."

"I never said I didn't understand why you wanted to keep Jared out of here!" he shouted as Frankie closed both morgue drawers. "I said you needed to go about it like a noncrazy person. I said I needed you—for once, just once—to rein in your lack of impulse control and act like a damn adult!"

"That's not fair."

"No, you know what's not fair? This. This is an official censure," Eric said, throwing his bundle of papers on the exam table. "From the county commission. They actually met in a special session at six this morning to discuss how I'm handling my responsibilities. Apparently I've been too 'heavy-handed' in how I'm dealing with certain youngsters within the community. It was also mentioned that I was letting my personal relationships affect my professional decisions."

Frankie scanned the pages, which looked awfully official. "Oh, big woo, they gave one of these to Ron Ludgate last year because he didn't smile as he emptied the trash cans behind the high school."

"Yeah, except instead of not applying enthusiasm to trash removal, I was noticeably absent from one of the biggest community events of the year, because I was busy hanging out in a parkin' lot, waiting to ambush a teenager. Oh, and in my absence, a massive fight broke out and a bunch of people got injured and kids got the crap scared out of them. And since it's kind of my job to provide law and order at community events, they officially sanctioned me a week before the election! And Vern Lewis went directly to his cousin-in-law to get the story on the front page of the *Ledger*. Landry might actually get elected sheriff of your county. Because of the threat to public safety alone, you should be concerned."

"Oh, no one in their right mind is going to vote for Landry. He shot himself in the foot."

Eric glared at her.

Frankie sighed. "I'm sorry. I'm sorry I asked you to come out here and keep watch for Jared, and I hate to point this out, but that's kind of part of your job, to keep watch over people and businesses in the county, particularly if that business has been the victim of a recent break-in."

"Well, not all of us have the luxury of working for our family. Some have to go out into the real world and get real jobs. We can't dress like a circus freak and get away with murder because Mommy and Daddy still baby the hell out of us."

Frankie's jaw dropped. Almost immediately, Eric's face turned white.

"Frankie, I'm sorry."

She raised a hand. "No, you said what you meant, the meanest, most low-down thing you could have said to me. Don't try to take it back now. I'm sorry that's what you think of me. I'm sorry that when you're stressed out, the first thing you do is lash out at me. And I'm sorry that you're a coward who doesn't know how to make a place for himself here, so you blame everybody else for not being able to hold on to *another* job."

"Looks like you're not too bad at the low-down insults, either," he said, before walking out of the morgue and slamming the door behind him.

And then Frankie did something she'd never done in her morgue. She sat on the floor and cried like a baby.

FRANKIE DID AS much work as she could possibly accomplish with her eyes nearly swollen shut from crying, and then she went home. She dodged her family as much as possible, using the intercom to tell Bob and E.J.J. that the smoke from the chili station the night before had made her congested and headachy. Bob immediately wanted to take her home, but she managed to duck into Duffy's truck and drive herself before he or her mama could spot her. And then she'd curled up on her bed and cried until she wanted to throw up. And she was pretty sure she was having a heart attack, because she kept feeling twinges in her chest. Or it was possible the pain was just from knowing that Eric not only thought those things about her but was able to say them.

She supposed this was some sort of karmic payback for never having a messy breakup in high school. And she wasn't even sure she could call it a breakup, because she and Eric weren't officially dating. They'd just slept together. And they hadn't gotten along particularly well. So why did this hurt so much? Why did she feel like there was no hope? Like this wasn't going to get better?

Grown-up feelings sucked.

"Frankie, open up!" Marianne called from outside her locked bedroom door. "Your mama called us. She's been really worried."

"Go away!" Frankie yelled. "I'm fine! I'm just sick and I don't feel like talking."

"Come on, Frankie," Duffy called. "We know you're not sick. You've got man trouble. Open up."

"Look, I appreciate you coming over, but just let me wallow, okay? Adult feelings are an awful tear-soaked hellscape, but I think it's better if I just feel them without someone trying to prop me up. It'll probably give me character or something."

"Frankie, I've got an hour before Nate is finished with basketball practice and comes home to break something. You're wasting precious time!" Marianne cried.

Frankie ignored her and pulled a pillow over her head.

"That's it! I'm using the hidden key!"

Frankie gasped, throwing off the pillow. "The hidden key is for emergencies only!"

"So you see how far you have pushed me!" Marianne called.

"You are breaking a sacred trust!"

The door popped open. Marianne bustled in, carrying takeout boxes from the Rise and Shine and a three-pound bag of Reese's Peanut Butter Cups. "And you are being a drama queen."

Duffy followed, carrying two twelve-packs of beer. "Et tu, Duffy?"

He pulled a sour face. "Discussing your romantic problems is literally the most uncomfortable I will ever be in your presence. All of this beer is for me."

"Yeah, 'cause your romantic problems with your ex-wife and her demon vagina are a walk in the normal park."

From the hallway, Frankie heard Margot yell, "I'm here! I'm here! Don't start without me!"

"Margot, too?" Frankie sighed.

"Oh my God," Margot cried when she saw her. "What happened to you?"

Frankie ran a hand through her hair, which she'd dyed a rich brunette shade in a fit of anger. Between that and the pink plaid cotton pajamas that had been a gift from Leslie's sister, she was practically unrecognizable. "Oh, yeah, I was trying something different."

"Was that part of your Halloween costume?" Margot asked. "I swear you had blue streaks last night."

"This is my natural hair color," Frankie said.

"Really?" Marianne poked at her thick mane. "I hardly remember."

"It looks nice," Margot told her. "Personally, I miss the rainbow of possibilities. But this is nice."

Marianne and Margot started unloading the food on Frankie's tiny bedside table. Duffy cracked open a beer and sat on her beanbag chair. Marianne and Margot sat on the bed.

"I'm sticking with this," Margot said, holding up a bottle of fancy French bubbly water. "I'm keeping the girls tonight. Kyle has parent-teacher conferences."

"Where did you get that?" Frankie asked.

"I stocked up at Whole Foods while I was in Atlanta this morning."

"Why did you go to Atlanta?" Marianne asked.

"Can I have one?" Frankie asked Duffy before Margot could answer.

"I told you, this is all for me," Duffy said, chugging his beer. "There has to be some payoff for my participation in all this lady talk. I begged my parents for a brother."

Marianne snorted. "So did I."

"Hey!" Duffy shot back. And then when Frankie snagged one of his beers, he said, "Hey!"

Margot snickered as she and Marianne divvied up burgers and fries. Frankie, who hadn't eaten since her candy bar binge in the wee hours, dove face-first into her double bacon cheeseburger. Margot picked at hers without much enthusiasm. Her cousins remained quiet as they chewed. Frankie knew they were giving her the floor so she could unload all her Eric angst. But what came out of her mouth was "Am I spoiled?"

Everybody stopped chewing and turned to her with somewhat guilty expressions on their faces.

"Aw, man, that means he was right." Frankie flopped

back on her bed and pulled the pillow over her head again. She felt the mattress dip under the weight of her cousins.

"You're not spoiled, hon," Duffy swore.

"You're a little self-involved sometimes, with the limited grasp of how your more . . . zealous behavior affects people around you."

"I mean, your parents do find every single thing you do to be the greatest thing ever. But I don't think it's made you go rotten," Marianne said. "You don't treat people badly. You don't take advantage. You're not lazy. You're just not used to a lot of obstacles being thrown your way."

"Isn't that how E.J.J. describes millennials?" Frankie sniffed.

"Yes, but that doesn't mean you're not competent or mature. You're just sort of used to getting your own wa— You know what? I am not helping," Margot said, shaking her head.

"Can you tell us where this is all coming from?" Marianne asked. "Maybe that would help us figure out what to say here."

"Eric's mad at me because I endangered his job with this whole Jared situation. He said I can't understand how he feels because I can't be fired. I work for my family. That *some people* have to go out into the real world and work for people who won't let them dress like circus freaks and baby the hell out of them."

Marianne winced. "He said 'circus freak'? Really?"

"Yeah, but Frankie, you've said that yourself, that your

parents don't pick at you about your clothes or your hair because they're just so happy you're here and you're well that they don't sweat the small stuff," Margot said.

"Yeah, but that doesn't mean I want *him* saying it!" Frankie cried.

"Fair enough," Marianne conceded.

"Was it the spoiling part or the circus freak thing that bothered you more?" Margot asked.

"He wasn't exactly callin' me a circus freak, he just said that he wasn't allowed to dress like one. And he apologized as soon as he saw how much it hurt me."

Marianne asked, "But is that why you dyed your hair? To try to look non–circus freaky?"

"No, mostly it was pouting. I thought, 'I'll dye my hair and I won't be nearly as cute and he'll see that I have to have the brightly colored hair, because it's what makes me so interesting.' But I'm still super cute. So I failed."

Margot burst out laughing.

"What?"

"It's just most people don't say things like that about themselves. Most people don't have that kind of confidence."

Frankie protested, "But I'm not confident!"

Marianne arched her eyebrows.

"About some things!"

"It's not a bad thing to be confident. Clearly, your personality is one of the things that attracted Eric to you in the first place. He's under a lot of stress right now, which doesn't make it okay to talk to you that way, but you might consider how a couple of your actions may have contributed to that stress," Marianne said. "Like busting out Jared's headlight."

"Which antagonizes Eric's boss," Duffy added.

"While Eric is dating you," Margot finished.

"So this is a dual-fault fight," Marianne said.

"Ugh, no, I thought you were supposed to come over and call him names and let me tell you awful secrets about how bad he is in bed while you fed me junk food," Frankie groaned. "Not convince me that I messed up and should apologize."

"Does Eric have awful secrets about how bad he is in bed?" Margot asked, feigning a casual tone.

"And I'm out," Duffy said, standing.

"No." Frankie sighed. "Not really."

"I'm back." Duffy dropped to the beanbag chair.

"He's awesome in bed. Just like everything else about him, it's perfect. His body is amazing and—"

Duffy stood. "I'm out again."

"If you don't stay, you forfeit the beer and food!" Marianne told him.

"You know my weakness," Duffy hissed. "Okay, but Frankie, I do not want any details about Eric in bed."

"Fine," Frankie muttered. "But just so you know, he's huge."

"Ew, no!" Duffy said, spitting out his beer. "Why?"

Margot cackled so hard that her fancy water dribbled out of her mouth. And then she started to cry.

"Oh, honey, is it the bubbles? Sometimes it burns when it goes up your nose."

"No," she said, wiping at the tears streaming from her eyes. "No, it's just . . . I had friends in Chicago. Friends I could meet for drinks or a concert or what have you, but never barbecue and peanut butter cups and laughing until water came out of my mouth. I had a little family, but no people I could be comfortable with. I never dreamed I would have people I could trust to know me so well and love me like this, and to think I could have missed it if those flamingos hadn't gone rogue and ruined a stupid gala. I'm just really, really happy."

"Aw, come here," Frankie said, hugging her. "You're a crazy person."

Margot responded by punching her in the side while hugging her closer with the other arm.

"You keep responding to stuff like that and people are going to think you're pregnant," Marianne told her.

Margot went pale. "Uh, yeah."

"I'm going to have to apologize, aren't I?" Frankie mumbled around a French fry.

"Probably."

"I've never done that before. Every other time some guy's had a problem with me, I just let him go and moved on to the next one." She wilted back against her bed. "Oh, Lord, I am spoiled, aren't I?"

"Willful," Margot suggested.

"Stubborn," Marianne added.

"You don't think that's forgivin' him a little too quickly and apologizin' even quicker?" Duffy asked. "He said some pretty rotten stuff to you, Frankie. And he should answer for those things."

"I agree," she said. "and I am still angry at him. I just don't think I want to live in a community where Landry is in charge of our safety."

"It wouldn't be that bad," Margot said. "It's not like he would have unlimited power."

"You watched him lock me in a cell overnight by dropping the keys down a vent."

Margot sighed. "Okay, fine."

FRANKIE'S COUSINS DISPERSED sometime around eight, leaving her with a full belly and the ability to get some sleep. The next morning, she walked downstairs to find her mama standing at the stove, flipping pancakes onto a plate. Bob was sipping coffee and reading the paper. Part of her wanted to march right back into her room, forget her whole plan, and avoid hurting their feelings. She'd already called her doctor this morning to schedule a discussion of her anxiety issues and semi-hypochondria. Maybe that was enough personal growth for one day.

"Mornin', sweetie," Leslie chirped. "Smiley face pancakes coming your way!"

Frankie sighed. No, this had to be done. The apron

strings had to be severed. Frankie McCready needed to grow the hell up.

"Leslie, Bob, I think we need to have a talk," she told them in what she hoped was a very serious tone.

"What did you do to your hair?" Leslie asked, sliding the pancakes in front of her.

"And what happened to 'Mama' and 'Daddy'?" Bob asked.

"I'm trying to approach you as adults," she told them. "And as an adult, I'm telling you that I'm moving out in a couple of weeks."

"What?" Leslie exclaimed, dropping into a kitchenette chair. "Why?"

"Margot is going to be movin' into Kyle's place pretty soon, and when she does, I'm going to move into her cabin."

Bob set his coffee aside. "Did we do something to hurt your feelings, honey?"

"No. I'm twenty-eight years old, and at my age, most people have lived on their own for quite some time. Besides, it's not like I'm movin' across the country. I'll just be a few doors down."

"So what's the point of movin' in the first place?" Leslie asked.

"Because I need privacy. I need my own space. I need to take care of my own clothes, my own meals, my own dishes."

Leslie's expression clouded over. "But that's how I show how much I care about you."

"And I really appreciate it, Mama, but wouldn't it be better for me to be able to take care of myself?"

"But I like takin' care of you. I like seein' you every day!" Leslie said, shaking her head. "I don't think this move is a good idea."

"Is this because of that boy? Did he make you feel bad about livin' with us?" Bob demanded. "Look, I didn't want to say anything about commission business, but we met about him yesterday and I'm not sure you should be datin' him. Vern had some real bad things to say."

"Okay, first of all, *that boy* is over thirty," Frankie told her father. "And no, it has nothing to do with him, but if I ever managed to have a successful relationship and decided to move in with my boyfriend—"

Bob made a disapproving noise.

"—or get married! How am I supposed to take care of my own household if I'm used to you doin' everything for me? Am I just supposed to move my husband into my childhood bedroom and let you fix us breakfast every morning?"

Leslie shrugged. "Well, it's not the worst idea in the world."

"Mama, no!" Frankie gasped. "I wouldn't want to be the kind of person who never took on adulthood, and you wouldn't want to have raised one. You wouldn't want me marryin' someone who was okay with sleeping on my little twin bed under your roof, either."

"She's right." Bob sighed. "Everybody's gotta grow up sometime. We've just put it off longer than we should have. You're our baby. We came so close to losing you, and I guess we just tried to grab on to as much extra time with you as we could."

Her mama wiped at her eyes. "I don't know what we would do without you."

"Well, you'll have less to do," Frankie said. "So maybe you can take up reading or knitting, or I don't know, have sex in the living room if you want, without me cramping your style."

Leslie made an indignant squawking noise. Bob pursed his lips as if he was considering it.

Frankie told them, "You two have earned some time together."

"You'll still come over every once in a while for dinner, won't you?" Leslie asked.

"I'm sure I'll have to at first. I'm probably going to burn half of what I cook."

"Well, I can get you through the basics before you go," Leslie said.

"I love you both, but I think it's time for a change. Before we become some creepy film noir cliché," she said. "And another thing: I want you to stop agreeing with me."

"What?" Bob exclaimed.

"When I do things that upset you, I want you to tell me. I don't want you to bite your lip because you're afraid of up-settin' me. I've seen what happens when parents treat their kids like that."

Leslie sat back in her seat. "Honey, you're not gonna turn out like Jared Lewis. For one thing, you're not a teenage boy."

"We don't parent you the way the Lewises parent Jared," Bob protested. "We've never scrambled around to hide something you've done. And do you know, I think Vern paid for all those posters for Landry around town. He was hinting at it pretty heavily at the special session yesterday. Saying he was takin' care of the problem."

"Yes, I do believe that. And please, just humor me and tell me when I've upset you," she said. "Also, I'm an adult, so the parenting, it's over now."

"No," Leslie said, shaking her head. "I won't speak ill of you to your face."

"I don't think it's healthy for resentment and hurt feelings to build up. So when you're upset with me, I want you to tell me."

Leslie's face scrunched up in refusal.

"Come on, let me have it."

"Frances Ann McCready!" Mama bellowed in a tone more forceful than Frankie could ever remember her using with her. "What in the Sam Hill were you thinking?"

Frankie craned back in her seat. "In regards to?"

"Smashing the Lewis boy's headlight!" Leslie hissed. "I didn't raise you to behave like this, Frankie."

"But that was . . . days ago . . . Have you been upset with me about that this whole time?" she asked. "See, this is what I'm talkin' about, you have to tell me . . . Oh, I mean, um, Mama, it wasn't that big of a deal. I smashed the kid's headlight. It's minor damage."

"You know I've always been supportive of you. I've encouraged your spirit and your energy because I believed you needed it. You have every right to be as lively as you want to be. But this? This is just crazy. And irresponsible. And point-less. You didn't prove anything by smashing that boy's car up, other than that he got under your skin. You're always saying that you're a grown-ass woman, so you can have orange hair. You're a grown-ass woman, so you can wear platform sneakers covered in dancing bears. Well, now I'm telling you, you're a grown-ass woman, act like it."

Leslie clapped her hands over her mouth. "Oh my."

"Dang," Frankie said, holding up her hand for a high five. "That was quality lecturing, Mama. Both pointed and guilt-inducing, without being over the top. Good job."

Her mama nodded primly. "Thank you."

"Also, you owe the swear jar seventy-five cents."

"Frankie."

Frankie snickered. "And you're right. I shouldn't have smashed up Jared's headlight. But if it led to him eventually gettin' disciplined and learning to behave better, which one could argue was true considering that he didn't break into the funeral home over Halloween, you could say that I actu-ally *helped* Jared."

"Frances Ann," Bob intoned.

"So I was stretching a little," she said, shrugging as she pushed back from the table. "Now, if you'll excuse me, I'm going to go talk to Tootie. And then, Daddy, you and I need to go to work so I can catch up on everything I missed yes-terday."

"I'm just glad I'm back to 'Daddy,'" Bob muttered as she walked out the kitchen door.

As she skipped toward Tootie's cabin, Frankie couldn't help but notice that Margot's seemed completely unoccupied. She hoped that meant her cousin had grown a pair of lady balls and told Kyle about their pending bun in the oven.

Frankie knocked on Tootie's door. The expected thunder of paws on the floor was followed by a cacophony of barking. No pizza man in his right mind would deliver to this house.

Tootie opened the door, chewing on one of those awful beige taffy things that only sold around Halloween. Tootie was the only one in the family who could tolerate them, which was why she bought about five pounds of them every year.

The dogs raced out, sniffing at Frankie's ankles.

"It's eight in the morning," Frankie told her, nodding at the taffy.

"You have a very serious expression on your little face," Tootie said. "I don't like it."

"Remember two years ago, when you dinged the hearse and I didn't say anything because E.J.J. had just fussed at you for parking too close to it?" Frankie said. "I'm calling in my favor."

"I knew this day would come." Tootie scowled at her. "What do you want?"

"I need you to activate the kitchen and beauty shop network," Frankie said. "I need you to bring up all of the stupid things Landry Mitchell has done since he was a toddler, particularly the bit about him shooting himself in the foot and that time he rammed a squad car into a light pole trying to get to the Dairy Queen drive-through. And then I want you to point out how well things have run since Eric took over. We haven't had any break-ins at homes or at the businesses—besides McCready's, that is. Our drunk driving arrests are up and we haven't had a fatal car accident all month. We are a safer and more stable community with Eric Linden in office."

Tootie crossed her arms over her chest. "What did you do?"

"Why do you think I did something?"

Tootie told her, pale gray eyebrow raised, "Because I've known you since the day you were born."

"Eric was officially reprimanded by the county commission because of me, in the week before the election. He thinks it's possible that he's going to lose. To Landry Mitchell."

Tootie shuddered. "Aw, that would be a shame. Landry is not ready for that sort of responsibility. Maybe he should start with a nice ant farm."

"Yes, so let's not put him in charge of the county and give him the key to the department's gun cabinet."

"I guess you feel pretty bad about this, huh?" Tootie asked.

"No. I have no particular feelings about it at all, other than being a good citizen. Plus, this reprimand on top of all the posters and stuff the Lewises paid for? That's not fair. Elections should be fair in our town."

Tootie smirked. "And it doesn't have anything to do with the fact that your shenanigans with Jared Lewis got him reprimanded in the first place?"

Frankie shook her head. "Nope."

"Or that you think Eric Linden is the bee's knees?"

"Nope."

"Frances Ann."

"I don't think that we need to bring my full name into this, *Eloise*."

"You like this boy. And that means something. You don't let yourself get involved. You are, as Duffy would say, a 'hit it and quit it' girl."

"Never let those words leave your mouth again," Frankie told her.

"Honey, it's just that you don't get emotionally attached to people outside the family circle. You treat everybody else like they're just stoppin' by and you can't wait to shove 'em back out the door, pie in hand. You're actually putting yourself out for him, tryin' to help him stay here. And right now, I think you need to stop worryin' yourself with busywork and try to figure out why."

"Does this mean you're not going to activate the kitchen grapevine?"

"Oh, I'm gonna do it. Because I don't feel safe havin' Landry in charge of us if somebody declares martial law."

"Well, on that note, I will be callin' Janey down at the sheriff's office, and if she happens to call you with some crime statistics information, maybe share that around town, too."

"What are you up to?" Tootie asked.

"Trying to grow up."

IT TOOK A lot of effort to dodge a prominent man in a small town.

It was difficult for her to stay away from Eric, to avoid calling or texting him. The town was only so big. Also, they were expected to communicate professionally, which she managed to do over e-mail. Fortunately, the citizens of their fair hamlet managed to die in purely natural ways for a week or so.

She'd voted for him. And she hoped that was enough.

Well, that and she'd activated every possible contact she had in the Good Ol' Girls network. She'd called in favors from the company that printed promotional materials for McCready's and had some emergency posters printed within twenty-four hours. She'd asked Stan to use the funeral home van to transport some of the older, less mobile voters to the polls. She had Marianne casually bring up Eric's enforcement of school zone speed limits at her room mom meeting.

Margot wanted to put a special thank-you to Eric in the e-mail blast to volunteers for the Trunk-R-Treat, but Frankie was afraid it would come across as sarcastic.

True to her word, Tootie had talked to all the most dedicated gossips in town. And Frankie's discussion with Janey had generated a tidy crime report listing all the statistic changes in the month since Eric had taken office. And if a copy of that report just happened to land in the hands of Jeanette Foy, Gary Thrope's chief rival down at the *Ledger*, so she could slip those numbers onto the front page days before the election, well, that was just a lovely coincidence.

And then, three days before Election Day, as an ecstatic Kyle had packed boxes of Margot's clothes into his truck, he'd dropped a piece of gossip on her.

"This is going to sound very convoluted, but one of my students told me that his babysitter's older brother's girlfriend said something about Jared Lewis planning to break into the funeral home while everybody's at the courthouse waiting for the poll results to come in. He figures that your guard is down now and since you won't be expectin' him to break in *after* Halloween, it will be even more of a gut punch."

"Jared Lewis," she growled.

"I don't know if it's true, but I figured if I didn't say anything and he broke in, you would shave off my eyebrows while I slept," he said. "And with Margot in her current delicate hormonal state, she would probably let you into the house to do it."

"You're right. She is a loyal thing," Frankie said. "Also,

you knocked up my cousin. Outside of marriage. If I had pearls, I would clutch them."

"She was so wound up when she told me, I thought she'd freaked out and taken a job in Alaska or something. A baby was much better news," he said, grinning to beat the band. "But I did give you the heads-up on your favorite teen vandal, so I think we're even."

"Could you ask Margot to call me? I have some stuff I really need her help with," Frankie said.

"Family stuff?"

"No, just . . . stuff."

"That's . . . cryptic."

"You'll get used to it," Frankie told him.

SO ON ELECTION night, Frankie found herself crouched in the back of the hearse. It was parked across the lot, in a shaded area by the dock. The funeral home windows were dark, as was the marina. Even the neon Snack Shack sign had been extinguished for the night. The only light spilling across the gravel of the parking lot was the streetlight over the Dumpsters. It cast a sickly greenish-yellow glow over the back bay doors.

Frankie watched from the hearse's hatchback as a black SUV with one headlight rolled into the parking lot. The driver's-side door opened and a dark figure snuck quietly across the lot, a black bag slung over his shoulder. Frankie's teeth clenched at the sight of him, wishing that Kyle had been wrong about Jared's plans. Why couldn't this kid be palling around with the other boys at the courthouse lawn, enjoying a burger from the diner, instead of committing several crimes at once? While wearing a cliché head-to-toe-black ensemble and greasepaint on his face? The little jerk was using his phone as a flashlight, for cripes' sake.

Sighing, she held up the night-vision game camera Duffy had provided and recorded Jared using a tire iron to bash off the door handle. He paused, as if waiting for an alarm to sound, and relaxed when nothing but autumn wind echoed across the lake. Because Frankie had turned off the alarm system for the night. And just in case Jared's parents tried to argue that her video could show any teenage boy breaking into McCready's, she zoomed the lens across the parking lot and took several seconds' worth of focused footage showing his car and license plate number.

When Jared entered the mortuary, Frankie slipped out of the hearse and walked quickly across the lot on feet she'd wrapped in burlap to muffle her steps. Within seconds, she heard Jared screaming his head off. She grinned, and continued to record from the shadows as he ran out of the mortuary, toward his SUV.

ACCORDING TO SEVERAL sources, Eric was sitting at the courthouse lawn with the rest of the locals, watching the marshals scribble election results on a whiteboard. He was winning in the polls, by a lot, while Landry's mama comforted him in the corner. As a write-in candidate, Landry scored twenty-three votes, most likely from people related to him.

As part of what Ike considered his patriotic duty, he served burgers and coffee from the Rise and Shine from a booth on the lawn. It was a pretty civilized way to handle politics, generally speaking.

Just as Eric was declared the unofficial winner of the election, Jared Lewis's SUV rolled up on the courthouse lawn, horn blaring. Jared Lewis hopped out, his face gray and sweaty, screaming for his father.

"Dad, Dad, we've got to get out of here. They're coming! The zombies are coming!"

Vern Lewis's eyes darted around, grimacing at the crowd that was gathering around them. He clutched his son by the arms. "Now, Jared, calm down, son, and just tell me what happened."

"ZOMBIES!" Jared shrieked. Several of the older parents rolled their eyes and redirected their children to their ice cream. "At the McCready place, that crazy bitch Frankie has been making zombies down in that basement of hers! I saw it. There was all this special equipment and this glowing green chemical stuff in beakers all over the counters. And there was a body on the slab and all of a sudden it started twitching and it sat up! It tried to grab me! And then the morgue drawers started opening and zombies started climbing out and they were moaning and growling and sniffing. Like they could smell me and they wanted to eat me!"

"Shhh," Vern Lewis hissed, looking around the crowd gathered in the lot. "Keep quiet, boy!"

"You've got to get me somewhere safe, Dad. The courthouse has a bomb shelter in the basement for the community leaders or something, right? Like a bunker? We need to hide out there until the army comes to save us."

"Jared, Jared, baby, what happened?" Marnette cried, pressing his head against her chest. "Shush, shush, now, don't get overexcited."

"Oh, hush, woman, stop coddling him. Can't you see he's high or drunk or something? He thinks zombies are walking around!" Vern yelled.

"They were!" Jared cried. "Go back to McCready's and you'll see them! Sheriff Linden! You need to take as many guys with guns as you can over to McCready's and start double-tapping those assholes."

"Jared, language!" Marnette whispered.

"Why don't any of you believe me?" Jared demanded. "I'm telling you, I know what I saw. Frankie probably wanted me to stay away from the basement because she didn't want me to find out that she was doing her sicko experiments on the bodies!"

It was at this point that Frankie strolled onto the courthouse lawn, cool as a cucumber. She smiled at the Lewises before giving a side hug to E.J.J., who was watching the scene with some confusion.

"Actually, I wanted you to stay out of the basement because it's private property and you don't have permission to be there. As a matter of fact, my family, the owners of said property, have asked you multiple times to stay away from that property," Frankie said.

"Tell them!" Jared shrieked. "Tell them that you made zombies, you crazy bitch."

"Oh, Jared. Poor, misguided, badly parented Jared," Frankie said, shaking her head as she opened up a video file on her tablet. "I didn't make anything, except for this videotape that shows you using a tire iron to break into the funeral home and then running out screaming a few minutes later.

"Sheriff, this should be all the evidence you need to press even more charges, which my family fully intends to file," she said as the action played out on the screen. "I have e-mailed a copy of the file to your work address. Also, this is an official application for a 'no trespass' order that would bar Jared from our property for the foreseeable future."

Eric cleared his throat. "Thank you, Ms. McCready."

"Now, wait, we don't have to bring criminal charges into this," Vern protested.

"Don't we?" Frankie demanded. "We asked you several times to keep your son from breaking into our place of business and committing vandalism. You said it couldn't possibly be him and refused to do anything, so now we have proof that he did it and there will be consequences for him."

Jared slumped against his mother. "So there were no zombies?"

"No, Jared, there were no zombies. I set that whole thing up with makeup and special effects and volunteers. Because I'm smarter than you. Deal with it and grow up."

He looked like he was on the verge of tears or throwing up, or both. "All right. All right. I did it," he said, looking at his mother, who was trying to hold her hand over his mouth. "No, I did it, Mom. She's right. I've been breaking into the funeral home for weeks, playing pranks and messing with her because I don't like her."

"Feelin's mutual," Frankie muttered.

"But I'm just glad there are no zombies," he said. "I'll take community service or probation or whatever. As long as there are no zombies."

"Mr. McCready, would you be willing to talk to the county attorney and agree to that sort of thing?" Eric asked.

"If he's willing to plead guilty to the charges, we're willing to cooperate with community service sentencing," E.J.J. said.

"Now, hold on," Marnette said, glancing around. "You don't have to sign anything. They can't prove—"

"Shut up, Marnette!" Vern thundered. "For once, let the boy take responsibility for what he's done! I should have done something years ago, should have told you no, but I just didn't want to hear you talk anymore. And now look at him, scared of zombies and losin' his mind in front of the whole town."

Marnette gasped and shot Vern a filthy look but didn't say anything else.

Eric sighed. "For right now, Jared, I'm releasing you on your parents' recognizance. Go home and don't be a little jerk for the rest of the week. You can come by and sign the paperwork tomorrow."

"Don't talk to my son that way!" Marnette screeched.

"Don't tempt me to file more charges," Eric told her. "Against you, for disturbing the peace."

Marnette swung her bag over her shoulder so hard it whacked Vern in the face. Vern and Marnette hustled Jared toward his SUV and drove home.

By the time they drove off, Eric turned to find that Frankie was gone.

FRANKIE SPENT THE following weekend moving her stuff from her parents' house to Margot's old cabin. She didn't need a truck, as the few items of furniture she was taking only had to move about thirty yards. But she'd had to ask her parents to go into Atlanta for a moving truck that she hadn't actually reserved so her unpacking wouldn't be interrupted by fond reminiscences of how cute she'd been when she'd used every single item in the two boxes of belongings she'd managed to smuggle out of the house.

She heard footsteps on her porch as she was setting out the last of her framed pictures. Without looking back, she said, "Okay, Mom and Dad, I feel really bad sending you on a wild-goose chase for a nonexistent rental truck reservation, but I think we can agree that my version of movin' involved a lot less cryin'."

"I like the version of moving that doesn't involve my pickup truck."

Frankie turned toward the male voice to find Eric standing at her open front door. Herc was sitting on his haunches.

"Hey, Herc!" she cried. The dog came trotting forward, allowing Frankie to scratch his neck, and then hopped up on her couch to make himself comfortable. Eric started to object, but Frankie waved him off.

"He's fine," she said. "Congratulations, Sheriff. I hear your election was a landslide."

"Yep. I get to keep my job for a few more years, at least. Do you know anything about this?" he asked, holding up a crime report filled with pie charts and numbers.

"Janey helped me crunch numbers from the papers she salvaged from the records room. It's got the statistics from the weeks you've been sheriff—showing everything: traffic accident response times, thefts, assaults, burglaries, vandalism, domestic disputes—and compares them to the same calendar weeks in the previous ten years. It was an absolute bitch to put together on a spreadsheet, but it shows a decline from the previous years, which is impressive considering that you haven't been in office for very long. If you show this to the county commission the next time you're up for a raise, it couldn't hurt."

"This is amazing, Frankie," he said. "I'm . . . I'm sorry for what I said. I know better than to call you names, and the things I said . . . It wasn't right. And for you to turn around and help me anyway shows that you're a better person than I am."

"I have my sucky moments, like everybody else. There are real-world consequences for what happens at your job, I recognize that. I do tend to get a little 'separated' from the outside world when I'm working, and I forget how sheltered I am. I won't do that to you again. I won't put you in the position where you have to choose between protecting me and keeping your job. And I'm so sorry that I did it in the first place."

"And I'm sorry for taking the whole thing so damn seriously and blaming you when it wasn't going the way I wanted. That was stupid and selfish. I had no right to talk to you like that. I'm not your daddy—it's not my job to try to change you. I don't want to change you. I wouldn't have fallen in . . . extremely deep like with you if you were anyone else."

"So we're both sorry and somewhat selfish."

Eric smirked. "I've been meaning to ask about the zombie thing. It's probably for the best if I don't, really, but . . . Your whole family was at the courthouse. Who'd you get to dress up as zombies?"

"Actually, it was your friends from the zombie walk group in Atlanta. Margot's friend put me in touch with them and they already had all of their makeup and costumes ready from Halloween. They felt really bad about what happened to you and were willing to put their best people to work if it was going to help the 'Segway guy.' Also, I think they wanted to prove that zombie scares could be used for good instead of evil. They even cleaned up the fake blood and lab equipment before they left. Very considerate zombies."

"Why go through the charade of the zombie apocalypse if you were just going to record him breaking in?" he asked.

"Two reasons. One, payback, which is always a noble pursuit. And two, because his parents needed to hear from Jared's own lips that he'd broken into the funeral home. I had to overcome his self-preservation instincts with fear."

"Well, I'm sure you'll be glad to know that Vern Lewis has decided to drop the charges against you, in light of you not throwing the book at Jared. Your record is now a clean slate."

"Aw, that means I have to remove the pins from my voodoo doll."

"If we're going to eventually date, you're going to have to stop saying things like that. I don't know if you're kidding."

She leaned close and whispered. "You'll never know if I'm kidding."

"True enough," he agreed.

"Besides, I don't know that I'll ever date you," she said, backing away. "The last time I slept with you, you arrested me."

"We can leave that part out next time," he promised. "Please go out on a date with me. We don't have to confess our undying love for each other or anything. I would just really like a chance to prove I'm not a selfish ass all of the time."

"What if I date you and it turns out that we still get angry at each other over things not related to Jared Lewis and we should be separated by several counties?"

"It's a risk I'm willing to take."

"What if I date you and you figure out that I just want access to your adorable dog?" she asked.

He grinned and kissed her soundly. "I'm willing to live with that."

15

FRANKIE RAN A comb over Ron Turner's age- and era-inappropriate pompadour, preserving the Elvis lookalikedom he'd maintained in life. Mr. Ron had been a sweet man with a never-ending stream of after-church knock-knock jokes when she was a kid. Frankie was pleased that she'd managed to preserve that little smile on his face. It's how his family and friends would want to remember him.

"It's a real shame that you had to leave before the holidays, Mr. Ron," she told him. "I know your family's going to miss the way you used to let them win the Thanksgiving wishbone pull every time. And how you used to measure how good a meal was by how far you had to undo your pants."

She dabbed a bit of Vaseline on Mr. Ron's lips to give them a more lifelike softness. "I would love to spend more time reminiscing on my favorites in your knock-knock joke repertoire, but I have plans tonight. I'm celebrating with my man-friend. He just got elected as sheriff; officially, not interim, which is a big deal. He's the first non–Lake Sackett native to win a landslide election for any county office in the county's history, you know."

The big celebration she had planned was actually a nice quiet dinner at her cabin, without jail cells or naked swimming or zombies. Or even discussion of zombies. They'd been skating the edges of a relationship for weeks and they hadn't had a normal, boring date yet. They might even watch Netflix and then actually chill.

For now, they were content with dating. Very cautiously. Frankie was not going to be moving into Eric's place anytime soon. Her toothbrush was there, and some of her Funko Pop! dolls, but she wasn't quite ready to make the full transition. She figured she would get there when she was ready. For now, she was content in Margot's cabin. She liked knowing that she could stumble about in the mornings without worrying about waking her parents up. She liked being able to walk around in her underwear if she wanted . . . if the curtains were closed, because she did live about ten feet from her cousin. She liked being able to watch the racier episodes of *Game of Thrones* without her mother walking through the room, covering her eyes, and saying, "Oh my goodness," over and over.

Frankie's work environment was also more relaxed, now that she didn't have to assiduously guard the mortuary. To avoid charges, Jared was going to be spending a lot of weekends picking up trash off the highway and volunteering at a grief counseling hotline for teens to help him appreciate how wrong it is to interrupt the grieving process with jerky shenanigans.

She stood back and smiled as she surveyed the full picture of Mr. Ron in repose. He looked just as he had in life, but quiet, for the first time since she'd known him.

She heard a knock on the door and Eric's voice calling, "Hey, in there! Everybody decent?"

"Come on in," she yelled back.

Eric walked into the morgue without hesitation. "Hi. You almost done for the day?"

"Just finishing up," she said, straightening Mr. Ron's cuffs.

"Very peaceful and lifelike," Eric assured her, gazing down at the casket.

"The four words every girl wants to hear," she said, kissing him lightly before wheeling Mr. Ron over to the elevator. "How was your day?"

"Traffic, tickets, the odd cat in a tree," he said. "Landry returned from his 'election bereavement leave' after I explained that wasn't a real thing."

"How's that goin'?" she asked, pushing the button to send the casket upstairs. "Is it awkward, him comin' back to work for you after tryin' to get your job?"

Eric shook his head. "Not really. I think he's kinda relieved, to be honest with you. I think the only reason he agreed to run is that he thought it would make his mama proud."

"Landry does love his mama," Frankie agreed, stripping

off her gloves. She gathered her things as she checked to make sure the occupied morgue drawers were secured. Leading Eric out, she used the newly installed thumbprint pad to lock the mortuary doors behind her. Only she and Uncle Stan and E.J.J. had access if the door was locked. Another pad was installed on the back bay doors. Anyone who tried to open either door without the right thumbprint would be treated to an earsplitting alarm that sounded like a British ambulance.

"Night, everybody!" she called as she closed the door.

"Still weird that you talk to them," Eric told her as they walked up the stairs.

"You'll get used to it."

"That will never happen."

Outside, Herc was waiting patiently by Eric's truck. He even let Frankie take his usual spot in the passenger seat. He did, however, rest his jaw on her shoulder and drool on her Avenger Cats T-shirt. And didn't take too well to Eric trying to hold her hand as they turned away from town.

"Herc is very disgruntled about not being allowed into the funeral home," Eric said. "He would like to file a formal protest against the health codes that prevent him from enterin' this building."

"Well, I just managed to convince Tootie that her 'emotional support animal' argument wasn't going to fly, so he's just going to have to live with it."

"I like the orange streaks," he told her, running his thumb over her braid, earning a huff from Herc. "Very festive."

"Well, I wanted to stay in the fall color family," she said. "So, does it feel safer, now that you're sworn in as the permanent sheriff? The county commission can only fire you for gross negligence!"

"I feel like we throw around the words 'gross negligence' a little too casually between us." He pulled out his wallet and showed her his badge. "But look, they gave me a new one made out of much heavier metal than the interim badge. They must be expecting me to stick around for a while."

While she was admiring this much more substantial badge, she glimpsed a tiny miniature of her face winking out at her from the photo portion of his wallet. "What is that?"

Eric's cheeks flushed pink as she shrugged out of her lab coat. "You're supposed to carry a picture of your girl around with your badge. It's tradition."

"Aw." She leaned in and kissed his cheek. Herc wedged his head between them. Frankie laughed and scratched Herc's ears. "That's so sweet. But did you have to use my mug shot from the Lock Down Hunger arrest?"

He shrugged. "Well, I didn't want to go on your Facebook page and steal a picture, like a stalker."

"This still seems weirder," she told him.

He cleared his throat. "Besides, I like the pose."

Frankie's brows shot up. "Do you?"

He tugged at his collar. "Yeah, the whole pinup-girl thing? I dig it."

"I'll have to remember that," she said, grinning and waggling her eyebrows.

"So what's the plan for the night?" Eric asked as they drove near the McCready compound.

"Well, as we have discussed, my cooking skills are limited, so I will be serving you Eggo waffles. But to make up for it, I will let you pick the movie. *Sharktopus* or *Sharktopus vs. Whalewolf.*"

"That doesn't seem like a choice," he said, shaking his head.

"We agreed when we started dating officially that you would become familiar with the mutant shark film oeuvre."

"Did we agree to that?" he asked, parking in front of Margot's old cabin with the cute little blue door.

"It was implied."

Herc jumped out of the truck after her and trotted into the house. He circled Margot's old couch and flopped onto the second personalized dog cushion she'd special-ordered for him as a sort of *Sorry I'm stealing Eric's spare time he used to spend petting you* peace offering.

It was almost dizzying, the freedom of having her own space to do with as she pleased. Her little house was cozy and colorful and comfortable, with her own quirky pop culture touches. She'd bought a new duvet, because that sounded more grown-up than sleeping under a quilt made from T-shirts she'd worn in high school. She'd found a company that made candles scented like *Game of Thrones* locations and chose to make her living room smell like the godswood of Winterfell. And she'd framed some very attractive prints for her wall. They were various versions of *Dr. Who*'s exploding TARDIS, but still, it was art.

"You better close the door before Tootie's pack comes barreling in here to play with Herc," she told Eric, opening her freezer to root around for the Eggo box.

Before Eric could close it, Bob "just happened" to walk out of her parents' cabin and "just happened" to notice that Frankie's front door was still standing open.

"Well, hey, kids. Congratulations on your election, Sheriff," Bob told him, giving Eric a firm shake of the hand. "I can't tell you how relieved I am that you got elected."

"You'd be surprised how many people have phrased it that way," Eric said, grinning.

"So, whatcha up to?" Bob said, apparently scanning Frankie's living space for unsecured sharp objects.

"Just having a little date night in," Frankie said. "Dinner and a movie. Lord help whoever tries to interrupt it by dyin'."

"I'm not sure that's something they can help, sweetheart," Eric told her.

"Honey, frozen waffles don't count as dinner. Why don't you just come over and join us? Your mama made fried chicken."

"No thanks, Daddy."

"All right. I'll just leave you here," Bob said, his voice cracking slightly. "Behind a door that closes. Unsupervised. With a man."

"Dad."

"And what time will you be heading home, Eric?" Bob asked.

"We don't know, and neither will you, because I am twenty-eight years old," Frankie told her father, while Eric did a careful inspection of the ceiling. "Now, scoot."

"I don't like this havin'-an-adult-daughter thing," Bob muttered as he walked toward the door. "G'night, Eric. I don't have guns, but I'll . . . figure out a scarier threat later."

Eric snorted. "Solid effort, sir."

"Good night, Daddy!" she said, gently but very firmly shutting the door in his face.

It was a good first step.